THE
Plainsmen

JACK SCHAEFER

Illustrated by Lorence Bjorklund

HOUGHTON MIFFLIN COMPANY BOSTON

THE RIVERSIDE PRESS CAMBRIDGE

PUBLISHER'S NOTE

Jack Schaefer's works appeal to readers of all ages. His first novel SHANE has already become something of a classic, and OLD RAMON was runner-up for the Newbery Award given by the American Library Association to the year's most distinguished contribution to children's literature.

The stories in this collection were written with no particular audience in mind but have been chosen for their special appeal to younger readers. By now it seems that more ink than blood has flowed over the OLD WEST and much that has been written has succeeded only in turning the real land into a garish stage setting. These stories have a strength and honesty that lead beyond the painted backdrop to the western plains themselves and show life both as it was and as it should have been.

THIRD PRINTING   R

CONTENTS

Books by Jack Schaefer

Shane
First Blood
The Big Range
The Canyon
The Pioneers
Out West (editor)
Company of Cowards
The Kean Land and Other Stories
Old Ramon
The Plainsmen

COOTER JAMES

And a Little Matter of Principle

COOTER JAMES rode in from the line camp blowing flakes of the first snow off his mustache and feeling sorry for himself. He was in no mood for light talk when he pulled up by the ranchhouse porch and found Jess Winslow standing there watching him approach.

"Jess," he said, "stock's all right and camp's tight. But you'd best send another man out. Can't winter it again."

"Trouble," said Jess Winslow. "I ought to know trouble's riding with you the way your mustache sags. What is it? Age getting you soft?"

Cooter James was too low to flare much at that. "Only turned forty last year," he said. "Just when a man's got his growth and a bit of sense in him. Three years running I've rode that line. Not doing it again."

"Money," said Jess. "That's what it is. You're hitting me for more money."

Cooter James sighed. "Not a matter of money. Matter of principle. Way back doing line work got worried being alone. Promised myself when I took to spooking easy and talking to myself I'd take fair warning. Last night an owl woke me shivering. This morning caught myself talking to the coffeepot. Saddled up and came straight in."

"Letting me down," said Jess. "That's what you're doing. Just when I need that line rode right you're letting me down."

"Sorry, Jess," said Cooter. "Man that can't keep a promise to himself's a peaked kind of mangy packrat."

"That's how you look to me this minute now," said Jess Winslow. "Jumping at owls and scared of your own voice. Packrat's too nice a word."

Cooter James sighed again. He wasn't much to look at and he knew it. Short and thickening around the middle with a limp from a bronc-thrown broken bone that never healed right. Scrambled features burnt and weathered with always-squinting, muddy-blue eyes and a hooked nose over a handlebar mustache that drooped to hide a short upper lip. But he was a good hand on any man's ranch and he knew that too.

"Easy, Jess," he said. "I'm quitting. Just made myself another promise. Going to winter warm and lazy in town. Thank you for my time quick as convenient."

Cooter James rode into town sighing soft into the drooping ends of his mustache. "Change," he said.

"That's what I need. Easy living for a spell." He had money to spend and he spent it, on thorough barbering and town clothes and genteel living quarters, a room at Mrs. Pearson's boardinghouse. Four days and he had his fill of that. The food was solid and staying, but he had an uneasy feeling that Mrs. Pearson disapproved of his table manners. The bed was too bouncy and the floor was too smooth, and he had difficulty navigating among the fussy scatter rugs that gave treacherous footing for a man used to unfinished planks. He was uncomfortable in his town clothes, and he felt shorter than ever in shoes lacking the high heels of his worn old boots. And he never could remember to scrape his feet on the mat before coming in the front door.

On the evening of the fourth day, Cooter took a long look at Mr. Pearson, who clerked ten hours at a stretch at the railroad freight office and came home to scrape his feet careful on the mat. Cooter sighed into what was left of his mustache and went upstairs to bed, mighty thoughtful. In the morning he rolled his town clothes into a neat bundle. He put on his old blue jeans and flannel shirt and work jacket. He struggled to get his feet again into his boots and jammed his faded Stetson on his head. He left an extra five-dollar bill on the bed and went downstairs and out the front door.

Two hours' walking found him what he wanted, a sagging shed at the edge of town abandoned when the railroad section gang moved on. Three days later he was snug and settled; the shed braced and tight, a bunk rigged, a cracked stove brought from the blacksmith shop and food on shelves along one wall. He could sleep late and putter around the place with not a thing pressing. He could wander around town and toss the time of day with plenty of folks and stop at the livery stable to visit his horse. He could spend as many hours as he wanted sitting by his stove reading through the stack of old newspapers he had found in a corner of the shed. Then late one night a board squeaked and he woke shivering and got up and made a pot of coffee and started talking to it.

"What's wrong with me?" said Cooter. "Took fair warning. Warm and lazy in town. Still there's an itch inside I can't get at. Might be I need something new to be doing."

That was why Cooter James went to working in Silas John Unger's general store and got himself involved with a barrel of flour.

Silas John Unger knew Cooter from the time they were Circle Bar hands together. He was lean with a lantern jaw and hair lightened with streaks of gray. He was maybe ten years older, and fatherly in his feeling for Cooter James. "Cooter boy," he said, "it pleases me to have you acquiring some smattering of sense at last. I'm doing well and putting money in the bank. You should be doing the same. When the sun's shining, get ready for a rainy day."

"Rain don't bother me," said Cooter. "And store-keeping's not my style. Want only to wear out the winter with it. If there's work enough to warrant."

"There's work enough," said Silas John. "During the selling times at least. When things are slack, we can play checkers like in the old days."

Several weeks went by, and Cooter was twenty-nine

games ahead on the chart they kept, when Silas John read a letter in one morning's mail. He chewed a pencil and made tracks on a piece of paper and came out of the cubbyhole he called his office.

"Cooter boy," he said, "the country hereabouts is getting thick with homesteaders and I'm thinking of adding a line of farm machinery. I'll have to go east to Chicago to tie the deal. Do you reckon you can handle things while I'm gone?"

"Reckon so," said Cooter.

Silas John tapped his nose with the pencil. "One thing worries me. You never had much head for figures. I like my books kept straight and neat."

Cooter blew air through the ends of his mustache that was growing out again the way he liked. "Set me on a corral rail," he said. "Drive steers past all day. Come night I'll have you the tally right with the swaybacks and bigjaws marked. Reckon I can keep figures on a cramped little store like this."

"Steers are one thing," said Silas John. "Store goods another."

"Take your trip," said Cooter. "Take your time. If my figures don't tot up exact, I'll teach you how to beat that checker game of mine."

Cooter James kept his figures clean and straight in the two books, one for cash and one for credit, and he lined down the pages neater than Silas John ever did. One day he tallied out fifteen cents ahead on the cash account. That bothered him till he undercharged a homesteader's wife fifteen cents on her winter dress goods and decided that balanced the account. Then reports came of a blizzard in the hills, and people began crowding into town by wagon to lay in quantity supplies for the hard months. He was busy as he had ever been at branding time, making up orders, packing goods into the wagons, and keeping the books posted. He was a tired man but a triumphant man when Silas John strolled in and sat down on a nail keg and set his satchel on the floor and looked around.

"You've been doing business," said Silas John. "My shelves look like people been buying."

"Been putting money in the bank for you," said Cooter. "Been protecting my checker game too."

Silas John went into his cubbyhole and bent over the books. After a while he came out and looked at Cooter perched on the rear counter and shook his head and went back in and chewed a pencil. Then he began coming out and counting articles and going back in to check the books. He kept at this till Cooter was blowing his mustache with chuckles.

"Enjoying yourself?" said Cooter. "Remind me of a chipmunk laying up nuts in a hollow tree." He slid off the counter and went up front to tend to a customer. When that was done he found Silas John occupying the perch on the rear counter and jutting his jaw at a high angle.

"Cooter boy," said Silas John, "you've lost me a barrel of flour."

"Crazy as a cracked teapot," said Cooter. "Couldn't lose anything that big."

"You could," said Silas John. "There were nineteen barrels out back when I left. There's four now. That means you sold fifteen. But there's only fourteen marked in the books, three cash and eleven credit."

Cooter's mustache sagged. His jawline stiffened. "Certain of those figures?"

Silas John slid off the counter and straightened tall. "That I am," he said.

"Right," said Cooter. His jawline stiffened even more and his muddy-blue eyes tightened at the corners in a serious squint. "Take the price out of my pay."

"That I'll not," said Silas John. "What's a little matter of a barrel of flour between you and me?"

"Not a little matter," said Cooter. "Matter of principle."

"Pay for it, then," said Silas John. "I know better than to try to stop you. But I'm giving you a bonus for taking care of my store while I was gone. I make it the price of a barrel of flour. You know better than to try to stop me."

Cooter sighed into the drooping ends of his mustache and his lips relaxed in a small smile behind it. "Reminds me of the old days," he said. He reached behind the counter and pulled out the battered checkerboard. "Got another debt to pay," he said, and began setting the checkers in place.

Two weeks went by, and Cooter James was only seven games ahead on the chart and fighting to hold his lead. That gave a mild tingle to the days, and it was pleasant wagging away the time with Silas John. It was pleasant too at his shed where he could be his own boss yet close to other folks within a nice neighborly reach. Then early one morning a train tooted faint and far off down the track, and he woke shivering and crawled out of bed in his undershirt and made a pot of coffee and started talking to it.

"Can't get to the bottom of this," said Cooter. "Doing something new and enjoying myself. Still there's that itch I can't scratch. Might be I need something to occupy my mind." That was why, in the middle of a game during the noon slack, he leaned back and looked at Silas John.

"Barrel of flour," he said.

"Gone and forgotten," said Silas John. "Get on with the game."

"Not forgotten," said Cooter. "Going to find what happened to it."

It was Silas John's turn to lean back and look interested.

"Cooter boy," he said, "how're you planning to do that?"

"Simple," said Cooter. "Add a barrel of flour to every bill. Man that got it will pay. Won't know we don't know. Others'll scratch it off or complain when they stop in."

"Sounds simple," said Silas John. "But simple-sounding things often ain't so."

"This one is," said Cooter. "Just keep out of my way and let me make out the bills."

Cooter James burned his kerosene lamp late over the bills and in the morning took them to the post office. "Only a matter of time now," he said, and went on to the store where there was plenty of work waiting. The

next three days, while Silas John handled the inside
business, he was busy building an open-face shed by the
store for the farm machinery that was coming. The day
after that he was busy uncrating the sample machinery
that had arrived. He was so busy he all but forgot that
barrel of flour. And Silas John said never a word about
it. During the afternoon of the second day, he stepped
outside and looked at Cooter wrassling shed timbers and
shook his head mournful and went back inside. Twice
on the third day he did the same. Late in the fourth
day he stood in the doorway and called. When they
were settled on the rear counter, he tapped his nose with
the pencil in his hand.

"Cooter boy," he said, "I have kept my mouth from
yapping so as not to disturb your muscular enthusiasm
with that shed. And I wanted to give your little lost-
barrel scheme plenty of play. But already it's had too
much."

"What now?" said Cooter. "Not working?"

"It's working," said Silas John. "It's working too
well. Thirty-seven people have paid their bills. Twenty
have complained about a barrel of flour."

"Told you they would," said Cooter. "Supposed to
work that way."

"Cooter boy," said Silas John, "you never were much
good at figures. Twenty from thirty-seven leaves seventeen. Up to and as of now seventeen people have paid
for that one barrel of flour."

Cooter's mustache sagged and he blew air through it.
He sucked in the drooping ends and chewed them
slow. His jawline stiffened and a serious squint formed
at the corners of his muddy-blue eyes.

"Need the names and the money," he said. "Reckon to be riding around evenings paying it back."

Three weeks went by, and Cooter James was nine games behind on the checker chart. The flour-barrel score stood at seventy with forty-two complaints and twenty-eight payments. These last had all been returned, and he was tired of crisscrossing the countryside in the evenings. But that worry was ended. He had sent out new bills to cancel the old and no more payments were coming in. He wasn't even bothered by the fact that his evening trips had let the town and most of the territory around know about the missing barrel and easy-tongued folk were beginning to rib him about it. He strolled along the plank sidewalks after store-closing and took the joshing and enjoyed the feel of being part of a community. He built a fire in his stove and had a lazy meal and sat warm and unworrying with his old newspapers waiting for the night freight to go past and tell him to go to bed. Then one morning about sunup a cat scrambled across his tin roof and he woke shivering and sat up in the bunk and stared at the coffeepot across the shed and began talking to it.

"Clean licked on this," he said. "Can't even locate that itch. Might be I need to settle this barrel business to settle my mind."

He was early at the store and busy with a can of paint, a small brush, and the cardboard bottom of an overall carton. He needed two cardboards before he was finished with his sign. He tacked them one under the other on the inside wall by the front door.

On or about the first week of December last one barrel of flour departed these premises leaving no record in S. J. Unger's account books. Person or persons giving information of aforesaid barrel's whereabouts will receive five dollars ($5) reward and the undying gratitude of

C. JAMES

Cooter James's sign provided plenty of amusement for Silas John and folks coming in, and it gave the ribbing a fresh boost. But it brought no news about the barrel. Cooter worried over that and was low in his mind. He began to think he would wear out the winter without tracing that barrel. Then one afternoon, when the sun was warming toward spring, a scrawny red-haired boy came in for a piece of patching cloth and stopped by the sign and kept staring at it.

Cooter eased alongside. "Like it, son?" he said.

"We got a barrel of flour this winter," said the boy.

"Know anything about that particular barrel?" said Cooter.

The boy shied away and started edging toward the door.

"G'wan," he said. "Suppose I did, I wouldn't tell you."

"Easy, now," said Cooter. "No way to talk to your elders."

"Go fry an egg," said the boy, and skipped out the door.

It was maybe an hour later that the boy came back and with him a little waist-high girl with the same red hair in pigtails, and both of them tagging a woman in a faded gingham dress with a man's coat on over it. This woman was plump and solid inside the coat and she had a lot of red hair pulled up with old celluloid hairpins haphazard on top of her head. Her plain round face would have been pleasant with the permanent smile crinkles around the eyes except that her mouth was pursed tight right now, so tight that it pulled her plump chin into little bumps. She swung around by the door and read the sign and she turned about and started toward Silas John in the rear of the store.

"Mr. Unger," she said, trying to hold her voice firm, "just what is the meaning of that thing on the wall?"

"Afternoon, Mrs. Moser," said Silas John. "Any questions pertaining to that peculiar piece of writing should be addressed to Mr. Cooter James here."

She turned to look at Cooter, and for some reason he began to feel fidgety and troubled in his mind.

"So that's C. James," she said. "I remember him. I did business with him last time I was in here." She glared at Cooter and the bumps on her chin started quivering. "Well, Mr. C. James," she said, "you open your mouth and explain that sign to me."

"Easy, now," said Cooter. "Ain't much. Was missing a barrel of flour and trying to find what happened to it."

"Well, it makes me do some wondering," she said. "I got a barrel of flour that week and I didn't pay for it or charge it either. You gave it to me."

Cooter's mustache sagged, and his voice came through it feeble and fumbling. "Did I now?" he said.

"That's right," said the boy. "We ain't ever eat so good."

The woman was talking straight along so fast the words were pushing each other out of the way.

"I came in here for my winter goods and I knew exactly what I had money for and you made out the list and I paid you and I asked for a bag of flour and when you brought it out to the wagon it was a barrel and ever since my man died last fall everybody's been so kind and I've been a good customer here because I can't afford much but what I buy I get here and I thought you were being kind and I thanked you for it and you said that was all right you were pleased to do it."

"Did I now?" said Cooter again. "Reckon I did. But I thought —" He shut off his talk and chewed the ends of his mustache slow and thoughtful.

"And what did you think?" said the woman. "It surprises me you can think at all. Making a woman feel maybe she's got something she wasn't supposed to have."

"Mrs. Moser, ma'am," said Cooter, "all my mistake. You were supposed to have it. So busy back then slipped my mind."

"Humph," said the woman. "Things like that don't slip minds easy. You stop squirming and tell me what you thought."

"No," said Cooter. "Won't."

The woman waggled her head at Cooter so hard the celluloid pins started loosening and he was afraid they might fall.

"It's not my fault I'm not a man," she said. "You treat me like one. You speak honest to me. You tell me what you thought."

Cooter was caught when she talked like that and he knew it.

"Thought you were thanking me for stowing things in the wagon," he said. He saw her chin quivering again, and he pushed his mind scurrying for words. "Easy, now, ma'am. So maybe I didn't mean to give it you then. Do now. Didn't know about your man passing on. Glad about it now. About the mistake, I mean. Wish it had been two. Two barrels. Give you the other one now." He started past her toward the rear of the store.

The woman's chin was quivering, but quivering mad.

"Mr. C.-for-Cooter James," she said, and stopped him in stride. She stared at him accusing, and the boy and the girl lined beside her and looked the same, and her words pushed each other out of the way in their hurry. "Mr. Mind-slipping James," she said, "I wouldn't take the tiniest speck of flour there ever was from you if me and mine were starving and you the last man on the whole earth. Doing a thing like that to a woman that's always paid her bills hard as it might be and making her find out the food she's been putting in the mouths of her babes ought to've been paid for and wasn't."

"Don't look like babes to me," said Cooter, beginning to be a bit peeved himself. "Got some size on them. Want to be treated like a man you do, so I will. Stop yammering at me and wobbling your chin. Barrel's been paid for. Know what I wanted to know and there's nothing more to it."

"Nothing more you think," said the woman. "I want to know who paid for it."

"I did," said Cooter. "In a way I did."

"Humph," said the woman. "So it's you I owe the price and just when I haven't got any cash money and don't know when I'll ever see any again with thinking

the pig and the garden that isn't plowed yet will take us
through the summer till I get some kind of a crop in and
sold and money's always been scarce with us anyways
and no extras for barrels that oughtn't to have to be
paid for but do because a fool man doesn't know a person
and lets his mind slip."

"Mrs. Moser, ma'am," said Cooter, getting a firm hold
on himself, "you don't owe me the least little bit of
nothing. Try to pay me a solitary single cent and I head
howling for the next county."

"Be good riddance," said the woman. "Howsomever,
I don't have a single cent. But I'm going to pay you. I
won't have a thing like that hanging on my mind, letting
a man do for me what he didn't mean to. A barrel of
flour costs fourteen dollars. Well, you owe me five
dollars reward money as that sign there says and I make
it nine dollars still owing and I'm going to pay it not
knowing how right now but that I'm going to." She
waggled her head emphatic at Cooter and two of the
celluloid pins fell bouncing to the floor. She stooped
and grabbed them and stuck them into the pile of red
hair and glared at Cooter and marched out the door. The
boy and the girl took turns according to size doing the
same, the glaring and the marching, and a silence settled
in the store.

Then the voice of Silas John came purring from the
rear. "Cooter boy," he said, "that woman's got a rope
on you."

"No rope," said Cooter. "How's she going to pay me
when I won't take it?"

"I wouldn't know," said Silas John. "But there's one
item I do know. I know the color of her hair."

Cooter James went home to his shed feeling sorry for himself. "Town life's mighty strenuous," he said. He burned his beans chewing his mustache and forgetting them on the stove. And he couldn't stay put in his chair with his newspapers. He pulled on his jacket and took a long hike along the tracks and return to weary his muscles and worried away some hours before he fell asleep. In the morning a metal-bumping sound woke him shivering, and he lay still listening to strange noises in his shed. The tasty smell of bacon grease tickled his nose and he raised his head to peer over the blanket. The woman was there by his stove, her back to him, bustling about in a knowing manner.

Cooter lay quiet for two minutes, maybe three. He held the blanket up under his chin and raised himself to a sitting position. He had trouble finding his voice.

"Mrs. Moser, ma'am," he said, "what in tarnation you doing here?"

"Fixing your breakfast," said the woman. "I figured I'd charge you a quarter each time till I was paid up. I've changed my mind and made it fifty. I'm a good cook and you keep your things dirty just like a man."

Cooter lay back down and tried to untangle his mind and was still trying when she snapped at him.

"It's ready," she said.

"It," said Cooter. "Not me. Can't get out of my bunk with you standing there."

"Humph," said the woman. "Wouldn't be the first time I saw a man in his drawers. If you're so delicate about yourself, I'll look the other way."

She did, and Cooter slipped out of the bunk and whipped on his old blue jeans and flannel shirt. With them on he felt better and able to work up the beginnings of a good mad.

"Blamed if I'm hungry," he said.

"Eat it or don't eat it," said the woman. "Anyways, I've fixed it, and a man that was a man 'stead of a mind-slipper that'd take the taste out of the food a woman that pays her bills puts in the mouth of her babes would eat it hungry or not hungry and I never knew a man that wasn't hungry in the mornings anyways."

Cooter was caught again and he knew it. He sat down and started to eat and the woman watching bothered him.

"Fixed it," he said. "Time to get out, and let me be."

"Where I come from," said the woman, "fixing a meal means cleaning up after."

Cooter sighed, and then his mad was boiling strong. He looked at the food, bacon and biscuits and coffee.

"Woman," he said, "where's my eggs?"

She jumped, and one of the hairpins fell and she stooped to pick it up and put it in place. "Didn't know you had any," she said.

"In that tobacco can," said Cooter. "Four I want. Fried and flipped."

He ate right through every snitch of bacon, every biscuit in the pan, the four eggs, and finished with a third cup of coffee. He pulled on his boots and jacket and jammed on his hat and slammed the door behind him.

Cooter James was upset and touchy all day. He kept busy by himself in the machinery shed and hurried home before closing time. He was worrying about what he might find and his worrying was justified. The place had a different feel the moment he entered. Everything was scrubbed and polished and so neat and orderly that he shuddered when he looked around. A flour bag had been ripped apart at the seams and the halves trimmed and put up at the side windows for curtains. A bunch of winter-ivy leaves from out by the tracks was in water in a coffee cup on the table. Beside it was a note written on the edge of a piece of newspaper.

> Mr. C. James — 50 cents for fixing breakfast. 1 dollar for scrubbing out dirt. 50 cents for fixing curtains and such. 7 dollars owing. Mrs. A. (Agnes) Moser.

Cooter stared at the note a long time. "Agnes," he said. "Was sweet on a girl named Agnes once. Didn't have red hair." He smiled into his mustache, remembering, and started to get his supper, and each thing he wanted was in a new place. "Women," he said. "Interfering things. Can't leave a man be." By time he was ready to eat, he had a good grip on his mad again. "Find a way to fix her," he said, and went to bunk early, determined to be up before she arrived, and slept only in cat naps worrying over the time. He was dressed and fed and had the place slicked, and he was by the window watching when she came in sight. He waited till she was near the door then opened it, and came out and shut it behind him.

"Morning, Mrs. Moser, ma'am," he said. "Had breakfast. Everything's clean."

He went off toward the store, leaving her staring at him, and felt fine for almost the whole morning.

Along about noon worry began creeping back into his mind. Silas John beat him two more games and the afternoon seemed unusual long. He hurried home early with the worry big inside him and the woman was there in his shed by the stove preparing his supper. He pulled off his hat and leaned against the wall and sighed into his mustache.

"Stop making that silly noise," said the woman. "Thought you were cute didn't you sneaking up early to get breakfast ahead of me leaving a woman that's determined to pay her bills feeling that she's owing to you and why don't you act like a man that's got more sense than a fieldmouse and take off that jacket where it's warm in here so you won't catch cold if you go out again."

Cooter James was licked and he knew it. He took off his jacket and hung it on a nail and the hat over it.

"Determined to pay the whole price?" he said.

"I am," said the woman.

"Do it friendly, then," said Cooter. "Sit down and eat with me each time. Can't chew right with you just watching."

"Maybe I might," said the woman. "But you mind to think straight and not go notioning that I don't get enough to eat at home because maybe we do only have bread and hominy grits most of the time with the other winter things about gone but that's filling and we'll have a garden soon — and, oh, I just thought you being the kind of mind-slipping man you are you'll likely expect me to pay for what I eat."

"Woman," said Cooter, blowing his mustache out straight, "man can provide food for a woman in his own

house without her having to pay for it. Stop yammering
and get supper ready." He sat on the bunk and watched
her bustling by the stove. He forgot the worry and
began remembering yesterday's breakfast. "Woman,"
he said, "might be we could have some of those biscuits
you make?"

Two days more, and it was the end of the week and
the woman didn't come on Sunday. Three days into
the next week and by her figuring, two meals a day at
fifty cents each, she owed Cooter only one dollar and
fifty cents more.

The following morning Cooter looked across the table
at her.

"Time's getting short," he said. "Want to know how
you make those biscuits."

"The way anyone does," she said. "Flour and water
and shortening and a pinch of this and a pinch of that
till it feels right."

"Been making biscuits many a year," said Cooter.
"Never taste like yours."

"A man can't make decent biscuits," she said. "But
about any woman could on that stove of yours."

"That stove?" said Cooter. "Just a fall-apart that was
lying around at the blacksmith shop."

"It's a better stove than I've had for years and years,"
she said. "And I don't mean to tell you it's not hard
cooking on a stove that's got to be patched all the time
and puts smoke in your face and gets you all sooty so
you have to scrub all the time to be fitten for seeing."

Cooter saw the little bumps forming on her chin and

the whole chin starting to quiver. He was embarrassed and looked out the window.

"Might be," he said, "you'd let me get you a stove."

She pushed up from the table and waggled her head at him so hard some of the red hair fell down by her face.

"I will not," she said. "I wouldn't let you give me anything. Not you. Not ever." She sat down again sudden, and several of the hairpins bounced on the floor and she stooped to get them. When her head came up again, her eyes were snapping hard. "Get on off to that store," she said. "And right away quick so I can clean this mess and get away from this place that minds me of you every time I see it."

Cooter took his hat and jacket off the wall and slipped out the door. He walked slow to the store. He was sharp-tongued to customers all morning, and during the afternoon he managed to work up a quarrel with Silas John. When he realized what he was doing, he clamped down on his tongue and stomped out. He wandered over by the town saloon and looked in. "Snapped me out of meanness when I was younger," he said. "Not now." He wandered on and far out of town along some road, and about suppertime he wandered back toward his shed. He waited and worried a moment about opening the door, and when he did the place was empty. It was scrubbed and polished again and empty except for another note on the table.

> 50 cents for fixing breakfast. 1 dollar for scrubbing out a week's dirt. Makes 9 dollars now. Not a cent owing.

Cooter stared at the note. "Fooled with that scrubbing," he said. "Thought a couple more meals coming." He had been afraid at the door that maybe her chin would be quivering inside to meet him, but now he was disappointed. "That's done, anyways," he said. "Done. Finished. Over with. No more of it." He started to prepare his own supper and burned the beans, and his biscuits, even with a pinch of this and of that, were lumpy in his mouth and heavy in his stomach. He fussed around the shed and out and in a half-dozen times and started to hike along the tracks and came back as many times more till he began to think that he could call it spring and the winter over and be heading for the range again. "Where I belong," he said. "In the open where figures ain't so important."

He pulled off his outer clothes feeling better and planning an early start in the morning. He lay on the bunk and closed his eyes counting steers and checking the bigjaws and swaybacks and drifted off, counting, into sleep. A light rain began to fall tapping on his tin roof and thunder talked in the distance, and the night freight went by and he didn't hear it. Then along about sunup a mouse skittled across a shelf and a cup made a small jangle, and he sat up in the bunk shivering and stared across the shed at the coffeepot. He stared a long time and the light grew stronger. He shook his head and sighed into his mustache. "No sense fighting it," he said. "Know about that itch. Time comes to every man. Mine's now." He sat still, thinking, and after a while a chuckle waggled the ends of his mustache. "Not so bad at figures after all," he said, and slipped out of the bunk and dressed himself in his town clothes. He looked down at himself and snorted and pulled the town clothes off and made himself neat as he could in his old jeans and flannel shirt.

He stopped by the door to pick up his axe, changed his mind and took the hand whetstone instead. He started toward the center of the town and then swung along the road the woman had walked each way morning and evening coming to his place, and after a while he saw it, the unpainted two-room shack with rips showing in the tar-papered roof. A sagging small barn was at one side and two gaunt draft horses were in a makeshift corral behind it.

Cooter studied the place in the early morning light. He sniffed the air. "Spring all right," he said. "Plowing time for them's got a mind for farming." He went to the sagging barn and around it to a pile of old wood. There was a rusty axe on the ground still wet from the night rain. He picked it up and felt the blade. "Just like a woman," he said, and went to work with his whetstone till he had an edge that could slice a hair of his mustache. He pulled wood off the pile and began cutting it into stove lengths. He was swinging the axe steady when he noticed the woman standing by the corner of the barn and staring at him. He stopped chopping and leaned on the axe.

"Morning, Mrs. Moser, ma'am," he said. "Nice morning."

"Maybe it's a nice morning," she said, "and maybe it isn't and I don't care what it is because I don't mean to tell you I'll not have you snooping around here and trying to make me owing to you."

"Me that's owing," said Cooter, taking a deep breath.

"Forgot back there you paid for a bag of flour when you got the barrel. Two dollars you paid. Means two dollars you're overpaid now. Figure to pay that back cutting wood. Twenty-five cents each morning for cutting a day's supply. Stubborn as you on things like that."

The woman stared at him, and then the bumps were forming on her chin. "Just like the man you are," she said, "to be finding ways to make fun of a woman that pays her bills and tries to get along best she can, and even so if maybe it's you that's owing it's silly with charging things back and forth all the time we might never be out straight and somebody'd always be owing somebody."

Cooter's head came up straight and his mustache sat out stiff. "That be so bad?" he said. "Always doing things for each other, I mean."

She stared at him and her chin began to quiver, and she tried to speak, but the words would not come, and Cooter swung the axe solid into a chunk of wood and left it there and faced her square on.

"Agnes," he said, "through talking about barrels and owing and getting things paid. Talking now like a man that's found his woman and aims to know will she have him."

He looked at her, and she looked at him, and her voice when it came was so low he could scarce hear it. "Babes," she said. "I've got two babes."

"What's wrong with babes?" said Cooter. "Grow up to be people, don't they?"

She looked at him a long moment and her chin stopped quivering and the pleasant wrinkles by her eyes showed plain. "Cooter," she said, "that's no christened name. What's it really?"

Cooter James sighed into his mustache. "Courtney," he said.

The woman looked at him, and she smiled just a little, and her voice was as soft and tender as one of her biscuits. "I think I'll call you Cooter," she said. "I like Cooter best."

CAT NIPPED

The Tale of a Valuable Cat

CORPORAL CLINT BUCKNER ambled slowly across the flat baked surface of what would some day be the parade ground of Fort McKay. He carried a stubby cavalry carbine in the crook of his left elbow and patted the stock affectionately with his right hand as he walked. The hot Kansas sun beat full strength upon him and upon the double row of tents that flanked one side of the level space and upon the three sod-walled structures that stretched at a right angle to mark another side. The sun beat with equal untiring fervor upon the sweating bodies of Sergeant Peattie and a crew of half-naked privates piling strips of sod one on another for the walls of the first of the structures that would line the third side.

Corporal Clint ambled in a slow curve to pass near Sergeant Peattie and his sweating crew. He paused to yawn and wipe imaginary dust from the carbine and ambled on. The dripping privates stopped their work to watch him move past.

"Ain't he the brave hunter, toting that big gun."

"Takes nerve to go after those critters like he does."

"Yep. Turrible dangerous when wounded."

Chuckles and a climbing guffaw disturbed the afternoon quiet. Corporal Clint paid no attention to them. "Envy makes a mighty strong poison," he remarked to no one in particular. He ambled on and to the doorway of the middle of the three sod-walled structures and into the shaded interior.

Outside the sun beat down with steady glare. Inside Corporal Clint widened his eyes to look through the relatively cool dimness. He stood in a semblance of attention and raised his right hand in a limp salute. Angled across from him in a corner Lieutenant Henley, acting commissary officer, was perched on a stool using an upturned packing box as a desk. Lieutenant Henley waggled a hand in what could have been a languid salute or a mere greeting and returned to pencil-figuring on a piece of wrapping paper. Corporal Clint perched himself on another stool with his back to the wall where he could look along the rough ground-floored aisle between two long piles of grain in bags. He set the carbine across his knees.

Partway down the aisle between the grain bags a prairie mouse crept out and into the open and darted back and crept out again. Corporal Clint raised the carbine and aimed with casual ease and fired. There was a smudge on the ground where the mouse had been. Over in his corner Lieutenant Henley looked up. Corporal Clint nodded at him. Lieutenant Henley reached with his pencil and made a mark beside many other marks on a piece of paper tacked to the side of his box desk. He sighed and returned to his figuring. Corporal Clint took out of a pocket a linen cartridge holding its lead ball and powder and reloaded the carbine. He inspected the percussion cap. He set the carbine on his knees and watched the aisle in quiet content.

Outside the sun beat down upon the laboring soldiers. Inside was shaded silence punctured only by the occasional sharp blast of the carbine and the sighs and some soft new anguished grunts from Lieutenant Henley. Corporal Clint smiled drowsily to himself. A mouse slipped into view. Corporal Clint raised the carbine.

"Stop that infernal racket!"

Corporal Clint jumped to his feet. He snapped to attention. Off in his corner Lieutenant Henley did the same. Captain McKay stood in the doorway mopping his face and peering into the dimness.

"How's a man to get a report written or even take a nap wondering when that damn thing's going off again?" Captain McKay waved Corporal Clint aside and sat on the stool by the wall and stretched out his legs. "An infernal nuisance."

"You're right, sir." Lieutenant Henley came forward with his paper in his hand. "And useless, sir. Utterly and completely useless."

"Yes?"

"Well, sir, I've been doing some figuring." Lieutenant Henley's voice was weighty with overtones of awe.

"According to that animal book these damn mice have four to ten young ones at a time and it only takes them six weeks to have them. Worse than that, they start breeding soon as they're six weeks old." Lieutenant Henley sighed and stared down in somber fascination at his paper. "Well, sir, you take a middle figure for that litter number to be on the safe side and you just say only half each litter is females and you say again only half those females live to breeding age and all the same starting with just one pair after ten generations you've got close to half a million of those damn mice ruining my commissary and all of them busy breeding when they're not eating and they're averaging about a bag of grain a day already and making holes in all the bags. They're multiplying fifty times faster than Buckner here could kill them if he was triplets and every one of him as good a shot."

Captain McKay mopped his face again. "A formidable enemy, the way you put it."

"Beg pardon, sir, but it's no joke." Lieutenant Henley waggled his piece of paper. "We'll run short of feed for the horses and they're getting into our own provisions. We could try wooden bins but we can't get any good wood out on this damned prairie and they'd gnaw through it anyway. I just don't know what to do."

"Cats," said Corporal Clint.

Captain McKay slumped in his chair and drummed fingers on the onetime kitchen table that was his desk. From behind the hanging canvas partition that marked off his one-room living quarters in the same sod-walled building came a soft melodic humming and other small bustly noises as his wife moved about engaged in some incomprehensible feminine activity. The humming annoyed him. Two months they had been out here on the empty prairie creating an Army post out of next to nothing with supplies always short and no new appropriation to draw on for things needed and he didn't even have decent quarters for her yet because he was an old-line Army fool who believed in taking good care of his men first and still she was cheerful and could hum silly tunes and never once complain. By rights she ought to complain. And because she wouldn't, he couldn't, not even in the bosom, so to speak, of his own family and had to go on pretending to be a noble soul who enjoyed hardship for the sake of duty nobly done.

His fingers stopped drumming and he looked down again at the canceled requisition that had been returned in the fortnightly mail. Clipped to it was a note in vigorous handwriting:

> Mac — Lucky I caught this before it went any higher. Cats! You're starting a post out there not a blooming menagerie. Next thing you'll be asking for slippers and dressing gowns and a squad of nursemaids.

The chair squeaked as he shifted his weight. "Nursemaids," he muttered. "I'll nursemaid that jackass when I see him again. Even if he does outrank me."

The finger-drumming began again. It stopped short as Captain McKay realized he was keeping time with the humming from behind the partition. He stood up and strode to the doorway and looked out where his sweating sod crews were raising the walls of the second barracks. "Buckner!" he bellowed. He saw the solid chunky figure of Corporal Clint Buckner turn and start toward him and he swung back to his table desk.

The side edge of the canvas partition folded back and the cheerful face of Mrs. McKay appeared around it. "You be nice to that boy. He found me some more flowers this morning."

"Boy?" said Captain McKay. "He's seen thirty years if a day. Spent most of them doing things a boy wouldn't. Or shouldn't. I don't mean picking flowers."

Sweat gleamed on the broad face and dripped from the broad chin and rolled in little streams down the bare peeling chest of Corporal Clint as he came to attention before the table desk. Not even the heat had wilted the jaunty manner that often stirred in Captain McKay brief memories of his own cocksure youth. "Rest," said Captain McKay and Corporal Clint relaxed all over and began to appreciate the shaded interior of the room.

Captain McKay clasped his hands behind his head with his elbows flung wide. He noted that the canvas hung undisturbed but there was no humming behind it. He noted too the wary what's-coming-now look on Corporal Clint's face. "Buckner," he said. "How many times have you been busted and had to earn that stripe all over again?"

"Not so often, sir. Only about four times, sir."

"And how many times have you been in line for a sergeantcy and missed it for some damnfoolishness or other?"

Corporal Clint had the tone pegged now. His face exploded in a grin. "Reckon I've lost count on that, sir. But I'll make it yet."

"Maybe," said Captain McKay. "At least I'm giving you a chance. I'm giving you ten days and fifteen dollars and telling you to go find me some cats. Go easy on the money. It's coming out of my own pocket. My guess is there ain't a cat yet in the whole of Kansas Territory. But it was your notion and now you're stuck with it. You bring me some cats and the other stripe's yours."

Corporal Clint Buckner woke with the first light of dawn through the open doorway of the dugout. He lay on a thin matting of straw on the dirt floor of this one place that offered any accommodations at all for thirty miles in either direction along the wagon trace outside. He was not alone. His host, a beard-matted trader, was snoring two feet away. A pair of lank and odorous mule skinners lay like logs on the other side of the doorway. And the straw had a moving multitude of its own inhabitants.

Corporal Clint sat up and ruffled bits of straw out of his hair. Four of his ten days and a large part of the fifteen dollars were gone. It was time to start looking for cats in earnest. He had covered considerable territory already and made casual inquiries but there had been no pressure in the search. Two whole days he had wasted in the one settlement within a hundred miles of the post. Well, not exactly wasted. The settlement boasted no cat but it did boast a pert waitress at the false-fronted building called a hotel. She had slapped him the first time he kissed her. She had forgotten to slap the second time. He might have been there yet if her husband had

not come home with a wagonload of potatoes and tur-
nips and a positive itch to lambast anyone interested in
her. Corporal Clint had no aversion to fighting, any
place and any time, but it was against his principles to
fight husbands.

Outside by the well he stripped himself bare and
sloshed himself thoroughly with several buckets of
water. While his skin dried in the early morning air he
conducted a careful search through his clothes to elim-
inate any visitors from the straw. "Wouldn't want to
kidnap any of these critters," he said. "Now if they
were only cats . . ."

Dressed again, he caught his horse in the small-pole
corral by the dugout and saddled and started off. He
was traveling light in boots and pants and shirt and hat.
His saddleroll consisted of a blanket, a razor, and an
empty grain bag with a few holes punched near the top.
He had a vague notion of carrying any cats he might
collect in the bag. His armament consisted of a standard
cavalry pistol in a snap-shut holster on his left hip and
the cherished carbine in a saddle scabbard. He had a
long day's route mapped in his mind to cover the far-
scattered squatters' roosts and ranch stations within a
wide radius.

The welcome slight coolness of evening found Corporal Clint Buckner atop a long rolling ridge that gave
him a view of several hundred square miles of catless
Kansas. He was a tired and downcast man. As usual the
more tired and downcast he was, the more determined
he became. "Legwork won't do it," he said. "Like hunting a needle in a hell of a big haystack without even

knowing a needle's there. This calls for heavy thinking."

He dismounted and let the horse graze while he studied the problem. There were several villages of friendly Indians within reaching distance but Indians didn't have cats. They likely wouldn't even know what a cat was. Only white settlers who might bring them from back east would ever have cats. At that only a few would do it. Cats weren't good travelers like dogs. They had to be carried in the wagons and were a nuisance. They wandered off and were left behind or got lost or some bigger animals made meals of them. But settlers offered the only possible chance. New settlers, those fresh out from back east a ways.

In the cool of the dark Corporal Clint dismounted and picketed his horse. He was ten miles farther south near the deepening road ruts of the main route of the emigrant wagon trains heading farther west to pick up the Santa Fe Trail. He lay quiet, rolled in his blankets, and watched the nearly full moon rise over the left-hand ridge. "Just one of the scratching little brutes," he said, "and I'll make the old man give me that stripe."

Refreshed and jaunty in the morning sun, Corporal Clint rode along beside the wagon ruts. As he rode he hummed a small wordless tune. He had breakfast with an emigrant family, exchanging advice on the best route ahead for his food and edging around at last to the subject in hand. "Cats?" said the man. "Why sure, we had one. Coyote got it two days back."

Corporal Clint rode on, jauntier than before. "On the right track now," he said. He began humming again and after a while his small tune had words.

I'm hunting a feline critter
Some people call a cat.
To me any day it's a sergeant's pay —
A new feather in my hat.

Ten hours, seventy miles, three wagon trains, and two
ranch stations later, no longer jaunty, Corporal Clint
dismounted by a small stream and unsaddled before he
led the horse to the water. There were several hours of
daylight left but the horse was done for the day. He
could have pushed it farther but he had the true cavalry-
man's respect for his mount. He fastened the picket
rope and sat on a slight rise near the stream and chewed
on the sandwiches he had collected at his last stop.
"There ain't a cat between here and Missouri," he said.
"Wonder if a gelded skunk might do."

He finished the sandwiches and plucked a blade of
grass and chewed this long and thoughtfully. Far to the
east along the rutted trail a small dust cloud rose and
grew and drifted in the freshening breeze. It came closer,
always renewed, and beneath it and moving in it were
men on horseback and oxteams straining into yokes to
pull a motley collection of wagons. They came closer
and swung past in an arc to line up and stop along the
bank of the stream.

Corporal Clint chewed on his grass blade and watched
the wagons swing past. The third wagon was driven by
a faded woman in a faded sunbonnet and beside her on
the seat sat a brighter, sharper-colored copy with no
sunbonnet to cramp a tumbled glory of dark brown hair.
Corporal Clint forgot to chew and stared at this second
woman. "Man alive," he said, "that's a mighty attractive

sight." He leaned forward and stared some more. "Yes, sir," he said. "Without any argufying or equivocating whatsomever that's the most attractive sight I ever sighted." The woman had seen him on his knoll and had turned to look at him as the wagon swung past. Curled in her lap was a cat.

Corporal Clint Buckner was helpful to have around. He helped the man unyoke the third wagon and water the oxen and picket them along with the man's horse by some good grass. He was expert at finding buffalo chips for the fire in places overlooked by previous overnight campers. And he was a contagious and shrewd talker. By time cooking smells were drifting around he had adequate information in hand. The man and the faded woman, his wife, were headed for California. The other woman was the wife's sister. Her name was Ellen. The cat belonged to her and it was a damn nuisance too. The man didn't think much of this sister business. She was too independent and she thought she knew all there was to know and she made too much fuss over animals and she was another mouth to feed, but his wife had nagged him into letting her come along.

Corporal Clint squatted on his heels and sniffed the cooking smells. "Why sure, ma'am," he said to the faded woman, "I've only had four meals so far today so of course I'll join you. Ain't often I get me real woman's cooking."

Corporal Clint squatted on his heels by the stream bank and watched the sister rinsing off the dishes. "Miss Ellen," he said, "that cat must be a trouble to you on a jaunt like this. If you're so minded I'd do you the favor of taking it off your hands. Give it a nice home at my quarters."

Corporal Clint leaned against a wagon wheel and looked down at Miss Ellen on a stool plying a needle with knowing skill. "Tell you what," he said, "I always was seven kinds a fool. I'll give you a dollar for that cat."

Corporal Clint stood straight and solid and indignant and glared at Miss Ellen shaking out blankets before making up beds under the wagon. He calculated what remained in his pocket. "Miss Ellen," he said, "you're the obstinatest female I ever met. That cat's just a scrawny, mangy, piebald sort of thing. But I'll give you four dollars and thirty-seven cents for it."

Miss Ellen faced him, not as solid but just as indignant. "Mr. Soldier. That's a good healthy cat and you're a mangy sort of thing to say it isn't. I've told you and told you it's not for sale. It's my cat. It stays with me. It goes where I go. Now you go do some soldiering and stop bothering me."

Corporal Clint lay sleepless in his blanket on his knoll and watched the almost full moon climb the sky. "Could sneak down there now they're asleep," he said. "Nab the critter, leave the money, make some tracks." The moon climbed higher. "No," he said. "Can't do that to a woman." He lay on one side for a while and then on the other and the ground seemed uncommonly hard. "If I'm going to get places in this damned army," he said, "I got to get started soon. I need that stripe." The moon arched overhead and started its downward sweep and still his eyes remained open. "So it goes where she goes," he said. "Got to keep that in mind." He squirmed on the ground and sat up and hunted under the blanket and removed a small stone and lay quiet again. "Awful lot to ask of a man," he said, "just to get hold of a cat." The moon dropped toward the horizon and he began figuring the time he had left. Four days. One would be needed for the return to the post. Three days. Nights too. It would work out about right. In that time, the way the train was headed, it would be close to a meeting with the regular mail wagon bound for the post. "Shucks," he said. "She's unattached and she's a woman. That's plenty of time. Even got me a full moon coming on schedule."

In the early light of morning Miss Ellen held fast to the handle of a bucket of water as Corporal Clint Buckner tried to take it from her. "I'm quite capable of carrying this myself. And if you say one word about my cat I'll dump this water right over your grinning head."

"Cat?" said Corporal Clint. "Oh, you mean that pet of yours. Shucks, ma'am, I was only pretending to be interested in that cat trying to please you, you're so fond of it. Took one look at you coming along in that wagon and haven't been able to think of a thing else ever since but trying to please you."

Corporal Clint Buckner was very helpful to have around. He was on hand wherever help was needed along the wagon line, particularly in the neighborhood of the third wagon. Neither heat nor dust dimmed his cheerfulness. He knew the best camping places. He knew every kink in the trail and a cutoff that saved ten miles. He rode away across the prairie and out of sight and Miss Ellen watched him go with a speculative look in her eyes. He rode back with the carcass of an antelope over the withers of his horse and Miss Ellen watched him come back with a half-smile on her lips and found her hands fussing with her hair. Corporal Clint knew his way around in many ways. Walking with her in the moonlight he wasted no time talking about cats.

In the relative cool of approaching evening Corporal Clint stood by the unyoked wagon and watched Miss Ellen and her sister making antelope stew. He felt a familiar warning prickling on his skin and looked down the arc of bedded wagons and saw two men coming toward him, the two men, youngish and healthy and hefty in the shoulders, who herded the milk cows and spare oxen that tagged the train. He had the notion from the way they had looked at him now and again that their opinion of him was not flattering. They were looking at him now and their forward tread was full of purpose.

"Soldier," said the first one, "me and Bert been talking about you. We been watching you. We don't like it. We decided a couple weeks back Miss Ellen was going to have one of us and she'd have to pick which when we get where we're going. We decided now it's time you —"

"Oh-h-h-h," said Miss Ellen. "I guess I have something to say about that."

No one paid any attention to her, not even Corporal Clint. He was inspecting the two men and his eyes were beginning to brighten.

"That's right," said Bert. "We just don't like it.

Three days you been hanging around Miss Ellen. Last night was my night and night before was Jeb's but when we come looking she wasn't around. She was gallivanting off with you somewheres. We decided you better start traveling."

"Well, well," said Corporal Clint. "Ain't it too bad I don't feel any traveling urge."

"We decided mebbe you wouldn't," said Bert. "We decided we'd just have to give it to you."

They stepped forward. Corporal Clint stepped to meet them. With a grin on his face and a gleam of joy in his eyes Corporal Clint moved into battle. He bent low and drove his broad head like a cannonball into Bert's middle and straightened and swung to work on Jeb with experienced fists. Bert rolled on the ground and groaned.

"Oh-h-h-h," said Miss Ellen and ran to bend over Bert, "you poor man. Did he break your ribs?"

Corporal Clint heard. He saw. His blows began to go wild. They missed Jeb entirely or when they hit they no longer carried a powerful jolt. He winced when Jeb struck him and began to retreat. Jeb rushed at him, hot with encouragement, and Bert struggled to his feet and gulped in air and plunged to join Jeb. Together they battered Corporal Clint. The air hummed with sweeping fists. Corporal Clint went down. He groaned. He staggered to his feet. He went down again. His groan was a plaintive and appealing sound. His body twitched and was still.

"Oh-h-h-h," said Miss Ellen. She stood beside his prone body and smacked at Bert and Jeb with her words. "You cowards! Two of you beating him!"

Bert and Jeb stepped backward. "Why, Miss Ellen," said Jeb. "We just decided —"

"Who cares what you decided?" said Miss Ellen. "I hate the sight of both of you. You get away from here and back with those cows which is just about all you're fit to associate with." As Bert and Jeb retired in confusion she ran to the wagon and dipped a cloth in the water bucket and ran back to raise Corporal Clint's limp head with one hand and wipe off his bruised dusty face with the other. Corporal Clint opened his eyes. "You have such nice hands," he said and groaned again, a small satisfied groan, and closed his eyes.

Half an hour later, limping painfully, Corporal Clint edged around the wagon. Out of sight behind it, he strode off toward the rear of the line of wagons. The limp disappeared and he strode with purposeful stride. He found Bert and Jeb squatted by a fire downing third cups of coffee in sullen discouragement. "Stand up, boys," he said. "We'll take up now where we left off." With a grin on his bruised face and a gleam of joy in his half-closed eyes Corporal Clint moved into battle. Seven minutes later he looked down upon Bert and Jeb reclining dazed and much more discouraged on the ground. "Take a bit of advice," he said. "Don't go deciding to interfere with the Army again." He strode back the way he had come behind the line of wagons and as he went the limp began once more and became more pronounced with each step and as he limped he caroled his small tune to himself with new words.

> I found me a feline critter —
> A lady's personal pet.

Goes where she goes but I'm one knows
It won't be hard to get.

Walking with Miss Ellen in the moonlight he endured
his limp with gallant fortitude. It forced him to lean
some on her for support and to put an arm over her
shoulders.

The light mail wagon rolled steadily over the prairie.
Fifty yards ahead the escort, two privates and a lance
corporal, trotted steadily forward and with them, happy
at freedom from constant sitting on a board seat, trotted
the regular driver astride Corporal Clint Buckner's horse.
In the wagon, jaunty and cheerful with the reins in his
hands, sat Corporal Clint and behind him, between the
mailbag and a box, was a woman's trunk and beside him
sat Miss Ellen and curled in her lap was the cat.

The miles slipped away under the wheels. "Clint,"
said Miss Ellen, "my head's been in such a whirl I didn't
think before. Is there a preacher at the post?"

"Preacher?" said Corporal Clint. "Whatever for?"

"Why, to marry us, silly."

"Shucks," said Corporal Clint. "We don't need a
preacher. The old man, that's the captain, he's got authority to do the job tight and even better."

"A military ceremony!" said Miss Ellen. "That'll be
fun. Will they cross swords for us?"

"Sabers," said Corporal Clint. "I ain't a commissioned
officer so it won't be too fancy."

More miles slipped away. "Clint," said Miss Ellen,
"you're a sergeant, aren't you? You said so. But there's
only one stripe on your sleeve."

"Well, I am," said Corporal Clint, not quite as jaunty as before. "In a manner of speaking I am. I mean I will be when I get back there."

"Oh," said Miss Ellen. "You're being promoted you mean. I knew you'd be the kind of man who gets promotions. What did you do to get this one?"

"Shucks," said Corporal Clint, "nothing much. Just a little special duty." He began to notice that it was a hot and dusty day.

They stopped for a midday meal and to rest the horses. Corporal Clint strutted some giving orders because he was the ranking man present but his voice lacked its usual confident clip. He chewed in a strange silence, very thoughtful. The cat wandered about forty feet away, intent on its own individual business. Corporal Clint leaped to his feet and raced to grab it and bring it back. He smiled weakly at Miss Ellen. "Dangerous country," he said. "Coyotes and things around."

They drove forward again and Corporal Clint was restless on the wagon seat. Miss Ellen did not notice. She had missed most of her sleep the night before and the slight swaying of the wagon as it rolled easily along the trace among the grass tufts made her drowsy. She pulled his right arm about her and snuggled close and rested her head, half dozing, on his shoulder. Corporal Clint could feel her hair blowing softly against his cheek in the breeze of their movement and his shirt suddenly felt too small around his chest and this was very nice hair brushing his cheek and he knew he should be pleased but he was too bothered by troublesome thoughts to appreciate the pleasure.

The miles dropped away beneath the hooves and the

wheels and they came to a shallow stream and splashed into it. The front wheel on Corporal Clint's side hit a stone and rose up on it tilting the wagon. Miss Ellen slid on the seat squealing and clutching at him and the cat tumbled out of her lap into the water. Corporal Clint yanked on the reins and dropped them and scrambled past Miss Ellen to follow the cat. He landed on all fours in the eight inches of water and scrabbled about in it and rose dripping with the cat in his arms.

"Good grief!" said Miss Ellen. "You didn't even bother about me but just that cat."

"Might have been a pool over on this side," said Corporal Clint, trying to smile at her and failing. "Might have been real deep water."

"Silly," said Miss Ellen. "Maybe cats don't like water but they can swim all right if they have to. Well, I suppose it's nice you worrying so about that cat just because I like it so. I hope you don't catch the sniffles now."

"It ain't sniffles I'm worried about catching," said Corporal Clint.

The afternoon sun was low on the left as the mail wagon topped the last swell of the prairie that gave a clear view of the beginnings of Fort McKay in the distance. "That's it," said Corporal Clint Buckner with little of a prospective bridegroom's joy in his voice. His eyes brightened. "Maybe I'd better get on my horse and hurry on in ahead to sort of prepare the way some."

"And leave me?" said Miss Ellen. "I think we should drive in together. I want to see how surprised everyone is, too. And don't worry what I'll think about how you behave. I know you have to salute and stand at attention and things like that."

The escort dropped respectfully to the rear to tail the wagon in. Corporal Clint's face grew pale as he saw they had been sighted coming and the entire personnel of the post was assembling for a good view. It grew paler as he saw that Captain McKay, contrary to custom at this hour, was not in his quarters but was standing outside with Mrs. McKay beside him. Corporal Clint sighed. Then he straightened on the seat and snapped back his shoulders and cocked his head at a jaunty angle. He urged the team into a faster trot. He pulled up close to Captain McKay with a flourish and jumped to the ground. His salute was a gesture of swift and precise perfection. "Reporting for duty, sir. Right on the tenth day, sir. Brought a young lady with me, sir, who has done me the honor of consenting to become my wife, sir. With your permission of course, sir. I'm asking for same now, sir. And to perform the ceremony yourself, sir. As soon as —"

"But —" said Captain McKay. "But — but —"

"Awfully sudden, sir," said Corporal Clint. "But it had to be that way. Begging your pardon, sir, but I can report later. Bring her around for official introduction later too, sir. Really ought to be fixing her some quarters right away, sir. It's been a long drive. And dusty. She'll want to rest first, sir, and clean up some before a formal meeting. If you'll just let me have a tent, sir, I can fix —"

"But —" said Captain McKay. "But — but I sent you out to get some cats."

"Oh-h-h-h-h-h," said Miss Ellen.

"I told you I'd report later, sir." Corporal Clint had taken another breath. "Explain everything then, sir. I've done my duty. Done the best I could, sir. Things kind of happened and turned out this way. All for the best all around, sir. If you'll just let me have a tent —"

"Shut up!" bellowed Captain McKay. "I don't know what particular breed of devilment you've pulled this time but I know it's all of a piece with past behavior. Send you out with orders to find some cats and you come back bringing another woman to this Godforsaken place that ain't fit —"

"But she's got a cat, sir," said Corporal Clint.

"Oh-h-h-h," said Miss Ellen. "So that's why you were so interested in my cat! And jumping after it all the time without caring what happened to me! Talking about marrying just to trick me into coming here so maybe you could steal it!"

"I did not," said Corporal Clint. "That's not right. That's —"

"I hate you," said Miss Ellen. "I just plain utterly despise you. Taking me away from the only folks I had and making it all sound so nice when it isn't at all. I wouldn't marry you now even if — well, I just wouldn't — I wouldn't —" Suddenly Miss Ellen was crying and she was ashamed to be crying in front of a group of startled and embarrassed men and she put her head down in her arms and the cat slipped out of her lap and retreated over the seat into the rear of the wagon and she was sitting there with her shoulders shaking.

"Humph!" snorted Mrs. McKay. "A fine mess you men've made now. But then you always do. Where a woman's concerned anyway. Yelling at each other.

Blathering about cats. A nice lovely girl like that too." She marched to the wagon and cooed soft reassurances at Miss Ellen and helped her down from the seat. In a silence made ominous by the expression on Captain McKay's face she led Miss Ellen into the captain's quarters. They disappeared from sight.

"Buckner," said Captain McKay. His tone was mild and deadly. "You have committed so damn many offenses under the military code from the moment you started yapping at me before I gave you permission to speak that I won't even try to list them now. God only knows what devilish things you've been doing while you were gone but I intend to find out. You're under arrest. Go to your quarters and stay there till I decide what to do with you. While you're there improve your time taking that stripe off your sleeve."

Captain McKay wiped his forehead and turned to go inside and face Mrs. McKay and Miss Ellen. Surrounded by his fellows and a babble of jeering and commiserating and even envious voices, Corporal Clint moved toward the double row of tents. The mail escort rode forward and one of them dismounted and climbed to the wagon seat to drive it over by the stable. "Wait a moment," said Lieutenant Henley, pushing out from the shade of one of the sod-walled buildings. He leaned over the backboard of the wagon and reached inside and lifted out the cat.

Private Clint Buckner sat on a three-legged stool in the end tent of the front row facing the stretch of level ground that would some day be the parade ground and stared out into the morning sun. Somehow it was hotter under the canvas than it would have been outside under the open sun with a sod crew. The heat was personal, oppressive, made so by the silence, the solitude of that particular corner of the post, and his complete ignorance of what was happening in Captain's McKay's quarters and adjacent areas.

He twisted on his stool to get a better view. Across the way there was a flurry of unusual activity. Sergeant Peattie appeared with a squad of fast-stepping privates carrying various things and walking beside him, pert and chipper with her dark brown hair a tumbled glory about her head, was Miss Ellen. Private Clint could see that Sergeant Peattie was unusually neat and natty and was strutting to good effect and barking orders with obvious relish. The squad stopped and began to erect a tent almost exactly opposite the one in which Private Clint sat in his solitude and close to the bend in the lazy almost-dried-up little river that ran alongside the post. The tent went up quickly and was pegged tight. Into it went a cot, a chair, a washstand made of a box set on end with a cloth covering the open side, and Miss Ellen's trunk.

The squad was gone. Even Sergeant Peattie, who had lingered long, was gone. The flaps of the newly erected tent were closed. "Can't any more than shoot me," said Private Clint. He crawled under the rear canvas of his tent and set off on a wide circuit, bent low and crawling at times, taking advantage of all possible cover. He came up behind Miss Ellen's tent. He lifted its rear canvas and poked his head under. "Good morning, ma'am."

Miss Ellen was busy at her trunk. She jumped around, startled. She stared at the broad face peering up turtle-wise. "Oh, it's you," she said.

"It's me all right," said Private Clint. He crawled the rest of the way under and perched himself on the chair. "I'm mighty peeved too. If you'd only had sense enough to keep your yap shut —"

"Mr. Buckner," said Miss Ellen, "all I have to do is yell and you'll be —"

"Go ahead and yell," said Private Clint. "Another charge or two won't mean much to me now. I want to know what the hell and-I-won't-ask-pardon-for-that-either is going on over here."

"Why, Mr. Buckner," said Miss Ellen, very sweetly. "I don't know as you have any right to know but I'll tell you. Everybody's being so nice to me. That Lieutenant Henley's taking good care of my cat and he says it's just a marvelous mouser. And this tent is all my own and I'm to have a better place soon as more buildings are up and it'll be fixed real nice and I'm to be the officers' laundress and have my meals with the McKays and get right good pay too."

Private Clint groaned. He tried to make his voice plaintive. "But what about me?"

"You?" said Miss Ellen. "I don't know as that's any concern of mine. I have myself to worry about, seeing as you got me in such a fix. I think I'm doing right well." Miss Ellen reached up and fluffed her hair. "Maybe you've not noticed, being a man, but that Sergeant Peattie is a fine-looking man himself."

"Peattie," moaned Private Clint. "You watch out for him, I've been on leaves with him and I'm telling you —"

"He's told me plenty about you," said Miss Ellen. "Now I remember what he's told me I think it's time you crawled out of here and stayed away."

"Shucks," said Private Clint. "Peattie always did stretch things too far. How about you remembering those nights when the moon —"

"I will not!" Miss Ellen stamped one foot and glared at him. "You get out of here now or I really will yell!"

"Damn woman," muttered Private Clint as he crawled under the canvas. "Always being so damn womanish." The last he saw before he let the canvas drop and departed on his return circuit was Miss Ellen standing straight and glaring at him and prettier than he'd remembered her all through the previous night. What he did not see and what Mrs. McKay did see five minutes later, as she pushed through the tent flaps with her arms laden with blankets and a mirror, was Miss Ellen slumped on the chair and crying.

Captain McKay stomped into his office hot and dusty from his afternoon jaunt to inspect his work crews at their labors. For an instant he thought he had been hearing voices from behind the canvas partition as he entered but now there was no sound. He listened. A soft melodic humming began and he relaxed. His wife indulged in that silly humming only when she was alone. He sat behind his table desk and wiped dust from his face. The canvas partition folded back at the front edge and Mrs. McKay's face appeared around it followed by the rest of her.

"Mac," she said, "you've left that Buckner boy sweating in that tent and wondering what you're going to do all last night and most of today. Don't you think it's time you had him over here to speak up for himself?"

"Speak up?" said Captain McKay. "He spoke up so

confounded much yesterday I've a mind to let him squat over there the rest of the summer. If we were back anywhere near civilization and he behaved like that and I didn't have his hide there's plenty other officers'd think I was losing my grip."

Mrs. McKay simply looked at her husband and smiled a small smile. "Oh, I know," he said. "We're way out here the end of nowhere and I'm top dog and I can do about anything I damn well please. So I'm just letting him sit there a while meditating on his sins. It'll do him good."

"Mac," said Mrs. McKay, "he's the only one out here, yourself included, ever thought to find me flowers. He's talked a girl you've been making sheep's eyes at yourself into coming here to marry him and now he's talked himself under arrest and into having her think mighty small of him. Sometimes I think you're not the same man I married twenty-too-many years ago." The canvas partition folded back again and Mrs. McKay disappeared behind it.

Captain McKay sat still, drumming his fingers and remembering many things. He rose and went to the doorway and out a short distance. "Buckner!" he bellowed across the level space and remembered bellowing that same name in that same voice when he and his command were pinned down in small scattered groups in a dry stream bed by many times their own number of hostile Indians and he needed a man who might be just reckless enough and tough enough to get through with a message for reinforcements. The thought flashed through his mind that likely he'd be bellowing that same name again when the settlers his post and others were supposed to protect began coming in real numbers to populate the Territory and the Indians got worried again about losing their lands and made trouble. He returned and sat again behind his table desk and made himself look stern and official.

Private Clint Buckner stood before him with that what's-coming-now look on his face.

"Buckner," said Captain McKay, "how much of my fifteen dollars have you got left?"

"Four dollars and thirty-seven cents, sir."

Captain McKay thumped a fist on the table. "Better'n ten dollars gone and you didn't spend a nickel on cats. I've heard the girl's story. By rights I ought to skin you alive and hang your hide out to dry. Maybe I will yet. First I want you to tell me how you got yourself in such a fool fix."

"Well, sir," said Private Clint, "you wanted cats. I couldn't find cats. Well, sir, I found one and it was attached to that Miss Ellen woman and she wouldn't sell it. I figured the only way to get it here was get her here. I figured the only way to get her here was to marry her. You're a man, sir. You know how it is. It seemed a kind of good idea at the time."

"Damned if I do know how it is," said Captain McKay. "It's never crossed my mind to marry a woman to get a cat."

"That's only how it started, sir. More I saw of her the more I figured it was a good idea all by itself. She's a mighty attractive woman, sir."

"In a sort of way," said Captain McKay, conscious of Mrs. McKay behind the partition. "But she says it's plain you've been interested mostly in that cat all the time. Says you paid more attention to it coming here than to her. Says you were willing to about knock her out of the wagon to save that cat from a little water."

"That's all backwards," said Private Clint. "That cat gives me a pain just thinking of it. You see, sir, when we headed here I got to thinking. I got to thinking what a real chunk of woman she is. Nerve enough to leave that wagon train and the only folk she knew and go to a place she didn't know a thing about and take a chance on a cross-branded Army mule like me. That's my kind of woman, sir. I got to thinking the only way I'd ever keep up with her and take care of her the way I ought was being a sergeant. That's the cat. I had to keep it safe. You promised me if I —"

"So-o-o-o," said Captain McKay. "A hell of a soldier you are. Conducted your campaign without thinking through to the finish. Forgot till too late how your fine talk would sound to her when she found out about the cat. Walked right into what I'd call a verbal ambush. Now you've lost out all around. Lost the girl. Lost the sergeantcy. I distinctly told you cats. Plural. You brought just one."

The partition folded back and around it came Mrs. McKay. Behind her and moving up beside her came Miss Ellen. Miss Ellen's head was held high and her eyes were bright. "Captain McKay," she said, "that cat is cats." Miss Ellen blushed very prettily and looked at Private Clint and looked away and blushed even more prettily. "That cat had an — well, an affair with another cat back in Springfield when we came through. It won't be long now. She always has four or five at a time."

Captain McKay looked at Miss Ellen blushing so prettily. He looked at Private Clint Buckner, who was looking at Miss Ellen with his head at a jaunty angle and a grin on his broad face. He looked at Mrs. McKay, who was looking at him with that expectant expression that meant he had better do something and it had better be the right thing to do. He cleared his throat. "Sergeant Buckner, you will report back here directly after mess in the neatest uniform you can beg, borrow or steal around this post. You may regard the fifteen dollars as a wedding present. The ceremony will be at seven o'clock."

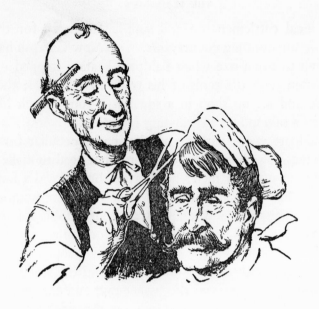

LEANDER FRAILEY

The Fabulous Barber of New Calypso

NEW CALYPSO was getting to be a real town when Bald-pate Frailey settled there. It wasn't tucked away so far in a corner of Nebraska that you couldn't find it on a map if you looked hard enough. On a big map. It bumped out with a fair quota of low buildings and squared-corner roads on each side of the railroad and twice a week a freight train stopped and when the station agent sold a ticket he could set the signals and one of the two-a-day one-each-way passenger trains would squeal to a halt instead of chugging straight through. The local farmers shipped there in harvest season and the local cattlemen too and supplies came in for the whole surrounding countryside. Yes, New Calypso had grown to town-size when Baldpate Frailey stepped off the train with the tools of his trade in a black leather valise and set up shop in a squat two-room shack between a saloon and a sprawling feedstore.

Baldpate was a barber. Maybe it was peculiar for a man without a hair on his own long thin head to make a living out of other men's head-crops, but he was a fair-to-middling barber who could trim your hair without nicking your ears and scrape away your stubble leaving most of the skin intact. His shop was on the wrong side of the tracks. Well, wrong side to some people. It was on the side with most of the saloons and the stockyard and the warehouse and the basket mill and the in-and-out squatters' shacks. It wasn't on the side with the saloon that had upstairs rooms to rent and called itself a hotel and the prosperous livery stable and the good retail stores and the solid respectable houses of the solid respectable townsfolk. That side already had a barber-shop that had already caught the fancy trade with its neatly painted pole out front and its big mirror behind the two chairs and its shiny brass spittoon that its proprietor called a cuspidor. Baldpate started with a makeshift chair that he could raise and lower with a wooden lever. He finally acquired a real barber chair second-hand out of Lincoln. He finally acquired a small mirror and a black-painted spittoon. But he couldn't compete with the other shop and he didn't try. He got the fringe trade, the men who worked on the same side of the tracks and an occasional cowboy nursing his nickels and trainmen stopping off and the squatters, who sometimes could pay and sometimes couldn't. He had to be content with that and he was. He didn't ask much out of life.

When Baldpate stepped off the train he wasn't alone. He had two boys with him, his sons, Leander and Greenberry. Leander was the older, already stretching long and thin in body and head with such a meager scraggly topknot of hair you could tell he wouldn't be wearing a man's pants long before he'd be bald as a bean. He took after his father. Greenberry was a pair of years younger, considerably shorter but plumper, with a waving tangle of hair that would have made a fine big floor mop. He must have taken after his mother, who had quietly checked out of the Frailey family and the whole of this world some years before.

The three of them lived in the back room of the shop. Baldpate did the barbering and Leander did the housekeeping and Greenberry did nothing. Nothing except eat hearty, wander around town with other boys, and sit lazy in the sun, which was what he liked best after the eating. Old Baldpate favored Greenberry, maybe because of that mop of hair, and was always telling Leander to take care of him and watch out for him. So naturally it was Leander not Greenberry who began to be snapping the shears at the chair in the afternoons when Baldpate grew tired and felt the arthritis creeping into his joints. And then one night along about the time the boys had their full growth Baldpate sat up on his cot in the dark and called across the little room, "Leander. You mind me now. You take care of your brother." And old Baldpate lay back down and rolled his head on the pillow and died.

You can forget about Baldpate Frailey now. He's not important to this story. He brought the family to New Calypso and started the family business and told Leander what to do and died and that's enough said about him. It's Leander and Greenberry we're interested in.

Leander first. He was a good boy, quiet and steady, so naturally he became a good man, quiet and steady still. The only thing unusual about his growing stage was the stretch he spent a lot of time drawing pictures with a thick surveyor's pencil he'd found somewhere, on any scrap of paper that came to hand. Nobody paid any attention to that. Nobody except Greenberry, who just looked and laughed and settled back to more lazing in the sun. But anyone who paid real attention might have noticed that Leander liked to draw heads, men's heads, with plenty of hair on them and sideburns and all kinds of mustaches and beards. Then he didn't have time for that because he was helping with the barbering as well as doing the housekeeping and then his father was dead and he had full-time barbering to keep him busy. He didn't need to draw heads after that. He had real ones to work with.

It wasn't long before folks on the wrong side of the tracks knew they had a prize barber there who wouldn't be worrisome about being paid on the dot as long as they brought him heavy manes of hair or thick crops of whiskers to be sheared. They gave him plenty of practice and by the time he had his techniques worked out it was a treat to be barbered by that Leander. He'd set you in that one chair and stand back and circle you slowly, studying your head from all around. Then he'd pick up the right tool and go to work. Sometimes it'd be the handclippers. He could do a whole handsome haircut with those clippers alone. Sometimes it'd be the heavy shears or again the light scissors or an alternating of them. Whatever it was, there'd be a wonderful snipping rhythm soothing about your ears. Leander had more than rhythm. He had positive melodies matching the work in hand. If your hair was coarse and strong, you'd hear a marching tune from the flying blades as the locks fell. If your hair was light and fluffy, you'd hear something like a delicate dance tune. His combing was right in time and his soft old brush with the powder on it would be dusting dainty about your neck at the exact second the cut tag ends of hair might be beginning to get itchy and threatening to slide down under your shirt. And when he'd lower the chairback and lather your face and take the right razor out of old Baldpate's box that had one marked for each day in the week, then you knew you were in the hands of a master. His razors were always so sharp the toughest whiskers surrendered without a struggle. His strokes were so deft you weren't certain you felt them. When he raised the chairback again and stepped away and circled you again, you sat still and waited for the verdict. Maybe he'd shake his head and snatch up his scissors and make a fresh attack on your hair or mustache or beard or even eyebrows and by that time you'd not even think of interfering because you knew that when he was finished you'd look better than you ever did before. Let him do it his way and Leander could make anybody look like somebody.

As good as his barbering, some people said, was the effect he had on his customers. He wasn't a talking barber and that marked him as different right away. He was usually so intent on the portrait he was making out of the raw material of features and hair and whiskers in his chair that he might not even hear you if you spoke to him. But if you listened closely you might hear him muttering to himself, not much and not often, just a few words now and then. "Interesting head to work on . . . now these are eyebrows . . . no sense hiding that chin," things like that. No matter how low and picayune you felt going into the shop, you had the feeling coming out that maybe the face you presented to the world had a point or two in its favor.

The first the folks on the right side of the tracks began to have some notion what had been developing over on the other side was when Osgood R. Buxton, proprietor of the Big Bargain Mercantile Establishment and president of the New Calypso Bank, was stranded there with a half hour to kill. The day had started bad for him. All through breakfast his wife had complained again about the wide drooping mustache that had taken him years to cultivate into the kind of upperlip canopy he thought impressive. "Makes you look like a seasick mastiff," she said and was so delighted at her comparison that he stomped out madder than usual. Then he went down to the freight office to check the shipment he was expecting and found it wasn't in and the train would be half an hour late. He stomped up and down the dirt street kicking at the dust, and the unfairness of it all hit him so hard he decided to strike back in some drastic way. Through the open door of Leander's shop he saw the barber chair empty and stomped in and planked himself in it. He took hold of his mustache with both hands. "Shave this damn thing off," he said.

Leander didn't pay any attention to the words. Leander was padding around him in a circle studying his head from all sides. Buxton slapped both hands on the chair arms. "You hear me?" he shouted. "I said shave this damn cookie duster off me!"

Leander focused on him as someone speaking. "No," Leander said. "It belongs there."

Buxton subsided with a blowing gurgle that waggled the mustache. "Belongs there?"

"Yes," Leander said. "It just needs a little pointing so it won't fight with your forehead."

"Fight with my forehead?" Buxton said in a small voice. He relaxed in the chair and a big piece of checkered cloth covered him up to the neck and was tied behind and a clipping rhythm began about his head and something like a cheery marching tune tickled his ears. When the cloth came off he stood up and peered into the little mirror. His hair had been thinned along the sides so suddenly it seemed thicker on top. His eyebrows had acquired a faintly quizzical air. His mustache was almost the same yet remarkably different. It had a slight upward twist suggestive of jauntiness without being aggressive and the side tips somehow pointed your glance upward to notice the broad forehead. The whole effect was that of a man who could do things in the world and was of consequence in his community. When he walked out the door Buxton was snapping his knees in long strides, and though the train was another half hour late he spent the time chatting cheerfully with the station agent and trying to catch the light right so he could see his reflection in a window.

With a beginning like that and a booster like Buxton only a few months were needed for Leander to have a steady clientele from the right side of the tracks. There were those who remained faithful to the other shop and that was sensible because even Leander couldn't have kept the entire masculine quotient of New Calypso in trim. But he had all the trade he could handle, fancy and fringe, and it was all the same to him. A customer was a customer regardless of where he lived or how full or empty his pocket. Leander would do as artistic a job on a stray tramp as on Osgood R. Buxton himself. He stayed right on in the same one-chair shop and made only the one change of buying a bigger mirror. New Calypso became real proud of him and Gus Hagelin, who ran the *New Calypsan Herald-Gazette*, ran items about his shop once in a while and kept notes on some of the stories about him to be included someday in a history of the township.

You've probably never heard the one about the hair-cutting contest with Polkadot City's best entry. New Calypsans rarely talked about that one. Some of them got to blowing boastful over Polkadot City way about Leander's speed with the shears, which was silly because speed with Leander was just a part of his skill and not a purpose in itself. But anyway that started an argument and the upshot was that the New Calypsans bet that Leander could trim down two shaggy heads before the best barber Polkadot City could find could finish one. The bets were heavy before Leander heard about it. He didn't like it but he couldn't let any of his regulars lose money on him by default so he said he'd make the race. They thought he ought to go into training, practice finger exercises and things like that, but he just said to tell him when and went on with his regular barbering. When they came for him on the day he just picked up his clippers and a comb and dropped them in a pocket and went along. They had three men lined up on kitchen chairs and those were really shaggyheaded. The other barber had a tray ready with half a dozen pairs of scissors laid out. Leander shrugged his shoulders and took out his own old clippers and waited. At the start-off gun the two of them went at it, and it was Leander's race all the way. While the other barber clacked his shears and tangled himself in the hair and nipped his own fingers in his hurry, Leander skimmed along, swift and sure, and a fine racing-fast jigtime tune played around the two heads he was working on, first one and then the other. There wasn't any waste motion. Each cut was exact and true. He was carving out neat haircuts with his clippers like a sculptor chipping a statue.

He was going strong and about finished when the in-evitable happened. He started muttering to himself. He had the two heads trimmed in a way that would have made any ordinary barber proud when he stepped back and made a circuit of his two men and shook his head. He didn't even hear the shoutings of his supporters and he stepped close again and started the final little delicate polishing strokes that would bring out the best-barbered points of those two men. While the New Calypsans groaned the other barber made a last jagged slice and claimed a finish, and considerable argument developed but the judges gave him the decision. And Leander wasn't even aware of the argument. He was quietly padding around his two subjects and nodding satisfied to himself. The New Calypsans paid their bets grumbling and in time most of them conceded that Leander couldn't have done anything else and still been Leander but they never talked much about that contest. They preferred telling the stories like the one about the time the Governor was worried over re-election and as a campaign stunt came all the way to New Calypso for some of Leander's barbering and Leander touched him up so noble and convincing that he won with a thumping majority. But you've heard that one. Everybody has.

It's Greenberry's turn now. Just as Leander kept on the way he had started, growing longer and thinner and balder and more energetic, so Greenberry kept on the way he had started too, growing plumper so that he seemed shorter, and thicker-haired and lazier. He sprouted whiskers at a remarkably early age and they weren't sparse and blond like Leander's, which had to be shaved off because they were such poor specimens. No, Greenberry's whiskers were stout and dark and close-sprouting and he showed prodigious power in producing them. By time he was old enough to vote, if he'd ever bother to do anything taking that much energy, he had the biggest, bushiest beard in New Calypso. And it kept right on growing. No razor, not even a pair of scissors, had ever touched the main body of it. The only clipping he gave it was a mere minor pruning around the mouth to keep the way clear for his frequent intake of food. It roamed around his face from ear to ear and down over his chest like a magnificent stand of underbrush and merged above into his dark waving hair crop so that his upper cheeks and eyes and forehead peeped out like someone hiding in a thicket. Maybe he clung to that wondrous beard because he realized it represented his one real accomplishment. Some backbiting folks said he did it because he was mean and worthless and was trying to shame his brother and in a figurative sense thumb his nose at the very family business that enabled him to stay so plump and well fed That couldn't have been true. Greenberry Frailey wasn't mean. Maybe close to worthless. But not mean. He was just lazy. He was just trifling. Matter of fact, he was as proud of Leander as anyone in New Calypso and if arguing hadn't been too much trouble he'd have been ready to argue with anyone that Leander was the best brother and the best barber in the country.

All the same it was peculiar to see the most amazing crop of hair and whiskers anywhere in civilized captivity sitting day after day in the sun on the little porch of a barbershop. That was what Greenberry did every day the sun shone. Nobody ever knew whether he would have tried to do any barbering if the shop had had another chair. Probably not, because Leander hinted about getting another one once and Greenberry promptly pointed out there wasn't room enough. So Greenberry took over the chore of meals, which was somewhat to his liking, and after breakfast he'd settle on the porch till time for his midmorning snack and then settle again till time for lunch and after that settle again till time for his midafternoon jaunt all the way next door to the neighboring saloon. Just before this last he'd go into the shop and around Leander by the chair and pull open the money drawer under the scissors shelf and slip into his pocket one dollar, never any more and never any less. When that dollar was in the hands of the bartender he would come back for the evening meal. If his taste had been for the good liquor at a quarter a shot, he'd still be able to navigate among the dishes and play a fair game of backgammon with Leander after supper. If it had been for the cheap liquor at ten cents a shot, he'd likely soon be snoring on his cot and Leander would have to be the cook. Those times Leander might begin to worry he wasn't doing right by his brother and shake him awake and try telling him he ought to get a job of some kind and Greenberry would simply say, "Why? We're doing all right, aren't we?" and Leander wouldn't know what to say because they were.

There they were, Leander doing his barber's magic inside the shop and Greenberry raising whiskers on the porch and they might have continued that way indefinitely if Leander hadn't acquired an obsession that started as a small notion and grew until it was so bad it could quiver in his fingertips. He had all his regular patrons in the New Calypso territory well in hand, each fitted with the hair style and whiskery facial adornments or lack of same that would make the emphatic most of their natural endowments. The task now was simply to keep them trimmed that way. There was no challenge left in them, no demand for fresh creative effort. He welcomed stray strangers who wandered in with positive delight. But they were few and long between. He began to feel frustrated and barren of inspiration. And then he stood on the little porch one afternoon and looked at Greenberry snoozing in the sun and a breeze waggled the long soft ends of Greenberry's beard and the small notion was born. By evening it was so big in him that he could hardly look at Greenberry across the supper table. During the next days it swelled to such proportions that it interfered with his barbering. He had to shake his head sharp to rid it of the image of that magnificent shock of raw material and the rhythmic melody of his cutting would break as his fingers quivered on the clippers. And then Greenberry all unknowing tripped the trigger of the trap awaiting him by taking on ten shots and coming home and falling asleep.

Leander closed his shop door at five o'clock as usual and padded into the back room and saw Greenberry gently snoring and a sudden little tremor ran through him. He rocked on his feet a moment and closed his mouth with a sudden snap. He padded into the shop and returned and laid out his tools on a chair by the cot, the clippers and the scissors, big and small, and a comb and the right razor and the brush and the soap mug. Carefully he raised Greenberry's shoulders with one arm and slipped two pillows behind them. Carefully he spread the checkered cloth over Greenberry's plump middle and raised Greenberry's beard to slide the upper edge of the cloth under it. For a long time he stood staring at the huge thatch of wondrous hair and whiskers framed against the cloth and the top pillow. He was not studying the head, because he did not need to. He knew every possible configuration hidden inside that thicket, every feature that everyone else in New Calypso had long forgotten. He was tasting the sweet tangy ecstasy of anticipation. At last he carefully set another chair by the cot side and sat down on it and leaned forward. With a soft sigh of complete contentment he picked up the clippers and went to work.

Greenberry stirred once at a slight tugging on his chin but a rich majestic melody of snipping blades was playing about his head and it soothed him even deeper into slumber. He woke late in the evening in the lamplight and was surprised that Leander had not roused him to supper. He was more surprised when he saw Leander limp on the other cot, asleep, and on his long thin bald-topped face the beatific smile of a man who has made a supreme effort and found it good. Greenberry heaved to his feet and was so befuddled he was not aware that he was a changed man. Out of sheer habit he ate five big sandwiches and did not notice the new freedom of access to his mouth and lay down again and slept once more. He was still unaware in the morning despite the secretive proud glances Leander gave him and awareness did not touch him until he went out the back door and took hold of the two-wheeled pushcart there and started off on his weekly food-shopping jaunt to Oscar Trittipoe's General Grocery Store.

He never reached the store. Not on that trip. He was accustomed to being ignored by most people passing and that pleased him because it saved the energy of a return greeting. He was accustomed to having those who did speak make humorous references to his beard. But this time neither thing happened. Everyone noticed him. Very definitely. They stared at him as if they had never seen him before and turned to watch him go by.

And no one spoke about his beard. No one spoke at all. Most of them nodded to him, respectful and deferential, and some of the men involuntarily tipped their hats. It was too much for Greenberry's somnolent mind to grasp all at once. He hurried back to the shop, went in and turned to Leander, puttering at his instrument shelf, and in the turning saw himself in the big mirror.

Not himself. Someone else. A man of amazingly impressive presence. A thick shock of hair tamed and disciplined to dignity yet with the inherent vitality plain in every faultless wave. Strong eyebrows subtly arched to emphasize the width and nobility of the brow. A sturdy mustache, firm and short-cropped, speaking of confidence and self-assurance and somehow also pointing out the outthrust power of the nose above. Rugged sideburns clipped close yet with a faint flaring that suggested breadth of mind. And a beard, deep under the chin and reliable, short but not too short, wide but not too wide, a solid foundation for the face proclaiming serenity and wisdom with every sturdy hair.

Greenberry shook with the shock. He threw Leander one look of frenzied reproach and fairly ran into the back room and closed the door. He sat on the edge of his cot and leaned the superb portrait that was now his head forward into his plump hands and let the frightening knowledge that he was marked with distinction sweep over him. It was characteristic that he never once thought that a few strokes with scissors could reduce him again to a scraggly nonentity. He would have had to make those scissor strokes. He sat motionless a long time. At last his head rose and he made a few exploratory motions with his hands around his chin and cheeks.

He stood up and placed himself in front of the little mirror that had once served in the shop and his mind was braced now for what he would see. He studied himself, turning his head sideways and rolling his eyes to catch the splendor from various angles. Unconsciously he stood straighter and pulled in his bulging waistline and puffed out his chest. By noontime the new Greenberry Frailey, fortified with a full lunch, was ready to face the world.

The new Greenberry Frailey. That is precisely what he was. A new man. A changed man. In all outward semblance at least. The very first day he discovered what his impressive appearance could accomplish in promoting prompt, actually scurrying service and the choicest cuts of meat from the formerly lackadaisical and almost contemptuous Oscar Trittipoe. On the third day he learned the ease with which he could obtain virtually unlimited credit at the Big Bargain Mercantile Establishment and forthwith arrayed himself in what was to be thereafter his unvarying uniform, black trousers and black frock coat and gorgeous gray vest and white shirt and celluloid collar and black string bow tie, unseen beneath that now disciplined matchless beard except when he thrust his chin outward and fluffed the beard up in a gesture calculated to draw attention to its perfect proportions. By the end of the first week he had even acquired a gold-headed cane and his voice had dropped several notes to a deepening resonance and he was developing a flowing almost courtly manner. By the end of the second week he was settled in his new role, rapidly becoming another New Calypsan institution, a monumental figure seen every clear day on the center bench between the town watering trough and the town flagpole across from the post office. You can assay the true measure of Leander's art when you understand that already the New Calypsans were forgetting the old Greenberry who sat in his ancient red plaid shirt and split-seam dungarees on the porch of the little shop and were drifting so completely under the spell of the new Greenberry that they accepted his benign nods as benedictions and felt that their town was a better place because such a towering testament to the dignity and nobility of the human race dwelt among them. When he had snoozed on the shop porch he had been a shiftless disgrace to be ignored. Now, when he drowsed on the bench, serene and nodding in the sun, he was a philosopher thinking deep thoughts and pondering grave problems and giving tone to the community. Why, it's a fact there was not even a noticeable chuckle when he began calling himself J. Greenberry Frailey.

It was Osgood R. Buxton himself who launched Greenberry on his public career. The time came when Buxton was a mite worried about the New Calypso Bank. More than a mite worried. The bank had overreached itself in granting loans and the cattle market was wobbly and a lot of the loans might have to be carried over and a few rumors got to skipping about and Buxton was worried what would happen if a run started. He sat at his desk by the bank's front window worrying and stroking the mustache Leander had saved for him and out the window he noticed with a sudden idea-prompted push the never failing impressiveness of Greenberry on the bench. Five minutes and a brief talk

later Buxton was on his way to Gus Hagelin with an
item for the *Herald-Gazette* to the effect that J. Greenberry Frailey had kindly consented to become a director
of the New Calypso Bank. The only immediate change
for Greenberry was the addition of ten dollars a month
to his pocket and a slight shift of sitting quarters, from
the bench by the flagpole to a bench in front of the
bank where the sun was even better and his presence
was a steady reassurance to troubled depositors. The
monthly meetings were no real chore. All he had to do
was attend and sit quiet and murmur "Hmmmm" in a
thoughtful tone when an important decision was posed,
and the other directors would proceed exactly as they
would have done without him, buttressed now with the
feeling that they were being wise and judicious indeed.
But this first gesture into the realm of actual activity
encouraged other people to draw him into other things.
He discovered the lure of speechmaking. The deep roll
of his voice combined with the overpowering benignity
of his appearance to produce hypnotic effect on his
audiences. The words were unimportant. It was the
impression that prevailed. He auctioned the box lunches
at town dances and could obtain good prices for those
prepared by the most unattractive unattached females.
He presided at the annual Strawberry Festival and the
Stockmen's Show and was the Fourth of July orator.
There was no doubt about it. With little real effort on
his part he had become an unofficial public functionary.

   And Leander? Well, Leander was content. He had
done what old Baldpate told him to do. He had taken
care of Greenberry in the most important way and what
remained of the taking care was merely a matter of

helping to maintain Greenberry in the style to which he had become accustomed. That was simple because Greenberry was not active enough to wear out clothes rapidly and ate, if anything, less than before and his drinks were almost invariably supplied by admirers more than willing to pay for the privilege. Leander now had constantly before him the inspiration of his finest masterpiece, the one perfect portrait that he never tired of retouching and keeping in perfect trim. And Greenberry, in his way, was properly grateful. His innocent trust that Leander would take care of him had been justified in a surprising and superlative degree. He never failed, when extolling the glories of New Calypso in his occasional orations, to include some mention of the tonsorial wizardry of that far-famed prince among barbers, my brother Leander. He continued to grace the little shop building with his presence as his eating and sleeping quarters. He continued to spend his spare evenings playing backgammon with Leander. So complete was his hold on the town that many people regarded this as somewhat of a condescension on his part.

Yes, Leander had worked out a way of life for himself and Greenberry that satisfied them both and was a double-weight asset to New Calypso. Then enter the serpent, Worthington P. C. Stimmel. That was the name in Old English lettering on his calling cards and he carried his cards in a cardcase. They also stated, in smaller but no less compelling type, that he was President and Corresponding Secretary, the Amalgamated Association for the Betterment of American Communities. This Stimmel had long since made an interesting discovery. He had learned that when towns attained some size they found themselves needing such modern improvements as sewers and cobblestone pavements and those ingenious means of public transportation, horsecars. He had discovered that sometimes the people of an ambitious small town could be persuaded that the process would work in reverse, that if they would sell bonds to themselves to raise the funds and draw plans for new streets and install sewers and pavements and horsecars, then their town would automatically attract newcomers and grow swiftly and become boomingly prosperous. It was unfortunate that the promotional expenses and the cost of this Stimmel's invaluable services always approximated most if not all of the funds raised. But by time the townsfolk learned that, in full eye-opening force, this Stimmel would be far away planning the improvement of another community in another part of the country.

A man of Worthington P. C. Stimmel's experienced discernment could see at once the splendid future that awaited New Calypso. He could recognize with equal facility the unusual opportunity offered by J. Greenberry Frailey's bewhiskered magnificence. He had not been in New Calypso ten days before stationery was printed and bonds were being engraved and both stationery and bonds proclaimed the fact that J. Greenberry Frailey was Chairman of the New Calypso Progressive Citizens' League, the latest chapter of the A.A.B.A.C. There was some opposition led by Oscar Trittipoe, who was by nature an obstinate individual, and Gus Hagelin, who had acquired from his newspaper work a suspicious trend of mind and some knowledge of human frailties. But obstinacy and suspicion could not prevail against the majesty of the Greenberry whiskers. The N.C.P.C. League gained momentum like an avalanche moving and the date was set for the public meeting that would launch the bond sale.

All this bothered Leander not at all. He never interfered in Greenberry's doings. His own doubts about the League project were overwhelmed by Greenberry's contagious optimism. To him the thought of a bigger and more booming New Calypso was pleasant because that might mean new and unfamiliar customers. He went quietly on with his barbering. And then Worthington P. C. Stimmel made a mistake. Operating on the principle of when in Rome doing what the Romans do, he went into the little shop for a hair trim.

"Heard about you from your brother," this Stimmel said in his best patronizing manner. There was no reply. Leander was circling the chair, studying him from all sides. The first eager small smile on Leander's face was fading into a tight-lipped frown. Muttonchop whiskers. Leander had never liked muttonchop whiskers and refused to permit them on any regular customer. They were not right for any decent human head. They could have only one purpose, to hide or draw attention away from other things. Correct. These muttonchops gave a broadness and solidity to this head that was not really there. They obscured the whole sinister, greedy, calculating cast of the countenance. Leander picked up his big scissors and they hovered about Stimmel's head, and the rhythmic tune they played in their first warming-up skirmishes in the air was a stern and resolute one. But they never touched a hair or whisker. Leander stopped and laid them down. He could not do it. He picked up the small scissors and for the first time since he was a boy relieving old Baldpate in the afternoons he gave an ordinary haircut, merely trimming into neatness the original portrait presented to him.

That was all that happened then in the shop. But afterwards Leander did what he had never done before. He closed the shop during working hours and went to see Gus Hagelin and what he learned there added more worry to what he had learned in the shop and he tried to talk to several League members and they laughed and told him to stick to his barbering and he tried to talk to Greenberry that evening and Greenberry laughed too and at last grew huffy and said he'd move to a room at the hotel if Leander didn't stop harping on something he knew nothing about. So Leander kept his worry to himself and it grew till it was a new obsession in him and he kept remembering what old Baldpate had said and realizing that Greenberry was in this slick Stimmel scheme and in a sense the kingpin of it, the asset that could push it through. And so at last when he had worried himself thinner and the time was short, he did something else he had never done before. On the day before the public meeting he went to the saloon next door and bought a bottle of the cheap liquor and had it on the table when he played backgammon with Greenberry that evening. He poured more into Greenberry's glass whenever that was empty and his own slick scheme succeeded. By eleven o'clock Greenberry was snoring soundly on his cot. Leander padded forward into the shop and returned and laid out his tools on a chair and spread the checkered cloth over Greenberry's chest. For a long time he stood staring down at the finest portrait he had ever achieved. With a soft sigh of torment he picked up his clippers and a slow sad melody of snipping blades began to play around Greenberry's head.

Greenberry slept straight through the night and well into the morning. He woke slowly and then focused suddenly on the old clock on a shelf. Five minutes past ten. The meeting had begun five minutes ago and he was not there. No time even for breakfast and that was a drastic thing to happen to him. He shrugged as quickly as he could into his frock coat and grabbed his gold-headed cane and hurried out through the shop past Leander sitting mournful in his own barber chair. He hurried out the front door disregarding Leander's calling to him, and hurried up the street and across the tracks and to the crowded space behind the flagpole where a bandstand had been erected and the four-piece New Calypso band was seated and Worthington P. C. Stimmel was standing erect delivering his practiced spiel.

There on the stand this Stimmel, talking against time, saw with relief the magnificent wavy shock of Green-berry's hair moving toward him through the assembled people. He shifted smoothly into remarks introducing that almost legendary repository of wisdom and civic foresight, that peerless pillar of New Calypsan com-munity life, J. Greenberry Frailey, and waved to the approaching pillar to ascend the stand. And Greenberry burst out of the crowd and went up the steps and took his dignified stance and thrust his head forward a bit and reached up in the strange hushed silence that had gripped the whole scene to fluff his beard.

It was that gesture that released the first of the sniggering chuckles into loud and contagious guffaws. Greenberry's hand came up in the familiar movement to fluff his beard and there was no beard for him to fluff. There was only what the New Calypsans had long ago forgotten, the ridiculous small and round little-boyish dimpled chin that the beard had hidden. As the laughter rolled around the flagpole and New Calypsans thumped each other on the back, Worthington P. C. Stimmel, that man of experienced discernment, slipped down from the stand and away and Gus Hagelin, that man aware of human frailties, leaped up on the stand and shouted at the band and raucous music began to blare. And through the midst of the over-all merriment came a long and thin and bald-headed figure, stoop-shouldered and sad and ashamed, to take care of his brother and lead him home.

All the rest of the day the little shop was closed. The next day it was open and time had gone backwards. A plump figure in a red plaid shirt and split-seam dungarees sat on the little porch in the sun. But inside there were no more snipping melodies. There was only the plain pedestrian plodding of routine cutting. Greenberry sat in the sun and some of the time actually snoozed and Leander went on with his barbering inside, but it was an ordinary barber's barbering. He had used his art to destroy and not to create and the magic was gone from his fingers.

In midafternoon Greenberry rose and went into the shop and pulled open the money drawer and took out a dollar and reached and took another and looked at

Leander patiently working his scissors in dull routine and put the second dollar back and plodded out. It was a ten-shot session for him and he returned barely able to navigate and lay down on his cot and in a few moments was sleeping, and almost anyone seeing him there would have said that was all he was doing.

But he was doing something else. All unaware he was doing the one thing that he could do better than anyone else in New Calypso. Leander saw it when he came into the back room from the shop and started to prepare some supper. He saw what he, a barber, had actually forgotten. He saw the dark stubble emerging on Greenberry's chin and remembered Greenberry's prodigious talent for raising whiskers. His eyes brightened and small rhythmic melodies began to stir again in his finger muscles. He had not failed old Baldpate. Not yet. He could try again and, if necessary, again. It would not take long, not with Greenberry so obligingly concentrating even in his sleep on that one wondrous accomplishment.

Already Leander could begin to see the next portrait. Not dignity and thoughtfulness and deep wisdom this time. No. A portrait built around a short, stubby, square-cut beard, the beard of a man steady and dependable and competent at whatever work he might have in hand.

JEREMY RODOCK

The Man Who Knew Horses

JEREMY RODOCK was a hanging man when it came to horse thieves. He hanged them quick and efficient, and told what law there was about it afterwards. He was a big man in a many ways and not just in shadow-making size. People knew him. He had a big ranch — a horse ranch — about the biggest in the Territory, and he loved horses, and no one, not even a one of his own hands — and they were careful picked — could match him at breaking and gentling his big geldings for any kind of roadwork. Tall they were, those horses, and rawboned, out of Western mares by some hackney stallions he'd had brought from the East, and after you'd been working with cow ponies they'd set you back on your heels when you first saw them. But they were stout in harness with a fast, swinging trot that could take the miles and a heavy coach better than anything else on hooves. He was proud of those horses, and he had a right to be. I know. I was one of his hands for a time. I was with him once when he hanged a pair of rustlers. And I was with him the one time he didn't.

That was a long ways back. I was young then with a stretch in my legs, about topping twenty, and Jeremy Rodock was already an old man. Maybe not so old, maybe just about into his fifties, but he seemed old to me — old the way a pine gets when it's through growing, standing tall and straight and spreading strong, but with the graying grimness around the edges that shows it's settling to the long last stand against the winds and the storms. I remember I was surprised to find he could still outwork any of his men and be up before them in the morning. He was tough fiber clear through, and he took me on because I had a feeling for horses and they'd handle for me without much fuss, and that was what he wanted. "You'll earn your pay," he said, "and not act your age more than you can help, and if your sap breaks out in sass, I'll slap you against a gatepost and larrup the hide off your back." And he would, and I knew it. And he taught me plenty about horses and men, and I worked for him the way I've never worked for another man.

That was the kind of work I liked. We always paired for it, and Rodock was letting me side him. The same men, working as a team, always handled the same horses from the time they were brought in off the range until they were ready and delivered. They were plenty wild at first, four- and five-year-olds with free-roaming strong in their legs, not having had any experience with men and ropes from the time they were foaled except for the few days they were halter-broke and bangtailed as coming two-year-olds. They had their growth and life was running in them, and it was a pleasure working with them.

Rodock's system was quick and thorough; you could tell a Rodock horse by the way he'd stand when you wanted him to stand and give all he had when you wanted him to move, and respond to the reins like he knew what you wanted almost before you were certain yourself. We didn't do much with saddle stock except as needed for our personal use. Rodock horses were stage horses. That's what they were bred and broke for. They were all right for riding, maybe better than all right if you could stick their paces, because they sure could cover ground, but they were best for stage work.

We'd rope a horse out of the corral and take him into a square stall and tie a hind leg to his belly so he couldn't even try to kick without falling flat, and then start to get acquainted. We'd talk to him till he was used to voices, and slap him and push him around till he knew we weren't going to hurt him. Then we'd throw old harness on him and yank it off and throw it on again, and keep at this till he'd stand without flicking an inch of hide no matter how hard the harness hit. We'd take him out and let the leg down and lead him around with the old harness flapping till that wouldn't mean any more to him than a breeze blowing. We'd fit him with reins and one man would walk in front with the lead rope and the other behind holding the reins and ease him into knowing what they meant. And all the time we'd speak sharp when he acted up and speak soft and give him a piece of carrot or a fistful of corn when he behaved right.

Hitching was a different proposition. No horse that'll work for you because he wants to, and not just because he's beat into it, takes kindly to hitching. He's bound to throw his weight about the first time or two and seem to forget a lot he's learned. We'd take our horse and match him with a well-broke trainer, and harness the two of them with good leather to a stout wagon. We'd have half-hobbles on his front feet fastened to the spliced ends of a rope that ran up through a ring on the underside of his girth and through another ring on the wagon tongue and up to the driving seat. Then the two of us would get on the seat and I'd hold the rope and Rodock'd take the reins. The moment we'd start to move, the trainer heaving into the traces, things would begin to happen. The new horse would be mighty surprised. He'd likely start rearing or plunging. I'd pull on the rope and his front legs would come out from under him and down he'd go on his nose. After trying that a few times, he'd learn he wasn't getting anywhere and begin to steady and remember some of the things he'd learned before. He'd find he had to step along when the wagon moved, and after a while he'd find that stepping was smoothest and easiest if he did his share of the pulling. Whenever he'd misbehave or wouldn't stop when he should, I'd yank on the rope and his nose would hit the soft dirt. It was surprising how quick he'd learn to put his weight into the harness and pay attention to the boss riding behind him. Sometimes, in a matter of three weeks, we'd have one ready to take his place in a four-horse pull of the old coach we had for practice runs. That would be a good horse.

Well, we were readying twenty-some teams for a new stage line when this happened. Maybe it wouldn't have happened, not the way it did, if one of the horses hadn't sprung a tendon and we needed a replacement. I don't blame myself for it, and I don't think Rodock did either, even though the leg went bad when I pulled the horse down on his nose. He was something of a hollow-head anyway, and wasn't learning as he should and had kept on trying to smash loose every time the wagon moved.

As I say, this horse pulled a tendon, not bad, but enough to mean a limp, and Rodock wouldn't send a limping horse along even to a man he might otherwise be willing to trim on a close deal. Shoo him out on the range, he told me, and let time and rest and our good grass put him in shape for another try next year. "And saddle my bay," he said, "and take any horse you'd care to sit, son. We'll ramble out to the lower basin and bring in another and maybe a spare in case something else happens."

That was why we were riding out a little before noon on a hot day, leaving the others busy about the buildings, just the two of us loafing along toward the first of the series of small natural valleys on Rodock's range where he kept the geldings and young studs. We were almost there, riding the ridge, when he stopped and swung in the saddle toward me. "Let's make a day of it, son. Let's mosey on to the next basin and have a look-see at the mares there and this year's crop of foals. I like to see the little critters run."

That's what I mean. If we hadn't been out already,

he never would have taken time to go there. We'd checked the mares a few weeks before and tallied the foals and seen that everything was all right. If that horse hadn't gone lame, it might have been weeks, maybe months, before any of us would have gone up that way again.

We moseyed on, not pushing our horses because we'd be using them hard on the way back, cutting out a couple of geldings and hustling them home. We came over the last rise and looked down into that second small valley, and there wasn't a single thing in sight. Where there ought to have been better than forty mares and their foals, there wasn't a moving object, only the grass shading to deeper green down the slope to the trees along the stream and fading out again up the other side of the valley.

Jeremy Rodock sat still in his saddle. "I didn't think anyone would have the nerve," he said, quiet and slow. He put his horse into a trot around the edge of the valley, leaning over and looking at the ground, and I followed. He stopped at the head of the valley where it narrowed and the stream came through, and he dismounted and went over the ground carefully. He came back to his horse and leaned his chest against the saddle, looking over it and up at me.

"Here's where they were driven out," he said, still quiet and slow. "At least three men. Their horses were shod. Not more than a few days ago. A couple of weeks and there wouldn't have been any trail left to follow." He looked over his saddle and studied me. "You've been with me long enough, son," he said, "for me to know what you can do with horses. But I don't know what you can do with that gun you're carrying. I wish I'd brought one of the older men. You better head back and give the word. I'm following this trail."

"Mister Rodock," I said, "I wish you wouldn't make so many remarks about my age. One thing a man can't help is his age. But anywhere you and that bay can go, me and this roan can follow. And as for this gun I'm carrying, I can hit anything with it you can and maybe a few things you'd miss."

He looked at me over his saddle and his eyebrows twitched a little upwards.

"Careful, son," he said. "That comes close to being sass." His jawline tightened, and he had that old-pine look, gray and grim and enduring. "You'll have hard riding," he said, and swung into his saddle and put his horse into a steady trot along the trail, and that was all he said for the next four-five hours.

Hard riding it was. Trotting gets to a man even if he's used to being on a horse. It's a jolting pace, and after a time your muscles grow plain tired of easing the jolts and the calluses on your rump warm up and remind you they're there. But trotting is the way to make time if you really intend to travel. Some people think the best way is to keep to a steady lope. That works on the back of your neck after a while and takes too much out of the horse after the first couple of hours. Others like to run the horse, then give him a breather, then run him again, and keep that up. You take it all out of him the first day doing that. Trotting is the best way. A good horse can trot along steady, his shoulders and legs relaxed and his hooves slapping down almost by their own weight, do it hour after hour and cover his fifty-to-sixty miles with no more than a nice even sweat and be ready to do the same the next day and the next after that, and a lot longer than any man riding him can hope to take it.

Rodock was trotting, and his long-legged bay was swinging out the miles, and far as I could tell the old man was made of iron and didn't even know he was taking a beating. I knew I was, and that roan I'd picked because he looked like a cowpony I'd had once was working with his shorter legs to hold the pace, and I was shifting my weight from one side to the other about every fifteen minutes so I'd burn only half of my rump at a time.

It was dark night when Rodock stopped by water and swung down and hobbled his horse and unsaddled, and I did the same.

"Might miss the trail in the dark," he said. "Anyways, they're moving slow on account of the colts. I figure we've gained at least a day on them already. Maybe more. Better get some sleep. We'll be traveling with the first light." He settled down with his saddle for a pillow and I did the same, and after a few minutes his voice drifted out of the darkness. "You came along right well, son. Do the same tomorrow and I'll shut up about your age."

Next thing I knew he was shaking me awake and the advance glow of the sun was climbing the sky, and he was squatting beside me with a hatful of berries from the bushes near the water. I ate my share and we saddled and started on, and after I shook the stiffness I felt fresh and almost chipper. The trail was snaking in wide curves southwest, following the low places, but rising, as the whole country was, gradually up through the foothills toward the first tier of mountains.

About regular breakfast time, when the sun was a

couple of hours over the horizon behind us, Rodock waved to me to come alongside close.

"None of this makes sense," he said, without slacking pace. "A queer kind of rustling run-off. Mares and foals. I've tangled with a lot of thievery in my time, but all of it was with stock could be moved fast and disposed of quick. Can't do that with mares and sucking colts. How do you figure it, son?"

I studied that awhile. "Mister Rodock," I said, "there's only one advantage I see. Colts that young haven't felt a branding iron yet. Get away with them and you can slap on any brand you want."

"You're aging fast, son," he said. "That's a right good thought. But these foals couldn't be weaned for three months yet. Say two months if you were the kind could be mean and not worry about getting them started right. What good would they be, even with your brand on them, still nursing mares that have got my J-tailed-R brand?"

"I'd be mighty embarrassed," I said, "every time anybody had a look at a one of them. Guess I'd have to keep them out of sight till they could be weaned."

"For two-three months, son?" he said. "You'd ride herd on them two-three months to keep them from heading back to their home range? Or coop them some place where you'd have to feed them? And be worrying all the time that maybe Jeremy Rodock would jump you with a hanging rope in his hand?"

"No," I said, "I wouldn't. I don't know what I'd do. Guess I just don't have a thieving mind."

"But somebody's doing it," he said. "Damned if I know what."

And we moved along at that steady fast trot, and my

roan dropped back where he liked to stay, about twenty
feet behind where he could set his own rhythm without
being bothered trying to match the strides of the longer-
legged bay. We moved along, and I began to feel empty
clear down into my shanks and I began to hunch forward
to ease the calluses on my rump. The only break all
morning was a short stop for brief watering. We moved
along and into the afternoon, and I could tell the roan
felt exactly as I did. He and I were concentrating on
just one thing, putting all we had into following twenty
feet after an old iron ramrod of a man on one of the
long-legged, tireless horses of his own shrewd breeding.

The trail was still stale, several days at least, and we
were not watching sharp ahead, so we came on them
suddenly. Rodock, being ahead and going up a rise, saw
them first and was swinging to the ground and grabbing
his horse's nose when I came beside him and saw the
herd, bunched, well ahead and into a small canyon that
cut off to the right. I swung down and caught the roan's
nose in time to stop the nicker starting, and we hurried
to lead both horses back down the rise and a good ways
more and over to a clump of trees. We tied them there
and went ahead again on foot, crawling the last stretch
up the rise and dropping on our bellies to peer over the
top. They were there all right, the whole herd, the
mares grazing quietly, some of the foals lying down, the
others skittering around the way they do, daring each
other to flip their heels.

We studied that scene a long time, checking every
square yard of it as far as we could see. There was not
a man or a saddled horse in sight. Rodock plucked a
blade of grass and stuck it in his mouth and chewed on it.

"All right, son," he said. "Seems we'll have to smoke

them out. They must be holed up somewhere handy waiting to see if anyone's following. You scout around the left side of that canyon and I'll take the right. Watch for tracks and keep an eye cocked behind you. We'll meet way up there beyond the herd where the trees and bushes give good cover. If you're jumped, get off a shot and I'll be on my way over ahumping."

"Mister Rodock," I said, "you do the same and so will I."

We separated, slipping off our different ways and moving slow behind any cover that showed. I went along the left rim of the canyon, crouching by rocks and checking the ground carefully each time before moving on and peering down into the canyon along the way. I came on a snake and circled it and flushed a rabbit out of some bushes, and those were the only living things or signs of them I saw except for the horses below there in the canyon. Well up beyond them, where the rock wall slanted out into a passable slope, I worked my way down and to where we were to meet. I waited, and after a while Rodock appeared, walking toward me without even trying to stay under cover.

"See anything, son?" he said.

"No," I said.

"It's crazier than ever," he said. "I found their tracks where they left. Three shod horses moving straight out. Now what made them chuck and run like that? Tracks at least a day old too."

"Somebody scared them," I said.

"It would take a lot," he said, "to scare men with nerve enough to make off with a bunch of my horses. Who'd be roaming around up here anyway? If it was anyone living within a hundred miles, they'd know my brand and be taking the horses in." He stood there straight, hands on his hips, and stared down the canyon at the herd. "What's holding them?" he said.

"Holding who?" I said.

"Those horses," he said. "Those mares. Why haven't they headed for home? Why aren't they working along as they graze?"

He was right. They weren't acting natural. They were bunched too close and hardly moving, and when any of them did move there was something wrong. We stared at them, and suddenly Rodock began to run toward them and I had trouble staying close behind him. They heard us and turned to face us and they had trouble turning, and Rodock stopped and stared at them and there was a funny moaning sound in his throat.

"My God!" he said. "Look at their front feet!"

I looked, and I could see right away what he meant. They had been roped and thrown and their front hooves rasped almost to the quick, so that they could barely put their weight on them. Each step hurt, and they couldn't have traveled at all off the canyon grass out on the rocky ground beyond. It hurt me seeing them hurt each time they tried to move, and if it did that to me I could imagine what it did to Jeremy Rodock.

They knew him, and some of them nickered at him, and the old mare that was their leader, and was standing with head drooping, raised her head and started forward and dropped her head again and limped to us with it hanging almost to the ground. There was a heavy iron bolt tied to her forelock and hanging down between her eyes. You know how a horse moves its head as it walks.

This bolt would have bobbed against her forehead with each step she took, and already it had broken through the skin and worn a big sore that was beginning to fester.

Rodock stood still and stared at her and that moaning sound clung in his throat. I had to do something. I pulled out my pocketknife and cut through the tied hairs and tossed the bolt far as I could. I kicked up a piece of sod and reached down and took a handful of clean dirt and rubbed it over the sore on her forehead and then wiped it and oozing stuff away with my neckerchief, and she stood for me and only shivered as I rubbed. I looked at Rodock and he was someone I had never seen before. He was a gaunt figure of a man, with eyes pulled back deep in their sockets and burning, and the bones of his face showing plain under the flesh.

"Mister Rodock," I said, "are we riding out on that three-horse trail?"

I don't think he even heard me.

"Not a thing," he said. "Not a single solitary god-damned thing I can do. They're traveling light and fast now. Too much of a start and too far up in the rocks for trailing. They've probably separated and could be heading clean out of the Territory. They're devilish smart and they've done it, and there's not a goddamned thing I can do."

"We've got the mares," I said. "And the foals."

He noticed me, a flick of his eyes at me. "We've got them way up here and they can't be moved. Not till those hooves grow out." He turned toward me and threw words at me, and I wasn't anyone he knew, just someone to be a target for his bitterness. "They're devils! Three devils! Nothing worth the name of man would treat horses like that. See the devilishness of it? They run my horses way up here and cripple them. They don't have to stay around. The horses can't get away. They know the chances are we won't miss the mares for weeks, and by then the trail will be overgrown and we won't know which way they went and waste time combing the whole damn country in every direction, and maybe never get up in here. Even if someone follows them soon, like we did, they're gone and can't be caught. One of them can slip back every week or two to see what's doing, and if he's nabbed, what can tie him to the run-off? He's just a fiddlefoot riding through. By weaning-time, if nothing has happened, they can hurry in and take the colts and get off clean with a lot of unbranded horseflesh. And there's not a thing we can do."

"We can watch the mares," I said, "till they're able to travel some, then push them home by easy stages. And meantime be mighty rough on anyone comes nosying around."

"We've got the mares," he said. "They're as well off here as anywhere now. What I want is those devils. All three of them. Together and roped and in my hands." He put out his hands, the fingers clawed, and shook them at me. "I've got to get them! Do you see that? I've got to!" He dropped his hands limp at his sides, and his voice dropped too, dry and quiet with a coldness in it. "There's one thing we can do. We can leave everything as it is and go home and keep our mouths shut and wait and be here when they come for the colts." He took hold of me by the shoulders and his fingers hurt my muscles. "You see what they did to my horses. Can you keep your mouth shut?"

He didn't wait for me to answer. He let go of my shoulders and turned and went straight through the herd of crippled mares without looking at them and on down the canyon and out and over the rise where we first sighted them and on to the clump of trees where we had tied our horses.

I followed him and he was mounted and already starting off when I reached the roan and I mounted and set out after him. He was in no hurry now and let the bay walk part of the time, and the roan and I were glad of that. He never turned to look at me or seemed to notice whether I followed or not. A rabbit jumped out of the brush and I knocked it over on the second shot and picked it up and laid it on the saddle in front of me, and he paid no attention to me, not even to the shots, just steadying the bay when it started at the sharp sounds and holding it firm on the back trail.

He stopped by a stream while there was still light and dismounted, and I did the same. After we had hobbled and unsaddled the horses, he sat on the ground with his back to a rock and stared into space. I couldn't think of anything to say, so I gathered some wood and made a fire. I took my knife and gutted the rabbit and cut off the head. I found some fairly good clay and moistened it and rolled the rabbit in a ball of it and dropped this in the fire. When I thought it would be about done, I poked it out of the hot ashes and let it cool a bit. Then I pried off the baked clay and the skin came with it and the meat showed juicy and smelled fine. It was still a little raw but anything would have tasted good then. I passed Rodock some pieces and he took them and ate the meat off the bones mechanically like his mind was far away someplace. I still couldn't think of anything to say, so I stretched out with my head on my saddle, and then it was morning and I was chilled and stiff and staring up at clear sky, and he was coming toward me leading both horses and his already saddled.

It was getting toward noon, and we were edging onto our home range when we met two of the regular hands out looking for us. They came galloping with a lot of questions and Rodock put up a palm to stop them.

"Nothing's wrong," he said. "I took a sudden mind to circle around and look over some of the stock that's strayed a bit and show the boy here parts of my range he hadn't seen before. Went farther'n I intended to and we're some tuckered. You two cut over to the lower basin and take in a pair of four-year-olds. Hightail it straight and don't dawdle. We've got that stage order to meet."

They were maybe a mite puzzled as they rode off, but it was plain they hadn't hit the second basin and seen the mares were missing. Rodock and I started on, and I thought of something to say and urged the roan close.

"Mister Rodock," I said, "I don't like that word 'boy.' "

"That's too damn bad," he said, and went steadily on and I followed, and he paid no more attention to me all the rest of the way to the ranch buildings.

Things were different after that around the place. He didn't work with the horses himself any more. Most of the time he stayed in his sturdy frame house where he had a Mexican to cook for him and fight the summer dust, and I don't know what he did in there. Once in a while he'd be on the porch, and he'd sit there hours staring off where the foothills started their climb toward the mountains. With him shut away like that, I was paired with Hugh Claggett. This Claggett was a good enough man, I guess. Rodock thought some of him. They had knocked around together years back, and when he had showed up needing a job sometime before I was around the place, Rodock gave him one, and he was a sort of acting foreman when Rodock was away for any reason. He knew horses, maybe as much as Rodock himself in terms of the things you could put down as fact in a book. But he didn't have the real feel, the deep inside feel, of them that means you can sense what's going on inside a horse's head; walk up to a rolled-eye maverick that's pawing the sky at the end of a rope the way Rodock could, and talk the nonsense out of him and have him standing there quivering to quiet under your hand in a matter of minutes. Claggett was a precise, practical sort of a man, and working with him was just that, working, and I took no real pleasure in it.

When Rodock did come down by the stables and working corral, he was different. He didn't come often, and it would have been better if he hadn't come at all. First thing I noticed was his walk. There was no bounce to it. Always before, no matter how tired he was, he walked rolling on the soles of his feet from heels to toes and coming off the toes each step with a little bouncy spring. Now he was walking flatfooted, plodding, like he was carrying more weight than just his body. And he was hard and driving in a new way, a nasty and irritable way. He'd always been one to find fault, but that had been because he was better at his business than any of us and he wanted to set us straight. He'd shrivel us down to size with a good clean tongue-whipping, then pitch in himself and show us how to do whatever it was and we'd be the better for it. Now he was plain cussed all through. He'd snap at us about anything and everything. Nothing we did was right. He'd not do a lick of work himself, just stand by and find fault, and his voice was brittle and nasty, and he'd get personal in his remarks. And he was mighty touchy about how we treated the horses. We did the way he had taught us and the way I knew was right by how the horses handled, still he would blow red and mad and tear into us with bitter words, saying we were slapping on leather too hard or fitting bridles too snug, little things, but they added to a nagging tally as the days passed and made our work tiring and troublesome. There was a lot of grumbling going on in the bunkhouse in the evenings.

Time and again I wanted to tell the others about the mares so maybe they would understand. But I'd remember his hands stretching toward me and shaking and then biting into my shoulders and I'd keep what had happened blocked inside me. I knew what was festering in him. I'd wake at night thinking about those mares, thinking about them way up there in the hills pegged to a small space of thinning grass by hooves that hurt when weight came on them and sent stabs of pain up their legs when they hit anything hard. A good horse is a fine-looking animal. But it isn't the appearance that gets into you and makes something in you reach out and

respond to him. It's the way he moves, the sense of
movement in him even when he's standing still, the
clean-stepping speed and competence of him that's born
in him and is what he is and is his reason for being. Take
that away and he's a pitiful thing. And somewhere there
were three men who had done that to those mares. I'd
jump awake at night and think about them and maybe
have some notion of what it cost Jeremy Rodock to stay
set there at his ranch and leave his mares alone with their
misery far off up in the hills.

When the stage horses were ready to be shod for the
last real road tests, he nearly drove our blacksmith crazy
cursing every time a hoof was trimmed or one of them
flinched under the hammer. We finished them off with
hard runs in squads hitched to the old coach and delivered them, and then there was nothing much to do.
Not another order was waiting. Several times agents had
been to see Rodock and had gone into the house and
come out again and departed, looking downright peeved.
I don't know whether he simply refused any more orders
or acted so mean that they wouldn't do business with
him. Anyway, it was bad all around. There was too
much loafing time. Except for a small crew making hay
close in, no one was sent out on the range at all. The
men were dissatisfied and they had reason to be, and they
took to quarreling with each other. Some of them quit
in disgust and others after arguing words with Rodock,
and finally the last bunch demanded their time together
and left, and Claggett and I were the only ones still there.
That's not counting the Mexican, but he was house-
broke and not worth counting. Claggett and I could

handle the chores for the few horses kept regularly around the place and still have time to waste. We played euchre, but I never could beat him and then got tired of trying. And Rodock sat on his porch and stared into the distance. I didn't think he even noticed me when I figured that his bay would be getting soft and started saddling him and taking him out for exercise the same as I did the roan. One day I rode him right past the porch. Rodock fooled me on that, though. I was almost past, pretending not to see him, when his voice flicked at me. "Easy on those reins, boy. They're just extra trimming. That horse knows what you want by the feel of your legs around him. I don't want him spoiled." He was right too. I found you could put that bay through a figure eight or drop him between two close-set posts just by thinking it down through your legs.

The slow days went by, and I couldn't stand it any longer. I went to the house.

"Mister Rodock," I said, "it's near two months now. Isn't it time we made a move?"

"Don't be so damn young," he said. "I'll move when I know it's right."

I stood on one foot and then on the other and I couldn't think of anything to say except what I'd said before about my age, so I went back to the bunkhouse and made Claggett teach me all the games of solitaire he knew.

Then one morning I was oiling harness to keep it limber when I looked up and Rodock was in the stable doorway.

"Saddle my bay," he said, "and Hugh's sorrel. I

reckon that roan'll do for you again. Pick out a good packhorse and bring them all around to the storehouse soon as you can."

I jumped to do what he said, and when I had the horses there he and Claggett had packs filled. We loaded the extra horse, and the last thing Rodock did was hand out Henrys and we tucked these in our saddle scabbards and started out. He led the way, and from the direction he took it was plain we were not heading straight into the hills, but were going to swing around and come in from the south.

I led the packhorse and we rode in a compact bunch, not pushing for speed. It was in the afternoon that we ran into the other riders, out from the settlement and heading our way — Ben Kern, who was federal marshal for that part of the Territory, and three of the men he usually swore in as deputies when he had a need for any. We stopped and they stopped, looking us over.

"You've saved me some miles," Kern said. "I was heading for your place."

Rodock raised his eyebrows and looked at him and was silent. I kept my mouth shut. Claggett, who probably knew as much about the mares as I did by now, did the same. This was Rodock's game.

"Not saying much, are you?" Kern said. He saw the Henrys. "Got your warpaint on too. I thought something would be doing from what I've been hearing about things at your place. What's on your mind this time?"

"My mind's my own," Rodock said. "But it could be we're off on a little camping trip."

"And again it couldn't," Kern said. "Only camping you ever do is on the tail of a horse thief. That's the trouble. Twice now you've ridden in to tell me where to find them swinging. Evidence was clear enough, so there wasn't much I could do. But you're too damn free with your rope. How we going to get decent law around here with you old-timers crossing things up? This time, if it is a this time you're doing it right and turn them over to me. We'll just ride along to see that you do it."

Rodock turned to me. He had that grim and enduring look and the lines by his mouth were taut. "Break out those packs, boy. We're camping right here." I saw what he was figuring and I dismounted and began unfastening the packs. I had them on the ground and was fussing with the knots when Kern spoke.

"You're a stubborn old bastard," he said. "You'd stay right here and outwait us."

"I would," Rodock said.

"All right," Kern said. "We'll fade. But I've warned you. If it's rustlers you're after, bring them to me."

Rodock didn't say a thing and I heaved the packs on the horse again, and by time I had them fastened tight, Kern and his men were a distance away and throwing dust. We started on, and by dark we had gone a good piece. By dark the next day we had made a big half-circle and were well into the hills. About noon of the next, we were close enough to the canyon where we had found the mares, say two miles if you could have hopped it straight. Claggett and I waited while Rodock scouted around. He came back and led us up a twisting rocky draw to a small park hemmed in part way by a fifteen-foot rock shelf and the rest of the way by a close stand of pine. It was about a half acre in size, and you'd never know it was there unless you came along the draw and stumbled into it. We picketed the horses there and headed for the canyon on foot, moving slow and cautious as we came close. When we peered over the rim, the herd was there all right, the foals beginning to get some growth and the mares stepping a lot easier than before. They were used to the place now and not interested in leaving. They had taken to ranging pretty far up the canyon, but we managed to sight the whole count after a few minutes watching.

We searched along the rim for the right spot and found it, a crack in the rim wide enough for a man to ease into comfortably and be off the skyline for anyone looking from below, yet able to see the whole stretch where the herd was. To make it even better, we hauled a few rocks to the edge of the opening and piled brush with them, leaving a careful spy hole. We brought a flat-topped rock for a seat behind the hole. The idea was that one of us could sit there watching while the other two holed in a natural hiding place some fifty feet back under an overhanging ledge with a good screen of brush. The signal, if anything happened, was to be a pebble chucked back toward the hiding place.

I thought we'd take turns watching, but Rodock settled on that flat-top stone and froze there. Claggett and I kept each other company under the ledge, if you could call it keeping company when one person spent most of the time with his mouth shut whittling endless shavings off chunks of old wood or taking naps. That man Claggett had no nerves. He could keep his knife going for an hour at a time without missing a stroke or stretch out and drop off into a nap like we were just lazing around at the ranch. He didn't seem to have much personal interest in what might develop. He was just doing a job and tagging along with an old-time partner. As I said before, he didn't have a real feel for horses. I guess to be fair to him I ought to remember that he hadn't seen those mares with their hooves rasped to the quick and flinching and shuddering with every step they took. Me, I was strung like a too-tight fiddle. I'd have cracked sure if I hadn't had the sense to bring a deck in my pocket for solitaire. I nearly wore out those cards and even took to cheating to win, and it seemed to me we were cooped there for weeks when it was only five days. And all the time, every day, Rodock sat on that stone as if he was a piece of it, getting older and grayer and grimmer.

Nights we spent back with the horses. We'd be moving before dawn each morning, eating a heavy breakfast cooked over a small quick fire, then slipping out to our places with the first streaks of light carrying a cold snack in our pockets. We'd return after dark for another quick meal and roll right afterwards into our blankets. You'd think we hardly knew each other the way we behaved, only speaking when that was necessary. Claggett was never much of a talker, and Rodock was tied so tight in himself now he didn't have a word to spare. I kept quiet because I didn't want him smacking my age at me again. If he could chew his lips and wear out the hours waiting, I could too, and I did.

We were well into the fifth day and I was about convinced nothing would ever happen again, any time ever anywhere in the whole wide world, when a pebble came snicking through the brush and Rodock came hard after it ducking low and hurrying.

"They're here," he said. "All three." And I noticed the fierce little specks of light beginning to burn in his eyes. "They're stringing rope to trees for a corral. Probably planning to brand here, then run." He looked at me and I could see him assessing me and dismissing me, and he turned to Claggett. "Hugh," he started to say, "I want you to —"

I guess it was the way he had looked at me and the things he had said about my age. Anyway, I was mad. I didn't know what he was going to say, but I knew he had passed me by. I grabbed him by the arm.

"Mister Rodock," I said, "I'm the one rode with you after those mares."

He stared at me and shook his head a little as if to clear it.

"All right, boy," he said, "You do this and, by God, you do it right. Hurry back and get your horse and swing around and come riding into the canyon. Far as I can tell at the distance, these men are strangers, so there's not much chance they'd know you worked for me. You're just a drifter riding through. Keep them talking so Hugh and I can get down behind them. If they start something, keep them occupied long as you can." He grabbed me by the shoulders the way he had when we found the mares. "Any shooting you do, shoot to miss. I want them alive." He let go of me. "Now scat."

I scatted. I never went so fast over rough country on

my own feet in my life. When I reached the roan, I had to hang on to the neck to get some breath and my strength back. I slapped my saddle on and took him at a good clip out of the draw and in a sharp circle for the canyon mouth, a good clip, but not too much to put him in a lather. I was heading into the canyon, pulling him to an easy trot, when it hit me, what a damn fool thing I was doing. There were three of them in there, three mighty smart men with a lot of nerve, and they had put a lot of time and waiting into this job and wouldn't likely be wanting to take chances on its going wrong. I was scared, so scared I could hardly sit the roan, and I came near swinging him around and putting my heels to him. Maybe I would have. Maybe I would have run out on those mares. But then I saw that one of the men had spotted me and there was nothing much to do but keep going toward them.

The one that had spotted me was out a ways from the others as a lookout. He had a rifle and he swung it to cover me as I came near and I stopped the roan. He was a hardcase specimen if ever I saw one and I didn't like the way he looked at me.

"Hold it now, sonny," he said. "Throw down your guns."

I was glad he said that, said "sonny," I mean, because it sort of stiffened me and I wasn't quite so scared, being taken up some with being mad. I tried to act surprised and hold my voice easy.

"Lookahere," I said, "that's an unfriendly way to talk to a stranger riding through. I wouldn't think of using these guns unless somebody pushed me into it, but I'd feel kind of naked without them. Let's just leave them alone, and if you're not the boss, suppose you let me talk to him that is."

I figured he wouldn't shoot because they'd want to know was I alone and what was I doing around there, and I was right. He jerked his head toward the other two.

"Move along, sonny," he said. "But slow. And keep your hands high in sight. I'll blast you out of that saddle if you wiggle a finger."

I walked the roan close to the other two and he followed behind me and circled around me to stand with them. They had been starting a fire and had stopped to stare at me coming. One was a short, stocky man, almost bald, with a fringe of grizzled beard down his cheeks and around his chin. The other was about medium height and slender, with clean chiseled features and a pair of the hardest, shrewdest, bluest eyes I ever saw. It was plain he was the boss by the way he took over. He set those eyes on me and I started shivering inside again.

"I've no time to waste on you," he said. "Make it quick. What's your story?"

"Story?" I said. "Why, simple enough. I'm footloose and roaming for some months and I get up this way with my pockets about played out. I'm riding by and I see something happening in here and I drop in to ask a few questions."

"Questions?" he said, pushing his head forward at me. "What kind of questions?"

"Why," I said, "I'm wondering maybe you can tell me, if I push on through these hills do I come to a town or some place where maybe I can get a job?"

The three of them stood there staring at me, chewing on this, and I sat my saddle staring back, when the bearded man suddenly spoke.

"I ain't sure," he said, looking at the roan. "But may. be that's a Rodock horse."

I saw them start to move and I dove sideways off the roan, planning to streak for the brush, and a bullet from the rifle went whipping over the saddle where I'd been, and I hadn't more than bounced the first time when a voice like a chill wind struck the three of them still. "Hold it, and don't move!"

I scrambled up and saw them stiff and frozen, slowly swiveling their necks to look behind them at Rodock and Hugh Claggett and the wicked ready muzzles of their two Henrys.

"Reach," Rodock said, and they reached. "All right, boy," he said. "Strip them down."

I cleaned them thoroughly and got, in addition to the rifle and the usual revolvers, two knives from the bearded man and a small but deadly derringer from an inside pocket of the slender man's jacket.

"Got everything?" Rodock said. "Then hobble them good."

I did this just as thoroughly, tying their ankles with about a two-foot stretch between so they could walk short-stepped, but not run, and tying their wrists together behind their backs with a loop up and around their necks and down again so that if they tried yanking or pulling they'd be rough on their own Adam's apples.

They didn't like any of this. The slender man didn't say a word, just clamped his mouth and talked hate with his eyes, but the other two started cursing.

"Shut up," Rodock said, "or we'll ram gags down your throats." They shut up, and Rodock motioned to me to set them in a row on the ground leaning against a fallen tree and he hunkered down himself facing them with his Henry across his lap. "Hugh," he said, without looking away from them, "take down those ropes they've been running and bring their horses and any of their stuff you find over here. Ought to be some interesting branding irons about." He took off his hat and set it on the ground beside him. "Hop your horse, boy," he said; "get over to our hide-out and bring everything back here."

When I returned leading our other horses, the three of them were still right in a row leaning against the log and Rodock was still squatted on the ground looking at them. Maybe words had been passing. I wouldn't know. Anyway, they were all quiet then. The hardcase was staring at his own feet. The bearded man's eyes were roaming around and he had a sick look on his face. The slender man was staring right back at Rodock and his mouth was only a thin line in his face. Claggett was standing to one side fussing with a rope. I saw he was fixing a hangman's knot on it and had two others already finished and coiled at his feet. When I saw them I had a funny empty feeling under my belt and I didn't know why. I had seen a hanging before and never felt like that. I guess I had some kind of a queer notion that just hanging those three wouldn't finish the whole thing right. It wouldn't stop me waking at night and thinking about those mares and their crippled hooves.

My coming seemed to break the silence that had a grip

on the whole place. The slender man drew back his lips
and spit words at Rodock.

"Quit playing games," he said. "Get this over with.
We know your reputation."

"Do you?" Rodock said. He stood up and waggled
each foot in turn to get the kinks out of his legs. He
turned and saw what Claggett was doing and a strange
little mirthless chuckle sounded in his throat. "You're
wasting your time, Hugh," he said. "We won't be using
those. I'm taking these three in."

Claggett's jaw dropped and his mouth showed open.
I guess he was seeing an old familiar pattern broken and
he didn't know how to take it. I wasn't and I had caught
something in Rodock's tone. I couldn't have said what
it was, but it was sending tingles through my hair roots.

"Don't argue with me, Hugh," Rodock said. "My
mind's set. You take some of the food and start hazing
the herd toward home. They can do it now if you take
them by easy stages. The boy and I'll take these three
in."

I helped Claggett get ready and watched him go up
the canyon to bunch the herd and get it moving. I
turned to Rodock and he was staring down the back
trail.

"Think you could handle four horses on lead ropes,
boy?" he said. "The packhorse and their three."

"Expect I could, strung out," I said. "But why not
split them? You take two and I take two."

"I'll be doing something else," he said, and that same
little cold chuckle sounded in his throat. "How far do
you make it, boy, to the settlement and Kern's office!"

"Straight to it," I said, "I make it close to fifty mile."

"About right," he said. "Kind of a long hike for those used to having horses under them. Hop over and take the hobbles off their feet."

I hopped, but not very fast. I was feeling some disappointed. I was feeling that he was letting me and those mares down. A fifty-mile hike for those three would worry them plenty, and they'd be worrying, too, about what would come at the end of it. Still it was a disappointment to think about.

"While you're there," Rodock said, "pull their boots off too."

I swung to look at him. He was a big man, as I said before, but I'd run across others that stood taller and filled a doorway more, but right then he was the biggest man I ever saw anywhere any time in my whole life.

I didn't bother to take off the hobbles. I left them tied so they'd hold the boots together in pairs and I could hang them flapping over the back of the packhorse. I pulled the boots off, not trying to be gentle, just yanking, and I had a little trouble with the hardcase. He tried to kick me, so I heaved on the rope between his ankles and he came sliding out from the log flat on his back and roughing his bound hands under him, and after that he didn't try anything more. But what I remember best about the three of them then is the yellow of the socks the slender man wore. Those on the others were the usual dark gray, but his were bright yellow. I've thought about them lots of times and never been able to figure why and where he ever got them.

Rodock was rummaging in their stuff that Claggett had collected. He tossed a couple of branding irons toward me. "Bring these along," he said. "Maybe Kern will be interested in them." He picked up a whip, an old but serviceable one with a ten-foot lash, and tested it with a sharp crack. "Get up," he said to the three, and they got up. "I'll be right behind you with this. You'll stay bunched and step right along. Start walking."

They started, and he tucked his Henry in his saddle scabbard and swung up on the bay.

By time I had the other horses pegged in a line with the packhorse as an anchor at the end and was ready to follow, they were heading out of the canyon and I hurried to catch up. I had to get out of the way, too, because Claggett had the herd gathered and was beginning to push the mares along with the foals skittering around through the bushes. Anyone standing on the canyon edge looking down would have seen a queer sight, maybe the damndest procession that ever paraded through that lonesome country. Those three were out in front, walking and putting their feet down careful even in the grass to avoid pebbles and bits of deadwood, with Rodock big and straight on his bay behind them, then me with my string of three saddled but riderless horses and the packhorse, and behind us all the mares and the skittering foals with Claggett weaving on his sorrel to keep the stragglers on the move.

Once out of the canyon we had to separate. Rodock and I and our charges turned southeast to head for the settlement. Claggett had to swing the herd toward the northeast to head for the home range. He had his trouble with the mares because they wanted to follow me and my string. But he and his sorrel knew their business and by hard work made the break and held it.

I guess he was a bit huffy about the whole thing because I waved when the distance was getting long between us, and he saw me wave and didn't even raise an arm. I don't know as I blame him for that.

This was midafternoon and by camping time we had gone maybe ten miles and had shaken down to a steady grind. My horses had bothered the roan some by holding back on the rope and had bothered themselves a few times by spreadeagling and trying to go in different directions, but by now the idea had soaked in and they were plugging along single file and holding their places. The three men out in front had learned to keep moving or feel the whip. The slender man stepped along without paying attention to the other two and never looked back at Rodock and never said a word. The bearded man had found that shouting and cursing simply wore out his throat and had no effect on the grim figure pacing behind them. The hardcase had tried a break, ducking quick to one side and running fast as he could, but Rodock had jumped the bay and headed him the same as you do a steer, and being awkward with his hands tied he had taken a nasty tumble. Not a one of them was going to try that again. Their feet were too tender for hard running anyway, especially out there in the open where the grass was bunchy with bare spaces aplenty, and there were stretches with a kind of coarse gravel underfoot. When Rodock called a halt by water, they were ready to flop on the ground immediately and hitch around and dabble their feet in the stream, and I noticed that the bottoms of their socks were about gone and the soles of their feet were red where they showed in splotches through the dirt ground in. I enjoyed those ten miles, not with a feeling of fun, but with a sort of slow, steady satisfaction.

I prepared food and Rodock and I ate, and then we fed them, one at a time. Rodock sat watch with his Henry on his lap while I untied them and let them eat and wash up a bit and tied them again. We pegged each of them to a tree for the night, sitting on the ground with his back to the trunk and a rope around so he wouldn't topple when he slept. I was asleep almost as soon as I stretched out, and I slept good, and I think Rodock did too.

The next day was more of the same except that we were at it a lot longer, morning and afternoon, and our pace slowed considerably as the day wore on. They were hard to get started again after a noon stop and the last hours before we stopped, they were beginning to limp badly. They weren't thinking any more of how to make a break. They were concentrating on finding the easiest spots on which to set each step. I figured we covered twenty miles, and I got satisfaction out of every one of them. But the best were in the morning because along late in the afternoon I began to feel tired, not tired in my muscles but tired and somehow kind of shrinking inside. When we stopped, I saw that their socks were just shredded yarn around their ankles and their feet were swelling and angry red and blistery through the dirt. With them sullen and silent and Rodock gray and grim and never wasting a word, I began to feel lonesome, and I couldn't go to sleep right away and found myself checking and rechecking in my mind how far we had come and how many miles we still had to go.

The day after that we started late because there was rain during the night and we waited till the morning mists cleared. The dampness in the ground must have felt better to their feet for a while because they went along fairly good the first of the morning after we got under way. They were really hard to get started, though, after the noon stop. During the afternoon they went slower and slower, and Rodock had to get mean with the whip around the heels of the hardcase and the bearded man. Not the slender one. That one kept his head high and marched along and you could tell he was fighting not to wince with every step. After a while, watching him, I began to get the feel of him. He was determined not to give us the satisfaction of seeing this get to him in any serious way. I found myself watching him too much, too closely, so I dropped behind a little more, tagging along in the rear with my string, and before Rodock called the halt by another stream, I began to see the occasional small red splotches in the footprints on dusty stretches that showed the blisters on their feet were breaking. The best I could figure we had come maybe another ten miles during the day, the last few mighty slow. That made about forty all together, and when I went over it in my mind I had to call it twelve more to go because we had curved off the most direct route some to avoid passing near a couple of line cabins of the only other ranch in that general neighborhood north of the settlement.

There weren't many words in any of us as we went through the eating routine. I didn't know men's faces were capable of such intense hatred as showed plain on the hardcase and the bearded man. They gobbled their food and glared at Rodock from their night-posts against trees, and for all I know glared without stopping all night because they had the same look the next morning. It was the slender man who suddenly took to talking. The hatred he'd had at the start seemed to have burned away. What was left was a kind of hard pride that kept his eyes alive. He looked up from his food at Rodock.

"It was a good try," he said.

"It was," Rodock said. "But not good enough. Your mistake was hurting my horses."

"I had to," the man said. "That was part of it. I saw some of your horses on a stage line once. I had to have a few."

"If you wanted some of my horses," Rodock said, "why didn't you come and buy them?"

"I was broke," the man said.

"You were greedy," Rodock said. "You had to take all in that basin. If you'd cut out a few and kept on going, you might have made it."

"Maybe," the man said. "Neither of us will ever know now. You planning to keep this up all the way in?"

"I am," Rodock said.

"Then turn us over?" the man said.

"Yes," Rodock said.

"You're the one that's greedy," the man said.

He shut up and finished his food and crawled to his tree and refused to look at Rodock again. I fixed his rope and then I had trouble getting to sleep. I lay a long time before I dozed and what sleep I got wasn't much good.

In the morning Rodock was grayer and grimmer than

ever before. Maybe he hadn't slept much either. He stood off by himself and let me do everything alone. I couldn't make the hardcase and the bearded man get on their feet, and I found my temper mighty short and was working up a real mad when the slender man, who was up and ready, stepped over and kicked them, kicked them with his own swollen feet that had the remains of his yellow socks flapping around the ankles.

"Get up!" he said. "Damn you, get up! We're going through with this right!"

They seemed a lot more afraid of him than of me. They staggered up and they stepped along with him as Rodock came close with the whip in his hand and we got our pathetic parade started again. We couldn't have been moving much more than a mile an hour, and even that pace slowed, dropping to about a crawl when we hit rough stretches, and more and more red began to show in the footprints. And still that slender man marched along, slow but dogged, the muscles in his neck taut as he tried to stay straight without wincing.

Rodock was mean and nasty, crowding close behind them, using the whip to raise the dust around the lagging two. I didn't like the look of him. The skin of his face was stretched too tight and his eyes were too deep-sunk. I tried riding near him and making a few remarks to calm him, but he snapped at me like I might be a horse thief myself, so I dropped behind and stayed there.

He didn't stop at noontime, but kept them creeping along, maybe because he was afraid he'd never get them started again. It was only a short while after that the bearded man fell down, just crumpled and went over sideways and lay still. It wasn't exactly a faint or any-

thing quite like that. I think he had cracked inside, had
run out his score and quit trying, even trying to stay conscious. He was breathing all right, but it was plain he
wouldn't do any more walking for a spell.

Rodock sat on his horse and looked down at him. "All
right, boy," he said. "Hoist him on one of your string
and tie him so he'll stay put." I heaved him on the first
of the horses behind me and slipped a rope around the
horse's barrel to hold him. Rodock sat on his bay and
looked at the other two men, not quite sure what to do,
and the slender one stared back at him, contempt sharp
on his face, and Rodock shook out the whip. "Get moving, you two!" he said, and we started creeping along
again.

It was about another hour and maybe another mile
when the hardcase began screaming. He threw himself
on the ground and rolled and thrashed and kept screaming, then stretched out taut and suddenly went limp all
over, wide awake and conscious, but staring up as if he
couldn't focus on anything around him.

Rodock had to stop again, chewing his lower lip and
frowning. "All right boy," he said. "Hoist that one
too." I did, the same as the other one, and when I looked
around damned if that slender man wasn't walking on
quite a distance ahead with Rodock right behind him.

I didn't want to watch, but I couldn't help watching
that man stagger on. I think he had almost forgotten
us. He was intent on the terrible task of putting one foot
forward after the other and easing his weight onto it.
Rodock, bunched on his bay and staring at him, was the
one who cracked first. The sun was still up the sky, but
he shouted a halt and when the man kept going he had

to jump down and run ahead and grab him. It was a grim business making camp. The other two had straightened out some, but they had no more spirit in them than a pair of limp rabbits. I had to lift them down, and it wasn't until they had some food in them that they began to perk up at all. They seemed grateful when I hiked a ways and brought water in a folding canvas bucket from one of the packs and let them take turns soaking their swollen bloody feet in it. Then I took a saddle blanket and ripped it in pieces and wrapped some of them around their feet. I think I did that so I wouldn't find myself always sneaking looks at their feet. I did the same for the slender man, and all the time I was doing it he looked at me with that contempt on his face and I didn't give a damn. I did this even though I thought Rodock might not like it, but he didn't say a word. I noticed he wouldn't look at me and I found I didn't want to look at him either. I tried to keep my mind busy figuring how far we had come and made it six miles with six more still to go, and I was wishing those six would fade away and the whole thing would be over. The sleep I got that night wasn't worth anything to me.

In the morning I didn't want any breakfast and I wasn't going to prepare any unless Rodock kicked me into it. He was up ahead of me, standing quiet and chewing his lower lip and looking very old and very tired, and he didn't say a word to me. I saddled the horses the way I had been every morning because that was the easiest way to tote the saddles along and tied them in the usual string. The slender man was awake, watching me, and by time I finished the other two were too. They were thoroughly beaten. They couldn't have walked a quarter of a mile with the devil himself herding them. I thought to hell with Rodock and led the horses up close and hoisted the two, with them quick to help, into their saddles. They couldn't put their feet in the stirrups, but they could sit the saddles and let their feet dangle. I went over to the slender man and started to take hold of him, and he glared at me and shook himself free of my hands and twisted around and strained till he was up on his feet. I stood there gaping at him and he hobbled away, heading straight for the settlement. I couldn't move. I was sort of frozen inside watching him. He made about fifty yards and his legs buckled under him. The pain in his feet must have been stabbing up with every step and he simply couldn't stand any longer. And then while I stared at him he started crawling on his hands and knees.

"God damn it, boy!" Rodock's voice behind me made me jump. "Grab that man! Haul him back here!"

I ran and grabbed him and after the first grab, he didn't fight and I hauled him back. "Hoist him on his horse," Rodock said, and I did that. And then Rodock started cursing. He cursed that man and he cursed me and then he worked back over us both again. He wasn't a cursing man and he didn't know many words and he didn't have much imagination at it, but what he did know he used over and over again and after a while he ran down and stopped and chewed his lower lip. He turned and stalked to the packhorse and took the pairs of tied boots and came along the line tossing each pair over the withers of the right horse. He went back to the packs and pulled out the weapons I'd found on the three and checked to see that the guns were empty and shook the last of the flour out of its bag and put the weapons in it with the rifle barrel sticking out the top. He tied the bag to the pommel of the slender man's saddle.

"All right, boy," he said. "Take off those lead ropes and untie their hands."

When I had done this and they were rubbing their wrists, he stepped close to the slender man's horse and spoke up at the man.

"Back to the last creek we passed yesterday," he said, "and left along it a few miles you come to Shirttail Fussel's shack. From what I hear for a price he'll hide out anything and keep his mouth shut. A man with sense would fix his feet there and then keep traveling and stay away from this range the rest of his days."

The slender man didn't say a word. He pulled his horse around and started in the direction of the creek and the other two tagged him, and what I remember is that look of hard pride still in his eyes, plain and sharp against the pinched and strained bleakness of his face.

We watched them go and I turned to Rodock. He was old, older even than I thought he was when I first saw him, and tired with heavy circles under his eyes. At that moment I didn't like him at all, not because he had let them go, but because of what he had put me through, and it was my turn to curse him. I did it right. I did a better job than he had done before and he never even wagged a muscle. "Shut up," he said finally. "I need a drink." He went to his bay and mounted and headed for the settlement. I watched him, hunched forward and old in the saddle, and I was ashamed. I took the lead rope of the packhorse and climbed on the roan and followed him. I was glad when he put the bay into a fast trot because I was fed up with sitting on a walking horse.

He bobbed along ahead of me, a tired old man who seemed too small for that big bay, and then a strange thing began to happen. He began to sit straighter in the saddle and stretch up and look younger by the minute, and when we reached the road and headed into the settlement he was Jeremy Rodock riding straight and true on a Rodock horse and riding it like it was the part of him that in a way it really was. He hit a good clip the last stretch and my roan and the packhorse were see-sawing on the lead rope trying to keep up when we reached the buildings and pulled in by a tie rail. I swung down right after him and stepped up beside him and we went toward the saloon. We passed the front window of Kern's office and he was inside and came popping out.

"Hey, you two," he said. "Anything to report?"

We stopped and faced him and he looked at us kind of funny. I guess we did look queer, dirty and unshaved and worn in spots.

"Not a thing," Rodock said. "I told you we could be taking a camp trip and that's all I'll say. Except that I'm not missing any stock and haven't stretched any rope."

We went into the saloon and to the bar and downed a stiff one apiece.

"Mister Rodock," I said, "when you think about it, that man beat us."

"Damned if he didn't," Rodock said. He didn't seem to be bothered by it and I know I wasn't. "Listen to me, son," he said. "I expect I haven't been too easy to get along with for quite a few weeks lately. I want you to know I've noticed how you and that roan have stuck to my heels over some mighty rough trail. Now we've got to get home and get a horse ranch moving again. We'll be needing some hands. Come along with me, son, and we'll look around. I'd like your opinion on them before hiring any."

That was Jeremy Rodock. They don't grow men like that around here any more.

THAT MARK HORSE

The Horse Who Knew Men

NOT THAT HORSE, mister. Not that big slab-sided brute. Take any or all of the rest, I'm selling the whole string. But not that one. By rights I should. He's no damn good to me. The best horse either one of us'll likely ever see and he's no damn good to me. Or me to him. But I'll not sell him . . .

Try something, mister. Speak to him. The name's Mark . . . There. See how his ears came up? See how he swung to check you and what you were doing? The way any horse would. Any horse that likes living and knows his name. But did you notice how he wouldn't look at me? Used to perk those ears and swing that head whenever he heard my voice. Not any more. Knows I'm talking about him right now and won't look at me. Almost ten months it is and he still won't look at me . . .

That horse and I were five-six years younger when this all began. I was working at one of the early dude ranches and filling in at the rodeos roundabout. A little riding, a little roping. Not too good, just enough to place once in a while. I was in town one day for the mail and the postmaster poked his head out to chuckle some and say there was something for me at the station a mite too big for the box. I went down and the agent wasn't there. I scouted around and he was out by the stock corral and a bunch of other men too all leaning on the fence and looking over. I pushed up by the agent and there was that horse inside. He was alone in there and he was the damndest horse I'd ever seen. Like the rest around I'd been raised on cow ponies and this thing looked big as the side of a barn to me and awkward as all hell. He'd just been let down the chute from a boxcar on the siding. There were bits of straw clinging to him and he stood still with head up testing the air. For that first moment he looked like a kid's crazy drawing of a horse, oversize and exaggerated with legs too long and big stretched-out barrel and high-humped withers and long-reaching neck. The men were joshing and wondering was it an elephant or a giraffe and I was agreeing and then I saw that horse move. He took a few steps walking and flowed forward into a trot. That's the only way to put it. He flowed forward the way water rolls down a hill. His muscles didn't bunch and jump under his hide. They slid easy and smooth and those long legs reached for distance without seeming to try. He made a double circuit of the corral without slowing, checking everything as he went by. He wasn't trying to find a way out. He just wanted to move some and see where he was and what was doing roundabout. He saw us along the fence and we could have been posts for all the particular attention he paid us. He stopped by the far fence and stood looking over it and now I'd seen him move there wasn't anything awkward about him. He was big and he was rough-built but he wasn't awkward any more even standing there still. Nobody was saying a word. Everyone there knew horses and they'd seen what I saw. "Damn it to eternal hell," I said. "That's a horse." The agent turned and saw who it was. "Glad you think so," he said. "It's your horse. This came along too." And he stuck a note in my hand.

It had my name on it all right. It was from a New York State man who ran some sort of factory there, made shoes I think he told me once. He'd been a regular at the ranch, not for any dude doings but once a summer for a camping trip and I'd been assigned to him several years running. It wasn't long. It said the doctors had been carving him some and told him he couldn't ride again so he was closing his stable. He'd sold his other stock but thought this horse Mark ought to be out where there was more room than there was back east. Wanted me to take him and treat him right.

I shoved that note in a pocket and eased through the fence. "Mark," I called and across the corral those ears perked stiff and that big head swung my way. "Mark," I called again and that horse turned and came about halfway and stood with head high, looking me over. I picked a coil of rope off a post and shook out a loop and he watched me with ears forward and head a bit to one side. I eased close and sudden I snaked up the loop and it was open right for his head and he just wasn't there. He was thirty feet to the left and I'd have sworn he made it in one leap. Maybe a dozen times I tried and I didn't have a chance. The comments coming from the fence line weren't improving my temper any. Then I noticed he wasn't watching me, he was watching the rope, and I had an attack of common sense. He was wearing a halter. This wasn't any western range horse. This was one of those big eastern crossbreds with a lot of Thoroughbred in them I'd heard about. Likely he'd never had a rope thrown at him before. I tossed the rope over by the fence and walked toward him and he stood blowing his nostrils a bit and looking at me. I stopped a few feet away and didn't even try to reach for the halter. He looked at me and he was really seeing me the way a horse can and I was somebody who knew his name out here where he'd been dumped out of the darkness of a boxcar. He stretched that long neck and sniffed at my shirt and I took hold of the halter and that was all there was to it . . .

That was the beginning of my education. Yes, mister, it was me had to be taught, not that horse. The next lesson came the first time I tried to ride him. I was thinking what a big brute he was and what a lot of power was penned in him and I'd have to control all that so I used a Spanish spade bit that would be wicked if used rough. He didn't want to take it and I had to force it on him.

The same with the saddle. I used a double-rig with a high-roll cantle and he snorted at it and kept sidling away and grunted all the time I was tightening the cinches. He stood steady enough when I swung aboard but when we started off nothing felt right. The saddle was too small for him and sat too high-arched over the backbone and those sloping withers. He kept wanting to drop his head and rub his mouth on his legs over that bit. At last he sort of sighed and eased out and went along without much fuss. He'd decided I was plain stupid on some things and he'd endure and play along for a while. At the time I thought he was accepting me as boss so I started him really stepping and the instant he understood I wanted him to move that was what he did. He moved. He went from a walk into a gallop in a single flowing rush and it was only that high cantle kept me from staying behind. I'm telling you, mister, that was something, the feel of those big muscles sliding smooth under me and distance dropping away under those hooves.

Then I realized he wasn't even working. I was traveling faster than I ever had on horseback and he was just loafing along without a sign of straining for speed. That horse just liked moving. I never knew another liked it as much. It could get to him the way liquor can a man and he'd keep reaching for more. That's what he was doing then. I could feel him notching it up the way an engine does when the engineer pushes forward on the throttle and I began to wonder how he'd be on stopping. I had an idea twelve hundred pounds of power moving like that would be a lot different from eight hundred pounds of bunchy little cow pony. I was right. I pulled in some and he slowed some but not much and I pulled harder and he tossed his head at the bit biting, and I yanked in sharp and he stopped. Yes, mister, he stopped all right. But he didn't slap down on his haunches and slide to a stop on his rump the way a cow pony does. He took a series of jumps stiff-legged to brake and stopped short and sudden with his legs planted like trees and I went forward, bumping my belly on the horn and over his head and hanging there doubled down over his ears with my legs clamped around his neck. That Mark horse was surprised as I was but he took care of me. He kept his head up and stood steady as a rock while I climbed down his neck to the saddle. I was feeling foolish and mad at myself and him and I yanked mean on the reins and swung him hard to head for home and that did it. He'd had enough. He shucked me off his back the way someone might toss a beanbag. Don't ask me how. I'd ridden plenty horses and could make a fair showing even on the tough ones. But that Mark horse wanted me off so he put me off. And then he didn't bolt for the horizon. He stopped about twenty feet away and stood there watching me.

I sat on the ground and looked at him. I'd been stupid but I was beginning to learn. I remembered the feel of him under me, taking me with him not trying to get away from me. I remembered how he'd behaved all along and I studied on all that. There wasn't a trace of meanness in that horse. He didn't mind being handled and ridden. He'd been ready and willing for me to come up and take him in the station corral. But he wasn't going to have a rope slapped at him and be yanked around. He was ready and willing to let me ride him and to show me how a real horse could travel. But he wasn't going to do much of it with a punishing bit and a rig he didn't like. He was a big batch of damned good horseflesh and he knew that and was proud of it and he had a hell of a lot of self-respect. He just plain wouldn't be pushed around and that was that and I had to understand it. I claim it proud for myself that I did. I went to him and he waited for me as I knew now he would. I swung easy as I could up into the saddle and he stood steady with his head turned a little so he could watch me. I let the lines stay loose and guided him just by neck-reining and I walked him back to the ranch. I slid down there and took off the western saddle and the bridle with that spade bit. I hunted through the barn till I found a light snaffle bit and cleaned it and put it in the bridle. I held it up for him to see and he took it with no fuss at all. I routed out the biggest of the three English saddles we had for eastern dudes who wouldn't use anything else and that I'd always thought were damned silly things. I showed it to him and he stood quiet while I slapped it on and buckled the single leather cinch. "Mark," I said, "I don't know how to sit one of these crazy postage stamps and I'm bunged up some from that beating. Let's take it easy." Mister, that horse knew what I'd said. He gave me the finest ride I ever had . . .

See what I mean, the best damn horse either of us'll ever see? No, I guess you can't. Not complete. You'd have to live with him day after day and have the endless little things happening tally up in your mind. After a while you'd understand as I did what a combination he was of a serious dependable gent and a mischievous little

kid. With a neat sense of timing on those things too.
Take him out for serious riding and he'd tend strict to his
business, which was covering any kind of ground for
you at any kind of speed you wanted. The roughest
going made no difference to him. He was built to go at
any clip just about anywhere short of straight up a cliff,
and you'd get the feeling he'd try that if you really
wanted him to. But let him loaf around with nothing
to do and he'd be curious as a cat on the prowl, poking
into every corner he could find and seeing what devilment he could do. Nothing mean, just playful. Maybe
a nuisance if you were doing a job where he could get
at you and push his big carcass in the way whiffling at
everything or come up quiet behind and blow sudden
down your shirt collar. Let him get hold of a bucket
and you'd be buying a new one. There'd not be much
left of the old one after he'd had his fun. He'd stick his
nose in and flip the thing and do that over and over like
he was trying for a distance record then start whamming
it around with his hooves, tickled silly at the racket. And
when there'd be no one else around to see how crazy you
were acting he'd get you to playing games too. He
liked to have you sneak off and hide and whistle low for
him and he'd pad around stretching that long neck into
the damndest places looking for you and blow triumphant when he found you. Yes, mister, that horse
liked living and being around him'd help you do the
same.

And work? That horse was a working fool. No.
There was nothing foolish about it. The ranch was still
in the beef business too in those days and he'd never had
any experience with cattle before. He was way behind

our knowing little cow ponies when it came to handling
them and he knew it. So he tried to balance that by
using those brains of his overtime and working harder
than any of the others. He'd watch them and try to
figure what they were doing and how they did it and
then do it himself. He'd try so hard sometimes I'd ache
inside, feeling that eagerness quivering under me. Of
course he never could catch up to them on some things.
Too big. Too eager. Needed too much room moving
around. He couldn't slide into a tight bunch of cattle
and cut out the right one, easing it out without disturb-
ing the rest much. And he wasn't much good for roping
even though he did let me use a western saddle for that
soon as he saw the sense to it. Lunged too hard when I'd
looped an animal and was ready to throw it. Maybe he'd
have learned the right touch in time but he didn't get
the chance. The foreman saw us damn near break a
steer's neck and told us to quit. But on straight herding
he couldn't be beat. He could head a runaway steer
before it even stretched its legs. He could scour the
brush for strays like a hound dog on a scent. He could
step out and cover territory all day at a pace that'd kill
off most horses and come in seeming damn near as fresh
as when he started. I used to think I was tough and
could take long hours but that horse could ride me
right out of the saddle and act like he thought I was
soft for calling a halt.

But I still haven't hit the real thing. That horse was
just plain honest all through. No, that's not the exact
word. Plenty of horses are that. He was something a
bit more. Square. That's it. He was just plain square
in everything he did and the way he looked at living.

He liked to have things fair and even. He was my horse
and he knew it. I claim it proud that for a time anyway
he really was my horse and let me know it. But that
meant too I was his man and I had my responsibilities. I
wasn't a boss giving orders. I was his partner. He
wasn't something I owned doing what I made him do.
He was my partner doing his job because he wanted to
and because he knew that was the way it ought to be
with a man and a horse. A horse like him. Long as I
treated him right he'd treat me right. If I'd get mean
or stupid with him I'd be having trouble. I'd be taking
another lesson. Like the time along about the second
or third week when I was feeling safer on that English
saddle and forgot he wasn't a hard-broke cow pony. I
wanted a sudden burst of speed for one reason or another and I hit him with my spurs. I was so used to doing
that with the other horses that I couldn't figure at first
what had happened. I sat on the ground rubbing the
side I'd lit on and stared at him watching me about
twenty feet away. Then I had it. I unfastened those
spurs and threw them away. I've never used the things
again ever, anytime on any horse . . .

Well, mister, there I was mighty proud to have a horse
like that but still some stupid because I hadn't tumbled
to what you might call his specialty. He had to show
me. It was during fall roundup. We had a bunch of
steers in the home corral being culled for market and
something spooked them and they started milling wild
and pocketed me and Mark in a corner. They were
slamming into the fence rails close on each side. I knew
we'd have to do some fancy stepping to break through

and get around them. I must have felt nervous on the
reins because that Mark horse took charge himself. He
swung away from those steers and leaped straight at the
near fence and sailed over it. He swung in a short circle
and stopped, looking back at those steers jamming into
the corner where we'd been and I sat the saddle catching the breath he'd jolted out of me. I should have
known. He was a jumper. He was what people back
east called a hunter. Maybe he'd been a timber horse,
a steeplechaser. He'd cleared that four-foot fence with
just about no take-off space like a kid skipping at hop-
scotch. I'm telling you, mister, I had me a time the next
days jumping him over everything in sight. When I was
sure of my seat I made him show me what he really
could do and he played along with me for anything
within reason, even stretching that reason considerable.
The day I had nerve enough and he took me smack over
an empty wagon I really began to strut. But there was
one thing he wouldn't do. He wouldn't keep jumping
the same thing over and over the same time out. Didn't
see any sense in that. He'd clear whatever it was maybe
twice, maybe three times, and if I tried to put him at it
again he'd stop cold and swing his head to look at me
and I'd shrivel down to size and feel ashamed . . .

So I had something new in these parts then, a jumping
horse bred to it and built for it with the big frame to
take the jolts and the power to do it right. I had me a
horse could bring me some real money at the rodeos.
I wouldn't have to try for prize money. I could put on
exhibition stunts. I got together with some of the old
show hands and we worked up an act that pleased the

crowds. They'd lead Mark out so the people could see
the size of him and he'd plunge around at the end of the
shank, rolling his eyes and tossing his head. He'd paw
at the sky and lash out behind like he was the worst
mean-tempered mankiller ever caught. It was all a joke
because he was the safest horse any man ever handled
and anyone who watched close could see those hooves
never came near connecting with anything except air.
But he knew what it was all about and he made it look
good. The wranglers would get him over and into the
outlaw chute with him pretending to fight all the way.
They'd move around careful outside and reach through
the bars to bridle and saddle him like they were scared
green of him. I'd climb to the top rails and ease down
on the saddle like I was scared too but determined to
break my neck trying to ride one hell of a bucking
brute. We'd burst out of the chute like a cannon going
off and streak straight for the high fence on the opposite side of the arena. All the people who'd not seen it
before would come up gasping on their seats expecting
a collision that would shake the whole place. And at
the last second that Mark horse would rise up and over
the fence in a clean sweet jump and I'd be standing in
the stirrups waving my hat and yelling and the crowd'd
go wild.

After a time most people knew what to expect and the
surprise part of that act was gone so we had to drop it.
But we worked up another that got the crowds no
matter how many times they saw it. I never liked it
much but I blew too hard once how that horse would
jump anything and someone suggested this and I was hot
and said sure he'd do it and I was stuck with it. He never

liked it much either but he did it for me. Maybe he knew I was getting expensive habits and needed the money coming in. Well, anyway, we did it and it took a lot of careful practice with a slow old steer before we tried the real thing. I'd be loafing around on Mark in the arena while the bull-riding was on. I'd watch and pick a time when one of the bulls had thrown his rider and was hopping around in the clear or making a dash across the open. I'd nudge Mark with my heels and he'd be off in that forward flowing with full power in it. We'd streak for the bull angling in at the side and the last sliced second before a head-on smash we'd lift and go over in a clean sweep and swing to come up by the grandstand and take the applause.

Thinking of that since I've been plenty shamed. I've a notion the reason people kept wanting to see it wasn't just to watch a damned good horse do a damned difficult job. They were always hoping something would happen. Always a chance the bull might swerve and throw us off stride and make it a real smash. Always a chance the horns might toss too high and we'd tangle with them and come down in a messy scramble. But I didn't think about that then or how I was asking more than a man should except in a tight spot that can't be avoided from a horse that's always played square with him. I was thinking of the money and the cheers and the pats on the back. And then it happened . . .

Not what maybe you're thinking, mister. Not that at all. That horse never failed in a jump and never would. We'd done our stint on the day, done it neat and clean, gone over a big head-tossing bull with space to spare and were just about ready to take the exit gate without bothering to open it. Another bull was in the arena, a mean tricky one that'd just thrown his rider after a tussle and was scattering dust real mad. The two tenders on their cagey little cow ponies had cut in to let the rider scramble to safety and were trying to hustle the bull into the closing out pen. They thought they had him going in and were starting to relax in their saddles when that brute broke away and tore out into the open again looking for someone on foot to take apart. While the tenders were still wheeling to go after him he saw something over by the side fence and headed toward it fast. I saw too and sudden I was cold all over. Some damn fool woman had let a little boy get away from her, maybe three-four years old, too young to have sense, and that kid had crawled through the rails and was twenty-some feet out in the arena. I heard people screaming at him and saw him standing there confused and the bull moving and the tenders too far away. I slammed my heels into Mark and we were moving too the way only that horse could move. I had to lunge forward along his neck or he'd have been right out from under me. There wasn't time to head the bull or try to pick up the kid. There wasn't time for anything fancy at all. There was only one thing could be done. We swept in angling straight to the big moving target of that bull and I slammed down on the reins with all my strength so Mark couldn't get his head up to jump and go over, and in the last split second all I could think of was my leg maybe getting caught between when they hit and I dove off Mark sidewise into the dust and he

drove on alone and smashed into that bull just back of
the big sweeping horns.

They picked me up half dazed with an aching head
and assorted bruises and put me on some straw bales in
the stable till a doctor could look me over. They led
Mark into one of the stalls with a big gash from one of
the horns along his side and a swelling shoulder so pain-
ful he dragged the leg without trying to step on it. They
put ropes on the bull where he lay quiet with the fight
knocked out of him and prodded him up and led him off.
I never did know just what happened to the kid except
that he was safe enough. I didn't care because when I
pushed up off those bales without waiting for the doctor
and went into the stall that Mark horse wouldn't look
at me . . .

So that's it, mister. That's what happened. But I
won't have you getting any wrong notions about it. I
won't have you telling me the way some people do that
horse is through with me because I made him smash into
that bull. Nothing like that at all. He doesn't blame me
for the pulled tendon in his shoulder that'll bother him
long as he lives when the weather's bad. Not that horse.
I've thought the whole business over again and again. I
can remember every last detail of those hurrying seconds
in the arena, things I wasn't even aware of at the time
itself. That horse was flowing forward before I slammed
my heels into him. There wasn't any attempt at lifting
that big head or any gathering of those big muscles under
me for a jump when I was slamming down on the reins.
He'd seen. He knew. He knew what had to be done.

That horse is through with me because at the last second I went yellow and I let him do it alone. He thinks I didn't measure up in the partnership. I pulled out and let him do it alone.

He'll let me ride him even now but I've quit that because it isn't the same. Even when he's really moving and the weather's warm and the shoulder feels good and he's reaching for distance and notching it up in the straight joy of eating the wind he's doing that alone too. I'm just something he carries on his back and he won't look at me . . .

NATE BARTLETT'S STORE

Dealer in Everything and Satisfaction Guaranteed

SOUTH LICKS was a nice town in those days. It couldn't compete with the boom cattle towns along the railroads, not in bustle and noise and general human devilment, so it didn't even try. It made out fair enough as supply and market center for a rising number of homesteads and small ranches round about and picked up extra business feeding folks passing through on the stage line. It was a nice town, not wide open and roaring like some but all the same not fussy about folks having their fun as they saw fit, and it had Nate Bartlett's store.

Nate was New England Yankee stock seasoned by a lot of grown-up years out in the new States and Territories where there was plenty of room for the spirit in a man to stretch and grow some and that was a combination hard to beat. He'd turned his hand to many a thing in his time and he'd made his pile, staked a claim on a rich ledge and sold out to a mining syndicate for a fine price, and he'd looked around and settled on South Licks as the place to do what he'd always wanted to do and that was run a store. All those years he'd remembered the one his grandfather had back east when he was a kid and he'd remembered the tangy smells and the neighborly feel and he'd never got over the notion that running a good store right was a pleasant way for a man to spend his slow-down days. He put up a solid frame building fronting on the main street with living quarters for himself at the rear. He stocked that building with anything and everything he could think of in the general merchandise line. He sent away to have a sign made and he hung that sign on a pole sticking out from the roof of the building and that was some sign.

NATHANIEL P. BARTLETT
Dealer in

EVERYTHING
Wholesale & Retail Satisfaction Guaranteed
"If we haven't got it we'll get it."

A sign like that was certain to make comment and liven a town's temper. It wasn't long before the South Licksians were proud of Nate and his store. They noticed it had special tangy smells and a special neighborly feel and they enjoyed themselves testing Nate's service. They'd stroll in chuckling and ask for some odd thing or other. More than likely Nate'd have it somewheres in his stock. Even if he didn't he'd never bat an eye but just remark he was fresh out of that particular item and would have it ready in a day or two. Smack after closing he'd be over at the stage office confabbing with the telegraph operator there and right enough, in a matter of days, he'd have that item ready and at a fair price, the straight cost plus his usual percentage. Like the time Al Foster who ran the Good Licks Restaurant came in and asked for a pair of red-white-and-blue suspenders. Nate looked up from the mail-order catalogue he was scanning for more things to put on his shelves. He never even cracked a smile. "Any particular design?" he said. "Why, certain," Al Foster said. "Red straps, white hooks, blue cross-hatches." Nate tapped his forehead thoughtful like he was studying over what he had. "Seems to me I had some like that," he said, "but I'm fresh out as of now. Come around next week." And right enough, when Al was passing the store one day next week, Nate hailed him from the door and Nate had those suspenders, just as ordered. He'd sent to the factory and had them made special. Al was so tickled with them and the talk they stirred he was down a while with pneumonia in the fall waiting too long to start wearing a coat over them.

It was about two-three months after Nate arrived in South Licks and opened his store that Kemp Ackley first saw that sign.

Kemp was a Texas-born-and-raised who'd been away from his home state long enough to have the usual brag

and horny layer rubbed off exposing the real man under-
neath and that was a hard combination to beat too. He
was somewheres in his early thirties, a hard-riding, hard-
working, hard-playing man who'd filled his pockets one
night bucking a faro game and right away put the cash
into good cows and started building himself a herd. He
had a ranch about eight miles out of South Licks, the
biggest spread in those parts. He worked the place himself, along with four-five riders who could keep pace
with him at whatever he might be doing whether that
was working or playing or just plain yipping at the
moon. The scale he operated, he didn't try to market
through South Licks. Roundup time he'd cut out his
beef stuff and drive cross-country to one of the railroad
towns. He'd collect his money there but he wouldn't
spend it there even though he and his riders'd be ripe
for a pay-off spree. He had local pride, Kemp Ackley
had. He figured that South Licks was his town. He
figured that if he and those who sided him were going
to take any town apart and fill the evening air with
the clink of glasses and the clatter of chips and the melody of song and gunshots, why then South Licks ought
to be so favored. He'd head up there from the railroad
and coming near he'd collect dry-throated gents from
the smaller ranches along the way till there was quite a
crowd of them raising dust on the road and they'd come
whooping into South Licks with him to help him spend
a fair share of the beef money and whatever they could
scrape out of their own pockets.

This time Kemp came whooping along in the lead
and when he swung into Main Street the first thing he
saw was that sign hanging bright and brave overhead.

He pulled his horse back on its rump and the others did the same and he looked that sign over. "Well, now," he said. "Here's something new to add to the merriment of men and nations and such. Ain't that a pretty target!" He pulled a gun and spun it fancy on a finger through the trigger guard and clamped his hand on the butt and was raising his arm to fire when out of the corner of one eye he caught sight of old Nate standing in the store door. Nate was leaning easy against one doorjamb and he was holding a double-barreled shotgun hip-high with both hammers cocked and both barrels bearing on Kemp. "I wouldn't do that was I you," Nate said.

Kemp stayed still, just as he was. "Is that thing loaded?" he said.

"I wouldn't take a chance on it was I you," Nate said. "I heard you coming the whole last mile."

"Well, then," Kemp said. "I expect you're right. You've got two mighty powerful arguments there." Kemp let his arm down slow, careful where his gun pointed, and slid that gun back into its holster. "Shucks," he said. "You ought to know popping signs is all part of the game. Likely you've peppered a few in your own time."

"Likely I have," Nate said. "But I've learned different too in my time. I'm learning you different right now."

"Well, now," Kemp said, "it kind of looks like you are at that." Something about that old rooster of a Nate leaning there quiet and easy and maybe deadly too seemed to tickle him. "Boys," he said. "This is one sign we leave strict alone." He slapped spurs to his horse and led the way on along the street to swing in by Ed Lafferty's Licks-That-Thirst saloon.

It was six-seven-maybe-eight drinks later, near the time Kemp and his crew'd be heading to feed at Al Foster's place and get up strength for a full evening's fun, that Kemp got to realizing he couldn't keep that sign out of his head. "Cocky old bird," he said to himself. " 'Dealer in EVERYTHING.' Puts that in capitals too. I expect we ought to give him a whirl." He downed the last in his glass and called out, "Come along, boys. We've got to find out does everything mean anything." Nate was tidying up his store for closing when the crowd came in. He set his broom aside and took his usual spot behind his main counter.

"No hard feelings on what was previous," Kemp said. "I was just wondering do you really stand by that sign outside?"

"Certain as sunrise," Nate said. "Each and every word."

Kemp chuckled low in his throat and tipped a wink around at his crew. "Well, then," he said, "me and the boys here have a hankering for some genuine one-dollar-per-each seegars."

Nate tapped his forehead thoughtful. "I'm fresh out of any at that precise figure," he said, "but maybe these might do." He rummaged under his counter and came up with a fancy box and slit the seal and lifted the lid and inside were fat cigars each wrapped separate and that lid said in curlicue letters they were super-extra-panatelas-de-luxe costing one dollar and twenty-five cents per each.

"I'm a flop-eared jackrabbit," somebody in the crowd said. "He's topped you, Kemp. You'll have to pay."

Kemp paid. He had to shuck his roll plenty to spread those cigars all around but he paid. He didn't mind that

much. What he minded was being capped so neat by
Nate. He lit his cigar and looked around and tipped
another wink at his crew. "Well, now," he said, "you
met me on that and I've paid. But now me and the boys
are thinking it would be nice to top off eating this evening with some of that stuff they call cavvy-yar."

"Are you certain you want some of that?" Nate said.
"That's powerful stuff for simple stomachs." There was
a twinkle deep in Nate's eyes but he was speaking slow
and hesitating like he was worried some.

"Certain I'm certain," Kemp said. "I want all you've
got — if you've got any."

Nate turned and went to pushing things aside on his
shelves and pulled out a flattish wooden box and pried
off the top. Inside were twenty-four flattish round cans.
"That'll be seventy-two dollars," he said.

"Yippee for Nate!" someone shouted. That was Al
Foster standing in the doorway and snapping his red-
white-and-blue suspenders. "He'll match you every
time, Kemp my boy. You'd better quit."

"Quit?" Kemp Ackley said. "I'm just beginning."
He stood there scratching the slight stubble along one
side his chin. He leveled a finger at Nate like it was a
gun. "I'm telling you what I want now," he said. "I'm
wanting me a pair of those fancy striped pants dudes
wear back east when they go strutting up the avenue
showing off for the ladies. I'm wanting me a forked-
tail coat to go with those pants. And some pearl-but-
toned spats and a — a —"

"Top hat?" Nate said.

"Certain a top hat," Kemp said. "And a gold-headed
cane and —"

"And I'm telling you," Nate said in a voice that showed he'd been a lot of things in his time and had stood on his own two feet wherever he was. "I'm telling you I've got all those items right here in my stock and more of the trimmings than you'd ever think of. And I'm telling you I'm not going to sell them to you. Fun's fun. But you don't need those things and you'd look like a misplaced jackass in them and it's closing time for this store anyway. And now," Nate said with the twinkle in his eyes shining plain, "I'm telling you too, son, there's a few aspects of your so-called disposition that remind me of the kind of fool I was at about your age. If you'll let me pay the tariff on food for the crowd, by which I mean up to and including that caviar, and then soak in some liquid refreshment to sort of catch up, why then I'll show you how we used to outhowl the coyotes on payday when I was a cowhand down on the Cimarron."

South Licks rocked some on its foundations those evening hours. There were folks used to date things before and after by that night. But the chief thing to be dated from it was the game played by those two, Nathaniel P. Bartlett and Kemp Ackley. Just about everybody else knew better than to keep betting against Nate about that sign but Kemp couldn't quit. Every time he came to town he'd try again. It got so he'd be out with his riders working his cattle and sudden he'd swing his horse and head for town and they'd know he'd hit another notion. He'd step into the store and say, "Still standing by that sign?" and Nate'd say, "Certain as sunrise," and Kemp'd spring his new one and sometimes Nate'd have it already and sometimes Nate wouldn't but he'd take the order without batting an eye and come through on it surprising quick. One time it was a genuine imported Swiss cuckoo clock. Nate located one in Chicago and had it out by special express and a pony rider in five days. Another time it was a live monkey with coconuts for feeding. Nate spent plenty on telegrams over that but all the same he had one there in a cage with a crate of coconuts too in a day over three weeks. Kemp was about sure he had Nate stopped the time he stepped in and said he wanted an engine, a locomotive like they used on the railroad. Nate just looked at him and said, "Eight-wheeler or ten-wheeler?" and Kemp had to say something and said, "Ten-wheeler, of course!" and Nate said he was fresh out of that particular kind but he'd have one soon and in five weeks there it was, standing solid on all ten wheels back of the store. He'd bought it from the railroad by offering more than they'd paid themselves and had it taken apart and carted up to South Licks in freight wagons and put together again. Kemp had to put his ranch in hock to meet the bill that time. He managed to sell the thing back to the railroad at a fair figure but even so he was hit with quite a loss plus the cartage.

That should have slowed Kemp down. It only made him more determined. He thought and thought and took to moping around in his bachelor ranchhouse thinking. He knew he'd have to get something mighty tricky and special and at last he had it. The more he thought about it and from fresh angles the more tickled he was. He slapped his thighs and laughed smack out loud. He saddled up and rode into town. He looked at that sign and read it over again and laughed some more. He stepped into the store and grinned at Nate. He waved a hand back out toward the sign.

"Everything?" he said.

"Everything," Nate said.

"Well, then," Kemp said, fighting to hold back the chuckles, "I'm here to order me a wife."

For a full moment, maybe two, old Nate really was stopped. He stared at Kemp and his mouth dropped open a little. Then that twinkle started deep in his eyes but his face stayed solemn. He waggled his head sorrowful and started to talk. "I've been here and I've been there," he said, "and I've been about everywhere in between. I've seen strange things and some stranger yet only a fool'd believe. But I never thought to see the day a white man of the male sex and cattle-handling persuasion would regard a woman of the female sex, a wife-to-be of his board and bosom, as a merchandisable item to be talked of as such across a storekeeper's counter. True, I've heard tell that in biblical times . . ." Nate kept on talking and Kemp kept on grinning, certain he had Nate licked at last and Nate was just stalling to avoid admitting he was licked.

". . . and I've bumped into an Indian tribe or two," Nate said, "that some folks might claim put a price tag on a squaw. But you ain't an Indian and I expect it ain't a squaw you have in mind." Kemp shook his head, still fighting the chuckles, and sudden Nate reached a pencil and order pad and popped quick words: "Any particular specifications?"

Kemp was startled some. He hadn't thought much past just putting his joke. Then he chuckled out loud.

Old Nate was trying to run a bluff on him. "Why, sure," he said. "I like me a woman that has good meat on her bones. Nice curves in the right places, up and down. Face that won't stampede a steer and — and —"

"Reddish hair?" Nate said.

"Why, yes, if you say so," Kemp said, near to busting inside at the way his joke was growing. "I'm kind of partial to reddish hair. And I like me a woman old enough to know better but —"

"Know better'n what?" Nate said.

"Better'n to marry a maverick like me," Kemp said, "but still young and giddy enough to take a chance." He couldn't hold the laughing in any more and he let it out in bursts between his words. "Oh, I know — you're fresh out — that particular item — but if I'll come around — next week — next month maybe — next lifetime'd be more like it. Shucks, you're licked — backed right off the board — just too ornery to say so." Kemp was staggering around, slapping his arms and weak with the laughing. He plain had to share his joke with others who'd appreciate it the way his boys would and he staggered out the door and climbed aboard his horse and went skittering toward his ranch.

For quite a stretch, maybe four-five miles, that was about the most enjoyable ride Kemp Ackley'd ever had. He was rolling in the saddle, figuring to get his boys and swing back for some real celebrating, tasting already how he'd tell his tale, about Nate's jaw dropping and Nate's long-winded stalling and Nate's trying to run a bluff and how he'd called it. Then sudden, for some reason, the whole business didn't seem so funny to him. He began remembering. He remembered things like one-dollar-and-a-quarter cigars and a cuckoo clock and a monkey and a locomotive. He yanked his horse around and headed larruping back to town. He pulled to a stop in front of the store. The door was closed tight and padlocked. He saw Al Foster coming along the side walk.

"Nate?" Al Foster said, snapping his red-white-and-blue suspenders in a way that seemed mighty suggestive to Kemp. "Nate's closed down for a few days. Caught the afternoon stage out of town."

There was a lot of talk around South Licks all the next weeks. People knew Nate had gone off to get something Kemp had ordered and since he'd gone off personal they figured it must be a tough one and they began laying bets would he get it. At the same time there was a lot of silence out at Kemp Ackley's ranch. Kemp sat around in his ranchhouse chewing his fingernails. Every now and then he'd stand up and try to kick himself clear across the room. He sent one of his riders into town each day in turn to loaf about and keep an eye open for Nate's coming back. He got so he shivered like he had the ague just at the sight of the day's rider coming home along the road. He thought some of selling out, maybe just leaving without bothering to sell out, fading away into the hills so he wouldn't have to face the town, but he'd never dodged off yet on a bet or a debt and he knew he'd have to play this through. Then it was late one afternoon and the one of his boys they called Skimpy because he couldn't raise much hair was fogging home in a hurry. Kemp made it to the porch and wilted there waiting.

"Nate's back," Skimpy said.

Kemp groaned. "Alone?" he said.

"Not exactly," Skimpy said. "There's something with him."

"Something?" Kemp said. "Is it alive?"

"Seems like," Skimpy said. "Leastwise it was moving under its own power."

Kemp groaned again. "Female?" he said.

"More'n likely," Skimpy said. "But I couldn't be sure. Nate had it wearing his long coat and his hat with a veil down hiding the evidence."

Kemp was getting expert with all his practice and he managed to kick himself clear across the porch.

"My oh me oh my," Skimpy said, grinning wide. "That's some fancy acrobatics. But you'd best save your strength. Nate says he believes in prompt closing of important deals so he'll be open this evening waiting for you."

Kemp Ackley came into South Licks that evening like he was coming to an execution for which he was slated principal performer. He kept thinking of the happy free-roaming days likely he was leaving behind. He kept seeing horrible visions in the air around him of the frightening things unfeeling folk might regard as marriageable critters of the female sex. His boys had the good sense to tag back a bit where their grins and undertone joshing were out of range. In town, he climbed off his horse and looked up at that sign shining in the light from the store window and he shuddered all over. It didn't help his spirit any when he went inside and found near all the inhabitants of South Licks perched at vantage points on counters and boxes about. He looked around, mighty fearful. There wasn't a woman in sight he didn't already know as the nailed-down wife of some South

Licks man. He saw Nate sitting quiet and easy on the usual high stool behind the main counter. He sighed.

"All right," he said. "I'm here."

"So you are," Nate said. Nate's face was solemn as ever but that twinkle was showing deep in his eyes. "Seems to me though," Nate said, "you're a mite pale as a man ought not be on a happy occasion such as this. Now before I produce the merchandise you saw fit to order through me and my store I want to tell you that so as to be able to produce same I've had to talk myself into a sore throat two weeks running and prognosticate things about you as an upstanding gentleman and citizen of this community that your own mother'd blush to believe. Be all that on my own head, but you came blowing in here with what you maybe thought was a good joke but nothing about this store of mine is a joke to me and I took what you said straight and I'm making good on it. I've got the merchandise and to be certain the service along with same is right I've had myself made a justice of the peace so as I can do the ceremony myself."

Nate stepped back to the door that led to his living quarters and opened it. "South Licks in general and Mister Ackley in particular," he said, "I'm making you acquainted with my ward and niece, Miss Barbara Bartlett, late of St. Louis and points east." And out through the doorway, stepping dainty as primed in advance by old Nate, with color high in her cheeks and the lamplight shining on reddish hair, came as fresh and shapely and hearty-looking a young woman as any South Licksian'd ever seen. There were cluckings from the other women present and foot-shufflings and a few whistles

from the men. Kemp Ackley stepped back like someone
had hit him. He reached up hesitating and took off his
hat and a sort of sick grin spread over his face. He pulled
himself together and stiffened some. "Howdy, ma'am,"
he said.

"Whoa, now," Nate said. "I intend to do this proper."
He motioned Kemp to come closer and all the while this
Barbara niece stood still as a statue with a twinkle like
old Nate's deep in her own eyes. "I ain't forgot those
specifications," Nate said. "I ain't going to have you
claiming misrepresentation any time later. You said
good meat on her bones. Any objections to the meat on
these bones? Step up and feel it if you've a mind to."

Kemp jumped back like someone had kicked him.
"Oh, no," he said, quick. "Looks all right from here
where I am."

"Nice curves too," Nate said, "and in the right places.
So you specified. Find anything wrong with these
curves?"

"Now, lookahere, Nate," Kemp said. "You've got no
call to —"

"My oh me oh my," someone said in the background
and it was Skimpy, grinning wide again. "If you're
scared out, Kemp, step aside and I'll take over."

"And give yourself a real good look," Nate went
right on. "Do you have any lingering suspicion that face
might stampede a steer?"

"Shucks," Kemp said. "Ain't you through riding me
yet? How'd you expect me to have any objections anyway with the woman herself standing right there listening? There ain't any need for all this talk. I'm caught
on my own fool play and —"

"Humph," this Barbara niece said. "So he feels caught, does he? Well, this specifying business goes two ways." She stepped out and around Kemp while he stood stock-still like he was fastened to the floor, only swiveling at the waist to keep an eye on her. "Uncle Nate," she said. "You claimed he was handsome. Well, maybe he is in a coarse, unwashed sort of way. You said he has a good ranch and is the kind of man could give a good home. I can't say I see much evidence of that in his present appearance looking like a sick calf that's afraid someone'll say boo."

Kemp jerked up straight. His color was high now too. He was getting his hell-raising legs back under him the way they hadn't been ever since Nate left town.

"Sick is it," he said, "and a calf? You just try saying boo and I'll —"

"Boo!" this Barbara niece said.

Kemp tossed his hat to one side and started for her and old Nate jumped between them. "Whoa, now," he said. "Don't you two go messing up this deal just because one's stiff-necked and the other's got reddish hair. This is a business proposition and for and as of now it's to be regarded as such. It's considerable irregular because in this case the merchandise can talk back so it's only fair it be a two-way deal. Barbara," old Nate said, "seeing him now and remembering the things I've told you, are you still willing?"

"Humph," this Barbara niece said. "Marrying a man who seems to think a wife is something you can pick up at a store like a barrel of flour is likely a poor risk." She was looking at Kemp mighty intent and speculative and seemed to enjoy watching him squirm. "But seeing as how the honor of our family seems to have got involved through that sign of yours, Uncle Nate, why maybe I can take a chance."

"Well, then, Kemp," Nate said. "Here's your merchandise as per order. How do you stand?"

"What's the price?" Kemp said. He was looking at this Barbara niece just as intent and speculative as she was at him and he seemed to enjoy watching her wince at that question of his.

"No price," Nate said. "Except your present freedom as a bachelor."

"All right," Kemp said. He wasn't going to let himself be outdone by any woman. "Seeing as how my own honor's got involved here too, why I'll just pay that price."

It was on that basis those two let old Nate marry them. It was on the same basis those two behaved, free and easy with everybody else except each other, all through the evening at Al Foster's restaurant where the South Licksians cleared away the tables for a noisy dancing jamboree. It was on the same basis they departed for the ranch about sunup in a buckboard from the livery stable with this Barbara niece sitting way over on one side of the seat and Kemp sitting way over on the other side and her trunk behind them in the wagon and Kemp's boys riding well out of earshot range.

Old Nate stood under his sign and watched them go. "Maybe I've pushed it too far this time," he said to himself, "but it still seems like a good notion to me. Once they're alone together they'll work it out. If I was either one I'd want me another one just about like the other."

But Nate had his doubts when he went out to call two days later and found those two acting like a brace of gamecocks walking around wary and ready to start clashing spurs over any little thing. Neither one could say much at all without the other snapping to twist it into something mean. Nate didn't stay long because he was too uncomfortable. Any way he looked at it, he knew he was really responsible for bringing them together and maybe, because of the way he'd handled it at the store, for setting them to striking sparks. He felt he ought to do something but he couldn't figure what.

Nate's doubts didn't improve with the rumors that began reaching town the following days. Kemp was said to be staying in the bunkhouse with his boys. This Barbara niece was said to be holed up in the ranchhouse. Nate was worried plenty when he heard that. He was just tidying things to go out there and see what he might be able to do when this Barbara niece came walking in the store door. She was mussed and dusty and right ready to cry any minute. She'd waited till Kemp and his boys were off somewheres out of sight and she'd wangled a horse out of the corral and made it to town.

"Uncle Nate," she said. "I'd hate to have that long-legged excuse for a husband you wished on me think I'd run away from anything but it can't go on like this."

Nate was mighty sorry for her but he remembered she was good Bartlett stock and he figured he could be brief and blunt.

"So maybe you'd like to get free of him, eh?" he said.

"Well, I don't know," she said and she was so close to crying that a couple of tears leaked out and started down through the dust on her cheeks. "Out there boss-ing around that ranch which is where a man like him belongs I can see maybe he's some of those things you said he is. But he isn't a real man. He's just a big chunk of wood. He's got about as much sentiment in him as one of those big steers of his. Every time he gets near me he can't seem to get past thinking of all that silly specification business and how he was caught and just had to marry me."

"I wonder now do you give him much chance to —" Nate started to say and had to stop quick because he saw something outside. He managed to push this Barbara niece into his living quarters and close the door and be back at his main counter when Kemp Ackley came in, walking slow and sorrowful and looking back at that sign outside.

"Nate," Kemp said. "When I think of that wife you pushed off on me holed up in the ranchhouse and me slipping off in the other direction and circling around to come here so she won't know what I'm doing, well, Nate, I feel plumb bad. Things can't go on like this. You take that sign of yours now. You still stand by it?"

"Certain I do," Nate said, stiffening some.

"Well, it says something I never paid much notice before," Kemp said. "It says 'Satisfaction Guaranteed.'"

"So-o-o," Nate said. "So you ain't satisfied with this last transaction." He felt a mite sorry for this Kemp too but he remembered Kemp was stock he'd thought could match the Bartlett and he figured he could be brief and blunt this time too.

"You want to turn the merchandise back?" he said.

"Don't be so all-fired hasty," Kemp said. "I ain't exactly complaining about the merchandise as such. It meets those specifications right enough and now I've seen it close maybe some we didn't even mention. But it acts most of the time something like a snapping turtle that tolerates living in the same country with me only because of that silly family-honor business. I ain't so cocky as I used to be. I'm not demanding a thing. I'm just wondering is there any way you could go about guaranteeing some of that satisfaction."

Nate looked at Kemp a long minute or two. Then that twinkle began to show in his eyes. "Kemp," he said. "If you acquired a windmill or a hay cutter or some such piece of machinery from me, there'd be instructions how to operate same and keep it operating along with it. You'd pay smart attention to those instructions, wouldn't you?"

"Of course I would." Kemp said. "That's simple sense."

"Precisely and exact," Nate said. "Well, you acquired a wife from me. There was some instructions supposed to go along with her that I forgot to give you. Wait a spell and I'll see can I remember what they were." And old Nate took a piece of paper and his old quill pen. He chewed the top end of the pen a while and then he dipped it in ink and started scratching with it. He finished and reached the paper across the counter to Kemp.

INSTRUCTIONS
to keep a wife happy
and derive satisfaction from same

Rule 1. Tell her you love her.
Rule 2. Tell her how pretty she is.

Rule 3. Think up three new ways each day for
following rule 1.

Rule 4. Think up three new ways each day for
following rule 2.

Rule 5. Mean what you say each time.

"And now," Nate said. "You just keep that paper out
of sight but not out of mind. And start following those
rules right away." He took Kemp by the arm and back
to the door of his living quarters and pushed Kemp
through and closed the door again. He stood there
listening a moment and then he nodded his head. He
returned to his main counter and perched himself on a
stool behind it and began looking through catalogues for
new things he might put on his shelves. He raised his
head and looked out the window at that sign and the
twinkle in his eyes was blazing bright. It wouldn't be
too long now before he'd be having some grandnieces
and grandnephews and they'd be in and out of his store
and maybe in later years they'd remember the tangy
smells and the neighborly feel of the place.

GENERAL PINGLEY

With His Own Brand of Honor

THE PINGLEYS came into our section of Wyoming to take over the claim of a cousin who made the mistake of trying to drive a buckboard over a mountain trail while tipping a bottle of whiskey. This cousin had proved up on the claim and the title was clear, and the Pingleys were the closest of kin. They were ready to leave their place in Nebraska for a middling-good reason. From what I heard they had left other times from other places for the same reason, one that walked on two legs, an old man, Bert Pingley's father, old J. Clayburn Pingley.

They were a mixed lot, these Pingleys. Bert was a big mild middle-aged man, about the hardest-working and easiest-natured I've ever known. His wife was some years younger, a pretty woman, fluttery in her actions, and so shy that sometimes you might think she was silly in the head. There were two children, a little girl just beginning to walk and trying to hide in her mother's skirts when strangers were near, and a boy, coming seven or eight, I'd say, fair-sized for his age and easy-natured like his father. And, of course, there was the old man, stiff-backed as a ramrod, still fighting the Civil War thirty years after the last shot had been fired.

The first time I saw him he was wearing his old gray uniform coat and campaign hat. It was a Saturday afternoon and I was in town to pick up any mail and rub elbows with other folks a bit. I saw him in Eiler's general store. He was ordering some tobacco and complaining about the price. He had a fringe of white chin whiskers that stood out straight when he talked.

"Double damn Yankees," he said. "Robbers. Every last one of you."

Eiler was surprised. He leaned forward on his counter. "Easy now, Pop," he said. "I was born back in Georgia myself."

"A renegade, eh? Lived so long among these thieving Yankees you're the same."

I saw this big man, Bert, hurrying over, a smile busting his face wide open.

"Don't mind my father," he said. "It's one of his bad days. Can't seem to learn the war's over and forgotten." He smiled at Eiler and shrugged his shoulders a little. "You see, Father hasn't surrendered yet."

"You're double damned right I haven't. I'll keep right on telling every yellow-bellied bluecoat I find just what —"

Bert's smile stayed the same, but his hand on the old man's arm stopped the words. "Father, wait for me at the wagon. I'll bring your tobacco."

I saw him later the same afternoon in front of the old stage post where folks liked to meet and swap neighborhood news and wait for the mail coach. The three or four other men there with him must have been working on him because he was hopping mad when I came along. The chin whiskers were sticking out stiff as hog bristles.

"— never was a time," he was saying, "any Federal troops could stand to one of our charges. I mind me once when General Pickett —"

"Choke it, Whiskers," said one of the men. "You rebs were licked before you started, only you didn't know it. Too many crazy old goats like you."

The old man pulled himself up even straighter. "Bert," he shouted, looking around. Right enough, Bert was hurrying over again, smiling again at the whole world. "Bert, you heard it. You going to —"

"Shucks," said Bert. "You'd want I should smack him just because you riled him into calling names?"

"My own son! A coward in my own family!"

Bert's smile didn't change. That was when I began to like him. As I say, he was a big man. He could have taken any two of us there and my money would have been on him.

"Shucks, Father," he said. "You forget when we're needing supplies we come in under a truce flag."

The old man subsided like a sudden thunderstorm ending. "You're right, son. So we do." He took off his ancient campaign hat and bowed to the rest of us. "I'm sorry, gentlemen. I forgot myself. But perhaps some other time —" He marched off erect toward their wagon, and I saw it there, a white cotton handkerchief tied to a buggy whip whose butt was stuck between the sideboards.

Someone was standing close beside me. That was our marshal, Clyde Eakins. He was watching the old man.

"Stubborn old coot," I said.

"Yes," Eakins said. "But his kind of fun ain't exactly enjoyable after a while. Beginning already to get some folks' nerves ruffled."

He was not really so bad, not at first anyway. You find some touchy ones anywhere you go. We had our share. But most of us were willing to let him talk his war. We couldn't be peeved at anyone who belonged to a man like Bert. I guess the old man had a right to a grudge at that. His other son, Bert's brother, had died at Shiloh, and the shock of that, together with Federal troop occupation of the family place in Virginia, had killed his wife, Bert's mother. Then he lost everything he owned in the early carpetbag days. There was not much left for him except to tag along when Bert struck out into the new Territories.

For quite a while people in town tolerated his talk. They liked to stir him a little and watch the chin whiskers wag. They could count on Bert to step in smiling before real sparks flew. And they had a kind of admiration for the old man's unwavering belligerence. They began calling him the General, and he liked that. Bert didn't. "Shucks," Bert would say, "he wasn't a general. He was only a sort of reserve captain. Managed a supply depot down in North Carolina and didn't even hear a gun go off." Bert himself had. Plenty. He had fought through the four years, starting as a green kid of seventeen and coming out a man. But he never talked about that. It was a job he had to do, and when it was done it was finished. Maybe he felt that the old man did enough talking for the whole Pingley tribe.

It was in July that the town's temper turned. July Fourth. We always celebrated the day. A town committee would make the arrangements, and those like me who lived out a ways would be on hand to make a respectable crowd for the doings. There would be shooting matches, rifle and revolver, and things like that, and about midmorning we would raise the flag on the town flagpole in the park space opposite the hotel and salute it with a lot of cheers and gunpowder. Then we would jam into the former storeroom we used for a courthouse and listen to the speechmaking and work up an appetite for the hot lunch some of the ladies always sold for the benefit of the volunteer fire department.

Judge Cutler usually made the main speech. He was dry and short with words on the bench, but his special orations were something to hear. This time he never got to finish. He was not much more than well unlimbered in the throat when someone standing by the door gave a shout and people turned to look where he was pointing, and there was a stampede through the doorway and across to the park space. Old J. Clayburn Pingley was standing stiff-backed by the pole. He had pulled down the flag and tossed it aside and run up an old Confederate flag instead.

People stopped in a half-circle around him and the pole gawking up at his faded old flag. And then things

happened fast. Young Pard Wheeler, who had considerable celebrating under his belt, pulled his gun and aimed
upward and started shooting. I think he was only trying
to cut the rope, but the bullets ripped through the flag
and the rents showed plain. The old man screamed and
started toward Wheeler, reaching in his side pocket and
his hand came out with an old-fashioned little derringer.
Marshal Eakins scrambled quick and caught him and
wrenched the arm, and the little weapon fell to the
ground, and he broke loose from Eakins and went at
Wheeler beating with his hands. Wheeler backed away
trying to fend off the blows and stopped and gave the old
man a push that sent him sprawling. And Bert Pingley
burst out of the crowd and crashed a big fist to the side
of Wheeler's head and Wheeler went down like a steer
when you poleaxe it.

Two things stick in my mind when I remember that.
One is the look of the old man lying on the ground. He
wasn't making any effort to get up. He was lying there,
quiet now, leaning on one elbow and watching Bert, and
mighty pleased about something. The other is the look
of Bert Pingley standing there, big as the side of a
mountain, not smiling, and disgusted with himself and
ashamed.

Maybe I ought to add a third thing. Young Pard
Wheeler, somehow acting for all of us, staggering a little
when he got to his feet and trying to make Bert see that
he understood what had happened.

The General wasn't amusing after that, not to most of
the people around. I guess they remembered his scream
and the little derringer coming out of his pocket. And

there were some who were shocked at his hauling down the American flag. He wasn't a joke, a neighborhood character any more. He was a nuisance that might cause trouble. But there wasn't any trouble because he was hardly ever in town again. That must have been Bert's doing. Bert was easy-natured. But he probably could be firm when he felt that he had to be.

The next I heard the old man was being sighted around the country, keeping out of people's way and getting about in a little buggy pulled by an old horse Bert let him use. Sometimes the boy would be with him and might wave a friendly arm, but the old man would drive right along, straight on the seat, not turning his head. He drove that buggy in the damndest places, where there were no roads and not even trails, smack across open range land and up into the mountains where you wouldn't think anything on wheels could go. When people spoke to Bert about it, Bert would just smile and shrug his shoulders. "Shucks," Bert would say, "he ain't worrying anybody, is he? Likes to camp out a few days at a time. Takes good care of the boy too." Then nobody was seeing much of him at all, and nobody seemed to know what he was doing, and Bert wasn't saying, even if he knew, and I was the first to find out what it was.

When the weather was right and no work pressing, I liked to saddle the gray and ride on up my valley and into the hills. After a few miles I'd be in the high country where the rock formations climbed and the bigness took you into itself in a comfortable quiet. Riding up there kept the horse in condition and my own mind too.

Sometime in late summer I was drifting along and

came out on the wide chunk of tableland that was the far edge part of Sam Piegan's range. During dry periods when grass was sparse near his home spread, Piegan ran some of his cattle on those high plateaus. One year he had tried wintering some there and had built a line camp on this stretch of tableland. By spring he knew better, and was lucky to have enough of the cattle still alive to pay his man's wages. The only mark left was the abandoned log cabin. I had passed it a few times and noticed that the door was gone and the walls sagging and holes beginning to show in the roof.

When I saw it in the distance this time, it had a different look. Smoke was rising out of the stone chimney. I rode closer, and saw it had a makeshift door with pieces of old harness nailed for hinges and the walls were being chinked and new slabs of bark were on the roof. There was a pole sticking up from one corner, and flapping out from this was an old Confederate flag.

The door opened and the old man stood in the doorway. He had a battered Sharps carbine in his hands. "Ought to blast you out of that saddle," he said. "Yankee spy. Nosing around my fort."

"Easy, General," I said, "you're no bushwhacker. I didn't know you were here."

"You know it now. So keep moving and don't come back." The chin whiskers stood out straight at me. "This is Confederate territory. By right of conquest." He waved the gunbarrel to point at the cabin wall beside the door and I saw stretched there by its paws the skin of a good-sized black bear.

I sat on the gray chuckling. I couldn't help it. But I wasn't chuckling after a warning bullet from his carbine sang uncomfortably close by my right ear. I swung the gray and went into retreat, about as scared as mad. I never had any fondness for bullets moving in my direction. But halfway home, I was chuckling again. When I told Sam Piegan about it, he chuckled too. "The old boy can use the place all he wants. Maybe it'll keep him out of trouble. We'll pass the word around so nobody'll bother him."

I didn't ride out much the next months. Having knocked off the rest of the summer and fattening my three-year steers for market on special rations took the fall. But I saw him a few times driving past my place in his little buggy. The best route to that rebel roost of his was up my valley and left along the trail that climbed through the notch to the tablelands. Even that must have been a hard pull for his old horse. I didn't know how often he made the trip because sometimes I'd miss seeing him and only know he had gone past by chancing on his fresh wheel tracks in the mud where the road forded the valley stream not far from my house. Then the cold edge of late fall began to creep into the air and I didn't see him or his tracks at all.

Winter hit us early that year. It hit us weeks ahead of the usual first snow with a surprise storm that whipped over the near line of mountains and caught plenty of us unprepared. I know because it caught me and shook me for a nice loss. I liked to keep my market-age steers as long as possible, putting on the last possible pounds with good grain, and move them out just before the winter snows when the price was at a peak. I hadn't even begun thinking about moving them that year when the storm hit. I had checked my fences and filled the trays in the feedlot again and come in and gone to bed early, and along before midnight I woke startled and heard the wind shrieking in the chimney. I crawled out of the bunk and went to the door and opened it and the snow struck me in a sheet and stung my face. It was the worst kind, dry and fine and driving. I was plenty worried, not about the cattle themselves because I had stout shelters, but about what a real blizzard could mean. Not many hours of that kind of snow would choke the trails and even the traveled roads. If the cold held and later snows kept building the drifts, I might have to feed my steers all winter and sell in a dropping spring market.

I pulled on clothes and went out to take care of the horses. They were bunched under the roof shelter out from the barn. I propped open the door to the stretch of stalls and didn't have to use any coaxing to get them in. There were knee-high drifts already by the time I pushed against the wind back to the house.

By morning I was snowed in tight, and the wind was still piling it down. I fought and floundered my way to the barn and saw the little path I made filling in fast again. I got one of the heavy work horses and climbed on him bareback and sent him plowing back and forth from the barn to the house and return till I had a real path showing. But this kept on filling in, too, so I took fence posts from my stock pile and stuck them in the snow on the wind side of the path about six feet apart and found enough planks in the barn to set against them for the beginnings of a barrier. The snow packed against the planks and held them firm and the drifts started this way protected the path quite a bit. Snow kept blowing over the top and into the path, of course, but not so bad that I couldn't clear it away every few hours without too much trouble. I was set then for as long a siege as that storm wanted to give me. There was fodder in the barn and food in the house, and my woodpile would last a whole winter.

Along in the afternoon of that first day, the snow slackened and almost stopped, but the wind kept at its battering, and sometime during the night it whipped in reinforcements from far up in the mountains and began piling down the snow again. When it finally eased during the third day, my path was almost a tunnel, shoulder high on one side and a foot above my head on the other. If there had been a strong crust on the snow, I could have walked right onto the roof of the barn from the big drift along one side. I settled into a nice routine, catching up on my sleep, fussing around the barn and adjoining feedlot morning and evening, walking the horses along the path to take the stall kinks out of their legs and the rest of the time loafing snug and warm in the house. When I didn't remember about missing the market, I even enjoyed the quiet laziness.

It was late in the morning of the fifth or sixth day, I'm not sure now which, that I heard faint shouts outside. I went out on the porch and there were two men bucking the drifts toward my house from where the road was under the snow. They were leading and almost dragging their horses by the reins. They were wrapped right for the weather with only a little of their faces showing, and I couldn't recognize them at first. They came closer, and I saw the big man in front was

Bert Pingley and the one plodding behind was Marshal
Eakins. They were beat, and no wonder. It was eight
miles out from town to my place. They dropped the
reins by the porch and nodded at me and went past me
into the house and collapsed on the nearest chairs. I
set a bottle on the table by Eakins and put the coffeepot
to warming on the stove and went out again to their
horses. I never knew two more grateful animals than
those were when I led them to the barn and worked
over them quick and pulled down some hay. They had
plugged through drifts so long that their legs were
quivering and could scarcely hold them up.

Back in the house I poured coffee around and waited
for the others to talk. Bert gulped his cup and sat still,
staring at the floor. Eakins finished his and poured
himself another.

"Thanks, John," he said. "Nothing like coffee ever."
He let the warmth work through him. He lifted an arm
and pointed it on up the valley toward the hills, and let
it drop. "The old man's up there," he said.

"Is he?" I said. "What the devil's he doing there?"

Bert raised his head briefly and let it drop again. "He
had to get his flag."

"Yes," Eakins said. "Bert finally made it to town this
morning for help and found me. The old fool left his
flag up there and got to worrying about it. Started for
it day before the storm. Must have been caught and
couldn't get back."

I thought around that. "Well," I said, "I'd let the old
coot hibernate there all winter. He's got shelter and
firewood's handy."

"No," Eakins said. He shook his head and gulped

his second cup of coffee and looked at me. "The boy's up there with him."

Bert raised his head again and almost shouted. "He had to get his flag, don't you see? His flag. And I couldn't go. Who knew about this storm anyway? It was his flag. Do you think I could say no?"

Eakins didn't pay any attention to him. Eakins just looked at me. "The boy's up there. They didn't take any supplies. Maybe a meal or two. Were coming back in the morning."

Eakins looked at me and I fidgeted on my chair. I felt the way you feel when there's something you know you have to do and don't want to do it.

"Hell, man," I said, "it can't be done. The notch will be plugged with drifts higher than this house."

Eakins just looked at me. "John," he said, "the old man's had his time. But the boy's up there. You know this country out here better'n about anyone else. Thought maybe you could figure a way through. An hour's rest and we'll start."

I left them in the house and went to the barn and put out plenty of feed for the cattle and hay for the horses. I fastened the door open so the horses could go out all right if I was a while getting home again. I passed by the gray and the big buckskin and the mare. She was with foal anyway. I looked over the work team and decided they were the ones. I didn't want speed or quickness or know-how. I wanted power and pull. I gave them a couple of quarts of grain each, and when they had eaten put on them the bridles with the long driving reins. I led them out by the porch and went in the house and wrapped myself good. I dropped the bottle in a side pocket and shook Eakins awake in his chair. I didn't need to shake Bert. He was up and had found my saddlebags and was packing them with food. He strapped them together and went out and slung them over the back of one of the horses and Eakins and I followed him.

"We'll use the horses to break trail as far as we can," I said. "We'll alternate them in the lead. Then we'll be on our own."

I took the reins of one horse and started him down the track already broken toward the road and Bert followed with the other horse and Eakins tagged us. When we reached the road, I swung toward town, keeping to the track they had made coming out. I heard Bert shouting behind me and he sounded angry, and I kept straight on and I heard Eakins' voice: "Shut up and follow him." I held to the track till we cleared the entrance to my valley, and then swung sharp right across the open land and the untouched whiteness of the snow.

I had it all clear in my mind, the one way we might have a chance. I kept the lead, trying to stay out of the hollows where the snow was too deep for movement and to follow the rolling rises that the wind had swept fairly clear and work my way through the foothills to the right place in the rimrock where the mountains soared into their high climb. It was hard going almost every yard of the way. The snow was dry and loose and gave no real foothold, and there were times when there was nothing to do except plow ahead and try to smash through. More than once the horse fought forward till he was helpless, unable to strike down through the snow to the ground, and I had trouble getting him back

out for a swing around to try another spot. After the
first twenty minutes, he was dripping sweat and in
about an hour he had enough.

I stopped and called back to Bert it was his turn and
gave him the general direction and he took the lead with
the other horse. He made a faster pace than I had, I
guess because it was his boy and his father up there and
not his horse fighting the drifts, and he was harsh urging
it ahead. I thought of calling him on that, then thought
better of it and kept my mouth shut. But I shouted
time on him quicker than I had on myself. If we were
going to kill my horses, we were going to do it the right
way and conserve their strength and get the most out of
them. We had a long way to go.

I don't know how many turns I called and alternated
the horses. Time got to be hazy as we plugged along.
Walking in that snow even with the trail broken by
those big hooves wasn't easy. And for the last couple
of hours we were moving uphill most of the time. I
know the horses were done, completely exhausted, with
the strength out of them, when we hit the steep rocky
slope, almost a cliff, I was looking for. I didn't dare tell
Bert where we would head next or he would have
started right on. I let him stew while I scraped the thick
sweat out of the horses' matted hair and tied them under
the shelter of an overhanging ledge and yanked down
some pine branches for them.

"All right," I said when I was ready. "It's not far
now. If we can scramble up here, we'll come out on
those flat stretches. They're like steps up the mountain.
Third one up's the place."

I was right that this was where we could make it.

That rocky slope was almost bare of snow except where outcropping ledges had caught it. We could zigzag up where the footholds were best and pull ourselves along by grabbing at the big rocks. Climbing took the breath out of us, but the flat stretches themselves were the really hard going. They had their own drifts and we had to break our own trail. I doubt whether Eakins and I could have crossed them without Bert smashing ahead of us. We were at the bottom of the last slope when we heard a shot somewhere above us. We shouted, but our voices would not carry, and then we couldn't shout because we needed all our breath for the final scramble to the top.

I wonder sometimes what exactly we expected to see when we reached the top. Not the peaceful scene we found. Everything was quiet and lovely in the late afternoon light. For some reason the quietness and the loveliness remain in my mind. All the long way we had been too busy fighting the snow to appreciate what was around us. Now it hit me suddenly. The cabin off in the distance, small and alone against the mountain wall behind it, was serene and untroubled in the midst of the white wonder and smoke was rising from its chimney. Close to us, where the wagon trail swung in an arc, was the little buggy, the wheels buried in a drift, and we could see the track it had made from the cabin and the spread snow where the horse had floundered and been caught and had been unharnessed and led back toward the cabin. And perched on the buggy seat was the boy, alive and alert and staring at us with the battered Sharps carbine across his knees.

Eakins was the first to speak. "What was that shot?" he said.

The boy gulped and found his voice. "Grandpa told me to shoot every so often, so somebody might hear. You took an awful long time. I've only got two bullets left." He stared at us, and suddenly he dropped the gun clattering on the buggy floorboards and jumped down and struggled through the snow toward us, and Bert leaped with long strides to meet him and gather him up, and the boy was crying and laughing in his arms and saying, "I knew you'd come." And after a moment he quieted and looked at Eakins and me. "Grandpa said some of you'd come too. He said even if you are Yankees, you'd worry about us and come get us."

Bert jerked his head toward the cabin. "Is he all right?"

"Oh, sure he is. I've kept the fire going like he said." Suddenly the boy was very serious. "He's broke his leg, though. But he says that isn't bad. He chopped and chopped an awful lot of wood and then he fell on something and his leg broke. But he says that'll get all right. He says he has good bones."

We started toward the cabin, Bert carrying the boy, and when we were almost there the boy was serious again.

"Please be quiet," he said. "Grandpa's awful tired and sleeps a lot. He hasn't waked up at all yet today."

We went in quietly, and when we saw the stillness of the thin old figure on the bunk, we knew that he would never waken. I saw Bert's face set in stern lines, and he put the boy down gently and went over and stood staring at the still figure. Eakins took the boy by an arm and led him outside, and I followed.

"Is Daddy going to wake him?" the boy said.

"No," Eakins said. "Not right now." He looked off into the distance and then at the boy again. "You hungry?"

"No," the boy said. "I don't think so. My stomach feels kind of puffy. We've only had a bag of dried apples that was here, and I only eat a little bowlful at a time and only twice a day the way Grandpa says. But dried apples make your stomach feel puffy."

Eakins looked off into the distance again, into the wide vast openness where the slope dropped away as if it were the edge of the world. "Your grandfather," he said, "has he been eating them too?"

"Oh, no," the boy said. "He doesn't want any. He says dried apples are bad for anyone with a broken leg."

I saw Bert in the doorway and Eakins did too and spoke quickly to him. "Take the boy, Bert, and back-track to where we left the horses. Get a fire going and rustle out some food. Start him in easy on it. John and I'll take care of things here."

We stood by the bunk and looked down at the wasted figure, at the thin old face with its sunken cheeks and pathetic fringe of chin whiskers.

"He was a stubborn old coot," I said.

"Yes," Eakins said, "he was."

I pulled the blanket up over the face, and together we made the best temporary grave we could to hold him till spring and proper burial in town. We scraped away snow and used the axe to dig into the hard ground. We yanked down part of the chimney to pile rocks over the grave so no animal could get at him. And just before we left, Eakins went inside again and came out with the torn flag and tied it to the pole from the corner of the cabin and stuck the pole firmly in among the rocks.

The last thing I saw in the fading light, as we went over the edge of the tableland and started down the steep slope, was that old flag whipping out straight and stiff in the mountain wind.

HARVEY KENDALL

A Father Who Grew Up

MY FATHER had two pair of boots. He had a pair of shoes too but he wore those only when my mother made him, to church on Sundays and to funerals and the like. The boots were what you'd call his regular footwear. One pair was plain, just rough and ready old-style cowboy boots, nearly knee high, made of stiff cowhide with canvas pulling-straps we used to call mule ears that dangled and flapped on the outside when he walked along. He wore those at work on weekdays. He was cattle inspector at the local stockyards, where the ranchers for quite a stretch around brought their stuff to be checked and weighed before being shipped out. He'd pull out of bed in the morning and pad around the house in his socks, or when Mother got after him, in the slippers she'd bought for him, until after breakfast and then he'd squat on the edge of a chair and heave and yank at those boots till they were on and tuck his work pants down inside the tops and stand up and stretch and say, "Another day, another dollar," which was sort of silly because he earned more than a dollar a day, and out the door he'd go with those mule ears flapping.

We lived a short ways out of town and sometimes he'd walk in those boots down to where the stockyards spread out beside and behind the station about a half mile away, and sometimes he'd saddle his old cow pony and ride down and maybe during the day circulate some through the pens helping the handlers move the stuff around, which he didn't need to do because he wasn't paid for that. "Can't let this Mark horse get too lazy and fat," he used to say, but that was only an excuse. The truth was he plain liked the feel of that horse under him now and again and the tickle of dust rising up in a man's nose saddle high and the fun of shooing a few steers through some tricky gates. It reminded him of the old days when he was a free-roaming cowhand with a saddle roll for a home before my mother herded him into the same corral with a preacher and tied him down to family responsibilities.

Those cowhide boots were just everyday knockabout working boots. The others were something else again. They didn't reach quite as far up the legs but they had high narrow heels that curved under in back

with a real swoop and they were made of soft calfskin
that fitted like a glove over the feet and ankles and then
opened out some to take care of the pants if those were
folded over neat and tucked in careful. The tops were
curved up on the sides with little leather pulling-straps
that stayed out of sight inside and those tops were made
of separate pieces of the calfskin darker brown in color
than the bottoms and they had a clever design of a rope
loop stitched into them. He wore those boots on Sundays after he came home from church and on special
occasions like meetings of the stockmen's association
and when he was riding old Mark near the front in the
annual Fourth of July parade. They reminded him of
the best part of the old days, the times he was represent-
ing whatever range outfit he was with that season in the
early rodeos and showing the other cowhands from the
whole country roundabout what a man could do with a
good horse and a good rope.

When he wore those calfskin boots my father always
wore the belt that went with them. It was made of
calfskin too and it was so wide my mother had to fix new
belt straps on every pair of new pants she bought for
him. It had a big solid slide-through silver buckle that
had three lines of printing engraved in the metal. The
first line said "First Honors" and the second line said
the one word "Roping" and the third line said "Chey-
enne 1893." That belt and that buckle, tight around his
waist above those calfskin boots, reminded him of the
best thing of all about the old days, the time he set a
record busting and hog-tying a steer, a record that
stood seven years before anyone beat it and then it
was beat only because they shortened the run some and

changed the rules a bit and fast work was really easier to do.

Anyone knows anything about kids knows which pair of boots I liked. Cleaning and polishing both pairs with good saddle soap to keep the leather in right condition was one of my regular chores every Sunday morning before church. I'd get out the soap and a moist rag and if my father wasn't around watching I'd give those old cowskin boots a lick and a promise and then I'd really go to work on those calfskins even though they didn't need much, not being worn often. Sometimes I wouldn't do more than just run the rag quick over the old cowskins and figure my father wouldn't notice I'd let them go because that old leather was rough and stiff all the time anyway and then like as not I'd be enjoying myself on the calfskins and sudden I'd look up and there my father would be watching me with his eyebrows pulled down till they about met over his nose. "Gee-rusalem, boy," he'd say. "One of these days you'll rub those boots clean through. It's the others need the limbering so my feet don't ache in them. Get busy on them now afore I sideswipe you one."

Mention of sideswiping points to maybe one reason I didn't like working on those old cowskins. Whenever I'd done something wrong, broke one of the rules my folks made for me or messed up some chore when I should've known better, my father would come after me from behind and hop on his left foot and turn his right foot toe outward and swing his right leg so that the side of his foot swiped me hard and hurting on my rump. He'd sideswipe me a good one or two or three according to how bad it was that I'd done and until I began to get some size there were times he raised me smack off the ground. Just about every time he did that he had those old cowskins on. But likely that didn't have too much to do with my feeling about them. I never was mad after a thumping or went around being sulky. My father sideswiped me only when I had it coming and he'd do it quick and thorough and tell me why, and then to show it was over and done and he was ready to forget about it he'd tell me to stick close around after supper and we'd saddle old Mark and he'd let me sit the saddle and get in some practice-throws roping a fence post before dark.

The truth was I didn't like working on those old cow-skins because they were tough and hard to do anything with and old-fashioned and pretty well battered and they didn't mean a thing to me. Working on those others, those fine-looking calfskins, meant plenty. I'd rub away on that soft dark-shining leather and talk proud to myself inside. Not many boys had a father who had been a roping champion and in country where roping was real business and a man had to be good at it just to hold an ordinary ranch job. Not another boy anywhere had a father who had made a roping record that stood seven years and might still be standing if changes hadn't been made. I could work on that leather and see in my mind what I never saw with my eyes because all that was over and finished before I was born, my father on old Mark, young then, firm and straight in the saddle with the rope a living thing in his hands, my father and young Mark, working together, busting the meanest toughest trickiest steer with the hard-and-fast method he always said was the best. I could see every move, as he had told them to me over and over, young Mark reaching eager for speed to overtake the steer and knowing what to do every second without a word or a touch on the reins and my father riding easy and relaxed with the loop forming under his right hand and the loop going forward and opening and dropping over the wide horns and Mark slowing as my father took up the slack and pulled the loop tight and Mark speeding again to give him slack again enough so he could flip the rope over to the right side of the steer and then Mark swinging left in a burst of power and speed and the rope tightening along and down the steer's right side and pulling its head around in an outside arc and at the same time yanking its hind legs out from under it and making it flip in a complete side-winding somersault to lie with the wind knocked clean out of it and then all in the same motion Mark pivoting to face the steer and bracing to keep the rope taut and my father using that pivot-swing to lift and carry him right out of the saddle and land on his feet and run down the taut rope with his pigging string in his hand and wrap it quick around three of the steer's legs and draw it close and tie it and Mark watching and keeping the rope taut ready to yank and make that steer behave if it started causing trouble and then easing some slack at the right instant so my father could cast the loop loose and stand up to show the job was done and walk casual back to Mark without even looking at the steer again like he was saying in the very set of his head on his shoulders that's that and there's a steer hog-tied for branding or ear-marking or anything anybody's a mind to do with it.

Well, what I'm telling about this time had a lot to do

with those boots and that belt and my father and old Mark too but mostly my father. It began the night before the sort of combination fair and rodeo at our town that year. The committee running things had some extra money available and they'd telegraphed and persuaded Cal Bennett to agree to come for the price and they'd plastered the town with bills saying the topnotch champion roper of the big-town circuit would be on hand to give some fancy exhibitions and everybody'd been talking about that for days. We were finishing supper, my father and my mother and me, and I notched up nerve enough and finally I said it. "Father," I said, "can I wear your belt tomorrow? Just a little while anyway?"

My father settled back in his chair and looked at me. "What's on your mind, boy? Must be something special."

"I'm sick of it," I said. "I'm sick of all the other kids talking about that Cal Bennett all the time. There's a new kid too and I was trying to tell him about you setting a record once and he won't believe me."

My father kept on looking at me and his eyebrows pulled down together. "Won't believe you, eh?"

"That's it," I said. "If I was to be wearing that belt and let him see it then he'd know all right."

"Expect he would," my father said and he leaned back further in his chair, feeling good the way he usually did with a good meal inside him, and he said in a sort of half-joking voice, "Expect he would even more if I was to get out there tomorrow and swing a rope in the free-style steer busting and show everyone around here a thing or two."

That was when my mother started laughing. She laughed so she near choked on the last bite she was chewing and my father and I stared at her. "Gee-rusalem," my father said. "What's so blamed funny?"

My mother swallowed down the bite. "You are," she said. "Why it's eleven years since you did anything like that. You sitting there and getting to be middle-aged and getting thick around the middle and talking about going up against young fellows that are doing it all the time and could run circles around you nowadays."

"Oh, they could, could they?" my father said and his eyebrows were really together over his nose.

"That horse of yours too," my mother said and to her it was still just something to chuckle at. "He's the same. Getting old and fat and lazy. He couldn't even do it any more."

"He couldn't, eh?" my father said. "I'll have you know being young and full of sass ain't so all-fired important as you seem to think. It's brains and know-how that count too and that's what that horse's got and that's what I've got and like riding a bicycle it's something you don't ever forget."

He was mighty serious and my mother realized that and was serious too. "Well, anyway," she said, "you're not going to try it and that's final.

"Gee-rusalem," my father said and he thumped a fist on the table so hard the dishes jumped. "Just like a woman. Giving orders. Tie a man down so he has to keep his nose to a grindstone getting the things they want and start giving orders the moment he even thinks a bit about maybe showing he still can do something."

"Harvey Kendall," my mother said, "you listen to me. I saw you near break your neck too many times in those shows before we were married. That's why I made you stop. I don't intend to have anything happen to you."

They were glaring at each other across the table and after a while my father sighed and looked down and began pushing at his coffee cup with one finger the way he always did when they'd been having an argument. "Expect you're right," he said and he sighed again and his voice was soft. "It was just an idea. No sense us flaring at each other over a little idea." He turned to me. "Wear the belt," he said. "All day if you've a mind to. If your feet were big enough you could wear the boots too."

In the morning my father didn't go to work because that day was a local holiday so we had a late breakfast and he sat around quiet like he was thinking things over in his mind the way he'd been all the evening before after supper. Then he pulled on the calfskin boots, looking a bit different in them without the belt on up above, and he went out and saddled old Mark and rode into town to help with the preparations there. I couldn't go along because just before he left he told me to stick close to my mother and watch out for her, which was a backhand style of putting it because she would really be watching out for me and that was just his usual little scheme to tie me to her so I wouldn't be roaming around and getting into any devilment. Soon as he was gone I got out the belt and put it on and it went around me almost twice but I could fix it so the buckle was in the middle in front as it should be and I stood on a chair

to admire that part of myself in the little mirror my
father used for shaving. I waited while my mother
fussed with her good dress and the trimmings, doing the
things women do to make themselves look what they
call stylish, and then the two of us, my mother and me,
walked the half mile into town and the day's activities.

We stopped at all the exhibits and saw who had won
the prizes for jams and jellies and raising vegetables and
the like and we spent some time looking over the small
pens where the prize-winning stock animals were. I
stood on one foot and then the other and chewed molas-
ses candy till my jaws were tired while my mother
talked to women and then more women and I didn't
get a chance to roam around much and show off that
belt because she was watching out for me just about
every minute. Three or four times we bumped into
my father busy circulating all over the place as the
cattle judge and one of the local greeters of out-of-town
folks and he'd stop and talk to us some and hurry away.
He was enjoying himself the way he always did at these
affairs, joshing with all the men and tipping his hat to
the women, and he was developing a sort of glow from
a drink or two with the other greeters.

He joined us for a quick lunch at the hotel. He was
feeling good again and he joked me over being about
half hidden inside that belt and as soon as we were
through eating he hustled us out and to the temporary
grandstand along one side of the main stockyard pen
so we all could have good seats for the rodeo doings.
He picked a place in the third row where he always said
you could see best and he sat in the middle with my
mother on one side of him and me on the other and it

wasn't till we had been there a little while and the two of
them were talking hearty with other folks around that
I had my chance to slip away by sliding through and
under the grandstand and go find some of the other
kids so I could strut and show off that belt. I went hunting them proud and happy as I'd ever been and I found
them and in maybe five minutes I was running back
under the grandstand as mad and near crying as I'd ever
been too. I knew where to crawl up through by my
father's boots and I did and he felt me squirming through
against his legs because the stand was filled now and he
took hold of me and pulled me up on the seat beside
him. "Quiet now, boy," he said. "We wouldn't want
your mother to know you've been slipping away like
that." He swung his head to look at her on the other
side and saw she was busy talking to a woman beyond
and he swung back to me and saw my face. "Gee-rusalem, boy," he said. "What's eating at you?"

"Father," I said, "he doesn't believe it about you."

"Who doesn't believe it?" he said.

"That new kid," I said.

"Did you show him that belt?" my father said.

"Yes," I said. "But he just laughed. He said it's a
fake. He said if it isn't you just found it somewhere or
got it from some old pawnshop."

"Found it?" my father said. His eyebrows were starting to draw down together but the people all around
were starting to buzz louder and things were beginning
out in the big pen that was the arena for the day. "All
right, boy," my father said. "We'll do something about
that when this shindig's over. Maybe a good sideswipe'd
do that kid some good. Be quiet now, the bronc riding's

coming up." He didn't pay any more attention to me because he was busy paying attention to what was happening in the arena but not all his attention was out there because he kept fidgeting on the plank seat and every now and then he was muttering to himself and once he did it loud enough so I could hear. "Pawnshop," he said and kept on fidgeting around and didn't seem even to know he was doing that.

Plenty was happening out in the arena, the kind of things I always enjoyed and got excited about, but I wasn't in any mind to enjoy much that day and then sudden there was an extra flurry of activity and the main gates swung open and the people began to shout and cheer. A man came riding through the gateway on a beautiful big buckskin that was jouncing with each step like it had springs in its feet and you could tell right away the man was Cal Bennett. He was slim and tall and straight in the saddle and he was mighty young-looking and mighty capable-looking all at the same time. He had on boots just like my father's calfskins, maybe not exactly the same but so close to it there wasn't much difference, and a wide belt like the one I was wearing, and sitting there so easy on that jouncing saddle like he was glued to it he was about the best-looking figure of a man I ever saw. He had a coiled rope in his hand and he shook out a loop as he came forward and began spinning it and it grew bigger and bigger and sudden he flipped it up and over and it was spinning right around him and that buckskin and sudden he flipped it again and it was spinning big and wide in front of the horse and he gave a quick little wriggle with his heels and the horse jumped forward and he and that horse went right through the loop and it was spinning behind them and then the people really went wild. They shouted and clapped and stomped their feet. Cal Bennett let the loop fall slack on the ground and bowed all around and took off his big hat to the women and put it back on and coiled in his rope and rode over to the side of the arena where he'd wait for time to do his real roping stunts and still the people shouted and stomped. And my father sat there beside me and pulled up straight with his head high, looking around at the shouting people, and his face got tight and red and he shrank down till he was hunched low on the seat and he sat very still. He didn't fidget any more or mutter to himself. He just sat still, staring out at the arena and things happened out there, and then the announcer was shouting through his megaphone that the free-style steer busting for the local championship was next and sudden my father turned and grabbed me by the arm. "Hey, boy," he said, "take off that belt."

I fumbled with it and got it off and handed it to him and he stood up right there on the grandstand and yanked off the ordinary belt he was wearing and began slipping that big belt through the special pants straps my mother had sewed for him. She saw him looming up there beside her and what he was doing and she was startled. "Harvey Kendall," she said, "just what do you think you're going to do?"

"You keep out of this," my father said and the way he said it would have made anybody shy away. He pulled the belt tight through the buckle and started down toward the arena, pushing through the people in the two rows ahead. He stepped to the ground and turned to look back at my mother. "Just keep your eyes on that arena," he said, "and you'll see something."

He squeezed through the fence rails into the arena and went straight to the little bunch of men who were acting as judges for the rodeo events. He was reaching in his money pocket as he went and he took out two dollar bills. "I'm in this one," he said to the men. "Here's my entry fee."

They all turned and stared at him. "Lookahere, Harve," one of them said. "You want to show us how you used to do it, that's fine. That's wonderful. We'll be proud to have you. But don't you go trying to do it racing against a stopwatch."

"Shut up, Sam," my father said. "I know what I'm doing. You just take this money." He pushed the bills into the man's hand and swung away hurrying and by time the other entries were lined up he was back leading old Mark and with a good rope he'd borrowed somewheres in his hand. He took a place in the line and the judges put all the names on slips of paper in a hat and pulled them out one by one to get a running order and my father's name was one of the last. He stood there among those younger men and their young horses, quiet and waiting by old Mark, just running the rope through his hands to see it had no kinks and coiling it careful and exact, and all the while the excitement was building up in me, and my mother sat still and silent on the plank seat with her hands tight together in her lap.

One after another the others made their runs, flipping their steers and dashing in to hog-tie them, and they used a lot of different methods, some forefooting the steers and some going straight for the heads and quick

pull-arounds, some risking long throws to save time
and some playing it safer and chasing till they were close
in, and some of them were good and some maybe better
than just good but you could tell easy enough none of
them were in the real champion class, and then it was
my father's turn. He led old Mark out and walked
around by old Mark's head and reached up a hand to
scratch around the ears and he whispered something to
that old horse nobody could hear and he came back
around and swung up to the saddle. Seeing him there,
straight and sturdy in the saddle, I couldn't hold it in
any longer. I jumped standing right up on the seat.
"Father!" I shouted. "Father! You show them! The
whole bunch of them!" My mother pulled me down
quick but she was just as excited because her hands
trembled and out there in the arena my father didn't
pay any attention to anything around him. He sat quiet
on old Mark checking the rope again and a hush spread
over the whole place and off to the side Cal Bennett
reined his big buckskin around so he could watch close
and sudden my father let out a whoop. "Turn that critter loose!" he yelled and the bars on the chute were
yanked away and a big rangy steer rushed out into the
arena and as it crossed the starting line the timer slammed
down with his hat and old Mark was leaping forward.
Not three jumps and there wasn't a person watching
didn't know that old horse knew what he was doing
and maybe he was a mite slower than the young cow
ponies that'd been performing but he was right up there
in the champion class with the know-how. The steer
was tricky and started twisting right away and old Mark
was after it like a hound on a hot scent, keeping just the

right distance to the left of it and closing in steady. My father was riding high in the stirrups and a loop was forming under his right hand and while he was still a ways back the loop whipped forward fast like a snake striking and opened out over the steer's head and the steer twisted and the loop struck on one horn tip and fell over the other horn and pulled off.

"Gee-rusalem!" My father's voice roared out over that whole arena. "Stick with him, Mark!" And old Mark was hard on that steer's tail with every twist and turn and my father yanked in the rope and whipped out another loop and it settled smack over the horns and head and he pulled it tight and flipped the rope over to the steer's right side and old Mark swung left, head low and plowing into the sudden strain coming, and that steer spun like a cartwheel somersaulting as it spun and was down flat and old Mark pivoted to face the steer and keep the rope taut and my father tried to use that pivot swing to lift him out of the saddle and his foot caught on the cantle going over and he went sprawling on his face in the dust. He scrambled up and scrabbled in the dust for the pigging string and started down the taut rope trying to run too fast and stumbled and went down again. He came up this time puffing with his face dark red and ran on and just about threw himself on that steer. He grabbed at the legs and got the string around three of them and tied it quick and jumped to the steer's head and old Mark eased some on the rope and he loosened the loop and threw it off and straightened up. He didn't even turn to look at the timekeeper. He didn't look around at all. He just looked down at the ground and walked slow toward old Mark. And while he was

walking there, slow and heavy-footed, the one thing
that could rule him out even if he'd made good time
and was the worst thing that could happen happened.
The steer had some breath back now and was struggling
and the knot had been tied in such a hurry that it slipped
and the steer got its feet free and pushed up hot and mad
and started after my father. Maybe it was the shouts
that warned him or maybe it was old Mark shying back
and snorting but anyway he turned and saw and dodged
quick and began to run and the steer was right after him
and sudden a rope came fast and low to the ground and
the loop in it whipped up and around that steer's hind
legs and tightened and the steer hit the ground again
with a thump and at the other end of that rope were Cal
Bennett and his big buckskin.

The people went wild again and they had a right to
because that was about as fast and tricky a job of roping
as they'd ever seen anytime and it wasn't just a show-
off stunt, it was serious business, but my father didn't
pay any attention to the shouting or even to Cal Bennett. He just stopped running and looked around once
and started walking again toward old Mark, slow and
heavy-footed with those calfskin boots all dusty. He
reached and took hold of the reins and went right on
walking and old Mark followed him and he remembered
the rope dragging from the saddle horn and stopped and
unfastened it and coiled it in and went on walking and
old Mark followed and together they went to the outside gate and someone opened it enough for them to go
through and he left the rope hanging on a gatepost and
they went outside and along around the fence toward
the road, the two of them alone together, my father

walking like an old man and sweaty old Mark tagging with his head low. I felt plain ashamed of being me, of being a boy with a father who'd made a fool of himself like he had, and I wanted to crawl away somewhere and hide but I couldn't do that because my mother was standing up and telling me to come along and starting down out of the grandstand right in front of all those people. She had her head high and she looked like she was just daring anyone to say anything to her. She marched along in front of the grandstand and around the side toward the road and I had to follow, trying not to look at anybody. She hurried a little and came alongside my father and he kept staring at the ground ahead of him and didn't seem to notice but all the same he knew she was there because he put out a hand and she took hold of it and they walked on along the road toward our house like that, neither one of them saying a word.

It was sad-feeling and mournful around our place the rest of that afternoon. My father was as silent as if he'd forgotten how to speak. After he took care of Mark he came in the house and pulled off those calfskin boots and tossed them in the hall closet with the other pair and put on his slippers and went out and sat on the back steps. My mother was just as silent. She hustled around in the kitchen and it looked like she was baking things but for once I wasn't interested in that. I didn't want to be anywhere close to my father so I took the front steps and I sat there whittling some and chewing on my knuckles and being miserable. I was mad at what he'd done to me, made me feel ashamed and fixed it so the other kids would have something to torment me about and so that new kid never would believe it about him.

"He ain't so much," I said to myself. "He's just an old has-been, that's all he is."

Then we had supper and we were all just as silent as before and Mother had fixed the things my father liked best, which was kind of a waste because he only picked at the food and didn't seem to be tasting it. But he perked some and at last he looked up at her and grinned a sick little grin and looked down and began pushing at his coffee cup. "I told you you'd see something in that arena," he said. "Well, you did."

"Yes," my mother said. "I did." She hesitated a moment and then she found something to say. "And I've been to a lot of those shows and I never saw a steer slapped down as hard and thorough as that one."

"That wasn't me," my father said. "That was Mark." He pushed up and turned away quick and went out again to the back steps.

It was only a while later and I was on the front steps again when I saw something that made me jump up and my heart start to pound and what I saw was a big buckskin coming along the road and turning in at our place and sitting easy in the saddle was Cal Bennett.

"Howdy, bub," he said. "Is your father handy?"

"He's around back," I said. He nudged the buckskin and started around the house and all at once it came rushing up in me and I had to shout it at him. "Don't you dare make fun of him! He was better'n you once! He made a record nobody's every really beat!"

Cal Bennett reined in his horse and leaned over toward me and his eyes were clear and bright looking down at me. "I know that," he said. "I wasn't much bigger'n you are now when I saw him make it. That's what started me practicing." He straightened in the saddle and went on around the house. I stood still in the surprise of his words and then I had to follow him and when I went around the rear corner of the house there was my father sitting on the steps looking up and there was Cal Bennett on that big buckskin looking down and they were holding a silence there between them for what seemed a long while.

My father shifted a little on the steps. "Nice of you to come around," he said. His voice was taut and careful. "I forgot to thank you for pulling that steer off me this afternoon."

"Shucks," Cal Bennett said. "That wasn't much. You've done it yourself many a time. There ain't a man ever worked cows ain't done it often for another man out on the range."

They kept looking at each other and the tightness that had been in my father's face all those last hours began to ease away and when he spoke again his voice was steady and friendly the way it usually was. "I sort of messed it up out there today, didn't I."

"Yes," Cal Bennett said. "You did kind of hooraw it some." He chuckled and sudden my father chuckled too and then they both grinned like a pair of kids.

"From what I hear," my father said, "you're good. You're damn good."

"Yes," Cal Bennett said and his voice was easy and natural and he wasn't boasting at all. "Yes, I am. I'm as good as a man named Harvey Kendall was some years back. Maybe even a mite better."

"Expect you are," my father said. "Yes, I expect you are." He leaned backward on his elbows on the steps.

"But you didn't come here just to chew that kind of fat, pleasant as that can be as I used to know."

"No," Cal Bennett said. "I didn't. I've been figuring. This rodeo business is all right for a young fellow long as he's young but there ain't any future in it. It's getting to be more fancy show for the crowds and less real roping all the time anyway. I've been saving my money. With what I collected in town a while ago I've got the tally I was aiming at. Now I'm figuring to get me a nice little spread somewhere in this territory and put some good stock on it and try raising me some good beef."

"Keep talking," my father said. "There's a lot of sense in what you're saying."

"Well, now," Cal Bennett said. "I figured to ask you to help me some getting started."

My father straightened on the steps and he cocked his head to one side, looking up. "Tell me something, Bennett," he said. "There's a woman mixed up in this somewhere."

"Yes," Cal Bennett said. "There is."

"And she wants you to quit risking your fool young neck showing off with a rope in front of a lot of shouting people."

"Yes," Cal Bennett said. "She does."

"And she's right," my father said. "And now you tell me something else. Why did you come to me?"

"Simple," Cal Bennett said. "I been asking questions round about for some months. Found out a few things. Found out there's one name signed to a checklist on a cattle shipment that'll be accepted without question anywhere the rails run and that name's Harvey Kendall.

Heard people say and for quite a ways around these parts that when you want good stock picked out and straight advice on how to handle them right you go find that same man. Heard them say that man never did another man dirt and never will. Heard them say —"

My father put up a hand to stop him. "Whoa, now," my father said. "No need to pile it on too thick. Of course I'll help you best I can. You knew that before you started all that palaver. Stop being so damn formal up there on that horse. Hop down and squat on these boards and tell me just what you have in mind."

And there the two of them were side by side on the steps talking quiet and friendly and the buckskin wandered off far enough to find a few grass tufts by our little pasture fence and whiffle some over the rails at old Mark and I was standing by the house corner with the strangest feeling in me. Somehow I didn't want to disturb them or even let them notice I was there and I stepped back soft and around the house again, wondering what was happening to me, and then I knew what I wanted to do. I went in through the front door and past my mother sitting quiet in the front room with our old photograph album in her lap and I went straight to the hall closet. I hardly even looked at those calfskin boots even though they were mighty dusty and could stand a cleaning. I took out the rough old cowskins and I got the saddle soap and a moist rag and I went over by the back door, where I could sit on a stool and hear them talking, and I really went to work on those old boots. I wanted to make that hard old leather comfortable as I could for his feet. I wanted to make those old boots shine.

THE OLD MAN

And the Last Ambush

JERRY LINTON was ten the year the old man came to live with them in the still-new house his parents had built the year before. He knew the old man was coming, knew it the day the letter came and his mother read it with her lips folding into a tight line and put it up on the mantelpiece and in the evening he sat cross-legged in his flannel nightshirt on the floor of the dark upstairs hall behind the top newel post of the still shiny front stairs and heard his parents discussing it downstairs in the parlor. He could even hear the faint rustling of paper as his father refolded the letter.

"Frozen his feet," said his father, dry-voiced and precise, nailing down the essential fact in invariable precise manner. "Well, something was bound to happen to the old fool sometime. I suppose this means we'll have to take him in."

"Trapped," said his mother. "That's how it makes me feel. Just plain trapped. If we don't, you know what they'll all say. We have the room. We're about the only ones can afford it right now. But if we do — well, you know what he is."

"Yes," his father said. "I know. But he's your kin and that's that."

So that was that as it always was when his father spoke and Jerry Linton knew the old man was coming, the not even imaginable old man who lived alone off up somewhere in the far mountains, whom he had never dared ask questions about because his parents and all the relatives, the few times the old man was ever mentioned, looked at each other as if even thinking about him was a mistake and hurried on to talk of almost anything else. But Jerry Linton did not know what to expect and the excitement in him that he kept hidden because his mother did not believe in noise and disturbance about the house reached a high pitch that Saturday morning as he and his mother stood on the front porch and watched his father, coming back from the station, drive their new Ford with its gleaming brass oil lamps into their alleyway and stop it and get out of it all alone and come toward them and shrug his shoulders in an exasperated way and say: "He wouldn't come in the machine. I've got him coming in a carriage from the livery stable."

Then the carriage came and stopped out front and the driver swung down and opened the door and Jerry Linton was disappointed at first because what climbed out, slow and awkward, backing out and down and leaning against the side of the carriage to turn around, was just an ordinary old man, thin and stooped in wrinkled and dirty clothes. The driver took him by one arm to help him up the front walk and he snapped out something in a sharp peevish old voice and shook the driver's hand from his arm and turned back again to reach inside the carriage and lift out a battered old carpetbag with something long strapped to one side and sticking out at both ends. He held the bag with one hand and leaned away from it to balance the weight and hobbled up the walk, taking slow short steps and easing down carefully on each foot in turn as if it hurt him to step on it. He hobbled up the walk without a look back at the carriage pulling away and he was a very old man with skin drawn tight over high cheekbones and a scraggly gray tobacco-stained mustache hanging down over his mouth and bright old eyes deep sunk below heavy brows. He stopped by the porch steps and set the old carpetbag down and what was strapped along its side was an old heavy-barreled rifle. He straightened and peered up at the three of them on the porch, at Jerry Linton and his mother and father.

"Made it," he said. "Bet ye thought I wouldn't. Mebbe hoped so. Ain't nothin' wrong with me 'cept these goldamned feet." He poked his head forward a bit at Jerry's mother. "Mary, ain't ye? Young Tom's girl."

"That's right, Grandpa Jonas," said Jerry's mother in

her careful company-manners voice. "It's so nice seeing you again. It'll be so nice having you with us."

"Will it now?" said the old man and he peered straight up at her and there was a short embarrassing silence and Jerry's mother broke it by turning to him. "Gerald. This is Jonas Brandt, your great-grandfather."

The old man turned his head a little and his bright old eyes peered at Jerry. "Looks like his father," the old man said and leaned and picked up the carpetbag and hobbled up the steps. "Where'll ye be puttin' me?"

But Jerry's mother had noticed the rifle. Her voice was normal again, with an extra little thin cutting edge. "Grandpa Jonas. We might as well get some things straight. One is I won't have any firearms in my house."

The old man stood still, caught, motionless, frozen in the midst of easing forward from one sore old foot to the other, penned between Jerry Linton on one side and Jerry's mother and father on the other. He looked at Jerry's mother and she looked right back at him and he lowered his head and looked down at the porch floor. "Ain't no hurt in it," he said. "It's broke. Won't work no more." He turned his head sideways towards Jerry Linton and put up his free hand as if to rub his cheek but the hand was there just to hide his face from the other side and far back in Jerry Linton's consciousness a slight tremor of shock and a kind of savage joy shook him because the old man was winking at him, the heavy old brow coming down and the high skin-stretched cheekbone seeming to rise to meet it until the bright old eye was lost between them, and then his father was making it that's that again by saying: "Well, then, Mary, there's no real harm in it. Just so he keeps it where the boy can't get at it."

So the old man was living with them and at first it was difficult because Jerry's parents didn't know what to do with him, what he could or would do to pass the long hours of just being alive. That was really Jerry's mother's problem alone most of the time, except on Sunday, because every other day in the week his father left the house right after breakfast exactly at half past seven to go to work at the bank and was away all day until the clock on the mantelpiece was striking six and he was opening the front door and coming in to hang his hat and coat in the front hall closet. But the old man solved that problem himself. At the supper table, after only a few days, he suddenly put down his knife, which he always held in his right hand all through the meal while he used his fork with his left hand, and poked his old head forward a bit diagonally across the table corner at Jerry's father and said: "Ye payin' that coalman much a anythin'?" He meant the man who stopped by three times a day to tend the big round furnace in the basement that sent hot air up through tin ducts and out through square registers into all the first and second floor rooms.

Jerry's father started a little in surprise. He pressed his lips together in a small frown because he disapproved of discussing financial matters at the table. "I'm paying him enough," he said. "Probably more than the job is worth."

"Get rid a him," said the old man.

"Now, Grandpa Jonas —" began Jerry's mother.

"These goldamned feet ain't that bad," said the old man. He picked up his knife again in his right hand and let the fork drop from his left hand and reached with it and took a slice of bread from the dish in the center of the table and began mopping at the gravy on his plate. Jerry's mother watched him shove the dripping bread through his drooping old mustache into his mouth and take half of the slice in one bite and chew it briefly and shove the rest of the slice in. She turned her head and saw Jerry staring in fascination as the old man pushed out his tongue and pulled it back in through the mustache hairs with a tiny sucking noise to get the traces of gravy there. She looked straight across the table at Jerry's father and raised her eyebrows and sighed.

"Bein' fancy ain't never made food taste better," said the old man and reached for another slice of bread and bent his head over his plate to concentrate on the last of the gravy and an almost imperceptible little shivery tingle ran down Jerry Linton's spine because he saw, just as the old head bent down, the glint, the unholy fleeting sparkle in the old eyes under the heavy brows.

So tending the furnace kept the old man busy much of the time. He was always up at the first light of dawn and this filled the early morning for him, hobbling his slow way down to the basement, shaking out the night's ashes, shoveling in the coal and fussing with the dampers until the fire was burning right for the kind of weather outside. After breakfast there was the job of taking the ashes and clinkers out to the growing pile behind the garage that would be hauled away in late spring. Then there was only an hour or two to sit smoking one of his stubby old pipes, in good weather when the sun was bright on the front porch steps, in bad weather in the parlor by the front window looking out on the street, before it was lunchtime and the furnace to be tended again and only a few hours more of sitting and smoking before it was suppertime and the furnace to be tended yet again. And when the warm weather really arrived there would be the other chores the coalman had done, cutting the grass of the neat rectangle around the house which was the yard, trimming the hedge along the side opposite the alleyway, cleaning out the basement and getting rid of accumulated trash. For an old man with frozen feet these things could consume many hours.

That left the evenings and at first these were particularly difficult because Jerry's parents tried to be polite and include the old man in at least some of whatever talk there was and he just couldn't or wouldn't fit into their kind of talk and almost always said things that seemed to irritate or embarrass them. But the old man solved that problem too. There was the evening they were all in the parlor, Jerry's mother with her sewing in her platform rocker under the overhead electric light and Jerry's father with his newspaper in his easy chair by the red-tasseled electric lamp and Jerry with his arithmetic homework on the high-backed sofa and the old man with his pipe on the straight ladder-back chair by the front window, and Jerry's mother looked up from her sewing and said in her half-joking voice that meant she was trying to make a point without any fuss about it: "Grandpa Jonas, don't you think it would be nice if you trimmed your mustache more often?"

The old man looked at her what seemed a long time. He looked at Jerry's father who was being very quiet behind the paper. He turned his head to look out the window where one of the town's carbon arc lights on its high pole cast a wide yellow circle along the street. "Mebbe so," he said and Jerry's mother took up her sewing again with a triumphant little half-smile curving her lips. And suddenly the old man turned his head back again and said right out into the middle of the room, his old voice cracking some: "Don't ye folks ever do anythin' diff'rent? Allus the same doin's the same time. Like a bunch a goldamned clocks."

Jerry's mother stopped sewing. She stared at the old man and two spots of color began to show on her cheeks. Jerry's father lowered the paper and looked over it at first one of them then the other. "Regularity," he said. "That's the secret of success." But for once Jerry's mother paid no attention to his father. She had her hands folded in her lap over the sewing and she stared at the old man. Her voice was prim and sharp. "Grandpa Jonas. We are decent, respectable people. The least you can do is try to understand that. You, of all people, trying to tell us how to live."

The old man pushed up from his chair and balanced himself on his sore old feet. "Wasn't tryin' to tell ye a goldamned thing," he said. "Was just wonderin' why." He hobbled across the room and into the front hall and they could hear him making his slow way upstairs.

And the very next day his deafness began to develop. It came on fast and within a few days he couldn't hear a thing that was said to him unless a person was close and shouted. That was peculiar because the way his eyes moved and the look in them changed off and on when there was talking going on around him made it seem as if he knew who was speaking and maybe even what was being said. But he kept quiet and when anyone spoke directly to him he poked his old head forward and cupped one hand by an ear and the remark or question had to be repeated in a loud voice before he would understand it.

So his being deaf made the evenings easier because there wasn't much sense in trying to talk to a person who couldn't hear. It wasn't long before none of them ever said much of anything at all to him except to shout things absolutely necessary. It wasn't long before his evening routine was settled too. After supper he hobbled down to the basement and took a time tending the furnace for the night and hobbled back up and sat by the parlor window and waited for Jerry's father to finish reading the paper. When the reading was done and the paper refolded and placed on the parlor table, he pushed up from his chair and hobbled over and took it and hobbled out into the hall and on up the stairs to his own room.

All the first weeks he was something new and strange to Jerry Linton and the boy couldn't help staring at him and watching him. Jerry's mother worried about that and had one of her talks with him about it. "Gerald," she said, "you're still a child and children are very impressionable. I don't want you ever to forget that you are a Linton and I intend you to grow up to be a gentleman like your father." That was a word his mother used often in these talks. Sometimes it seemed that she thought there was nothing worse than not being a gentleman. But this time she was not talking about how a gentleman behaved and what a gentleman did or did not do. She was talking about the old man. "Jonas Brandt," she said — she usually spoke of him not as if he were her grandfather, Jerry's great-grandfather, but someone removed who had no real connection with them — "well, Jonas Brandt is, well, he is just not a very nice person. That may not be altogether his fault because he didn't have a very good upbringing and, well, he just couldn't be after what he did. I don't want you watching him all the time and maybe learning bad habits —"

"But, Mother, what was it that was so bad that he did?"

"Gerald. It's not nice to interrupt. Jonas Brandt just wouldn't ever settle down and take care of his family the way a decent man would. Expecting a woman and with children to go off into wild country and not live decent when there was nice work he could do at home. He was always going off by himself and doing what he wanted and not even thinking of them and getting just cruder and coarser all the time. And then he — well, I'm sorry, Gerald, but you're not old enough yet to know about that. You just have to take my word about him. After all, I'm your mother. He has to stay with us because there's no place else for him to go and after all he is related. The least you can do for my sake is just not pay much attention to him at all."

And after the first weeks that was not hard to do. The newness of the old man was gone. He was there, but he was less and less there in actual seeing and noticing, somehow quietly slipping or being pushed ever

further into the background of household affairs. He
never ate with them when they had company and used
the dining room and Jerry's mother had out a linen
tablecloth and linen napkins in honor of people from
the bank or members of her Book and Thimble Club.
He took to using the back stairs all the time, the narrow
enclosed flight of steps that led from the rear of the
upstairs hall down to the kitchen. He was no longer
sleeping in the other back bedroom across the hall from
Jerry's room. When Aunt Ella came to stay a few
days he moved up into the little finished room in the
attic so she could have his room and after she left he
stayed on up there where he didn't have to bother so
much about Jerry's mother wanting things neat and
tidy even though being there meant another flight of
narrow steps to climb.

He was no longer on the front porch steps when Jerry
came home from school, just before lunch and again in
midafternoon. Jerry's mother worried about him sitting
there, what people would think, seeing him dirty and
disreputable sitting there, drawing on his bubbly old
pipe and spitting sideways into the shrubbery. She
bought him a nice new suit that first Easter, one with
matching coat and pants and vest, and he grumbled
some and at last began to wear it but within a week it
seemed as wrinkled and dirty as his old clothes had been.
She must have said something then because he shifted
around to the back steps and, later, to a bench he built
behind the garage.

He was no longer even in the parlor, even in bad
weather, except the brief silent time each evening when
he waited for the paper. There was the rainy afternoon

Jerry's mother was upset because Jerry had tracked mud into the front hall and the old man was sitting by the parlor window with his pipe in his hand and his old head cocked a bit to one side as if he could really hear what she was saying to Jerry and she caught a glimpse of him and swung around and marched into the parlor and said in a sharp voice: "Grandpa Jonas. Do you have to smoke that horrible pipe in my house? It's ruining my curtains." She didn't wait to see if he heard her. She swung around again and marched out to get a broom and dustpan and sweep up the drying mud. But the old man must have heard because after a few minutes he pushed up and hobbled off and down into the basement and after that, in bad weather when he couldn't be on his bench behind the garage, he stayed down there, sitting and smoking on an old kitchen chair with an old cushion pad on it in the recess between the coalbin and the basement stairs where a window up behind him just above the ground level gave some light.

So he was just there, something familiar now and receding even further into the taken-for-granted background of daily living. Jerry Linton hardly ever even thought or wondered about him any more. Every morning, for some reason, lying in his bed in the second-story back room, the boy would suddenly be awake and the first light of dawn would be creeping in his window and he would hear, overhead, slow hobbling footsteps, quiet and muffled, that would fade away then be heard again coming down the narrow attic stairway and going past his door and fading out again down the back stairway to the kitchen. But even then he would not think of the old man, not as another living person separate and discernible apart from all the ordinary almost unquestioned everyday surroundings. The hobbling steps were simply another sound out of the familiar round that measured existence and they simply meant there would be time for more sleep and somehow the best sleep before his mother would be calling to him to get dressed and come down to breakfast.

Jerry Linton was two weeks past his fourteenth birthday when the man from the historical society came to call. He came on a Saturday afternoon in a dust-covered green Maxwell that he had driven all the way from the state capital. Jerry answered the door because he was in the stage of being taught how a gentleman greeted strangers and he did very well, inviting the man in and showing him into the parlor before running to get his mother.

The man sat in the platform rocker facing Jerry and his mother on the high-backed sofa. He introduced himself as a Mr. Finley, as the secretary of the state historical society, and said he was assembling information for an article he was writing for the society's quarterly publication. Jerry's mother sat up straighter with a proud little smile on her face and then suddenly she looked as astonished as Jerry felt because Mr. Finley was saying that he wanted to talk to a Jonas Brandt.

Jonas Brandt?

Why certainly. Of course, what was happening nowadays in the state, the tremendous strides forward of economic and social progress, was what was really important. But still it was interesting to get down facts about the past and the time to do that was now while some of the old-time settlers and pioneers were still alive. Of course, their memories were not always to be trusted but the scholarly approach, checking this against that, sifting out the probable truth, often yielded excellent results.

Mr. Finley was somewhat self-important as he explained his work. Jerry's mother listened and seemed a bit worried as she listened and she gave a soft little sigh of relief when Mr. Finley said his article was about the Sioux outbreak of 1862, about one aspect of it, one incident, that had been generally overlooked in the wealth of material available. He had his article well in hand. In fact, he was quite satisfied with it. But his scholar's conscience told him he should check his facts with every source and, after all, he liked traveling about and so where was Jonas Brandt?

He was out on his bench behind the garage but Jerry's mother did not tell that. She simply excused herself and went out to get him and in a few minutes he had hobbled in after her and was sitting, of all places, in the big easy chair by the red-tasseled lamp. He sat on the edge of it, hunched forward in his wrinkled and dirty clothes, his old hands on his knees, peering at Mr. Finley from under his heavy old brows.

"Mr. Brandt —" began Mr. Finley.

"You'll have to speak up," said Jerry's mother. "He doesn't hear very well."

"Mr. Brandt —" began Mr. Finley again in almost a shout.

"What ye shoutin' fer?" said the old man.

"Well," said Jerry's mother quickly. "This must be one of his good days."

"Mr. Brandt," began Mr. Finley again. He spoke slowly, separating the words, almost as if he were speaking to a child. "In August of 1862 you were living in a little crossroads settlement about ten miles from the town of New Ulm."

"Nope," said the old man. "Just passin' through. Freightin'."

Mr. Finley cleared his throat. "In any event, you were there when the Santee Sioux under Little Crow went on the warpath and began massacring defenseless women and children."

"Men too," said the old man. "Fightin' men." His old eyes were beginning to brighten.

"Well, yes," said Mr. Finley. "In any event, you were one of the party, all the people there, who set out to slip through those massacring Indians and get to Fort Ridgely."

"Yep," said the old man.

"Thirteen of you, including the children."

"Sixteen," said the old man.

"Very good, Mr. Brandt. I was just testing your memory. And who was in charge?"

"Feller named Schultz. Marty Schultz."

"Splendid, Mr. Brandt. And this Martin Schultz was an excellent leader, was he not? Took charge and —"

"Nope. Seven kinds a fool. Didn't know much. About Injuns anyway."

"Now, Mr. Brandt." Mr. Finley seemed somewhat irritated. "Let's not permit personal feelings or perhaps even jealousy creep in here. The facts prove otherwise. There were only five of you men and the rest were women and children and Martin Schultz was in charge and you were three days getting to the fort with just about no food at all and unable to make a fire with murdering Indians all about — and yet you all got through safely. Now, didn't you?"

"Yep."

"And on the last day you wouldn't have. You were hiding in a ravine and an Indian way off on a hilltop sighted you and if he had got word to the rest of his band or been able to signal them you would all have been slaughtered. But he didn't because —"

"Ye're goldamned right he didn't!"

Mr. Finley was excited now. He jumped up from the platform rocker and began pacing back and forth in front of it. "There you are, Mrs. Linton. That is my article. With full details added of course. I got it first from Martin Schultz himself. And two of the women are still living. They check it on most points. Can you see it? Of course you can. What a climax. That murdering Indian off on the hilltop and sixteen innocent white people hiding in that ravine. And Martin Schultz takes his rifle and steadies it on a rock and takes his aim. It was all of nine hundred yards, Schultz claims, but of course that's exaggerated. Those old guns you know. But it was quite a distance anyway. And sixteen lives dependent on that one shot. And Martin Schultz knows that and maybe offers up a little prayer and —"

"Quit yappin'," said the old man. "Marty allus was one to hog it. Never made that shot." The old man raised his old hands and slapped them down on his old knees. "I did."

Mr. Finley stopped pacing. He raised one hand and looked down at it and turned it over and studied his neat fingernails. He cleared his throat. "Yes, yes, of course, Mr. Brandt. After all these years and thinking about it so much, perhaps it seems —"

"It was better'n a thousand yards too!"

Mr. Finley looked at Jerry's mother and raised his eyebrows and shrugged his shoulders. He cleared his throat again and followed this with a little cough and turned toward the old man. "Well, thank you, Mr. Brandt. You have been most helpful. At least I'm sure you meant to be. Perhaps sometime I will want to consult you about some of your other —"

The old man was not even trying to hear him. The old man was pushing up from the easy chair and hobbling toward the hall. "Thought ye wanted facts," he said and disappeared toward the back of the house.

So Jerry's mother was out in the front hall with Mr. Finley by the front door and she was saying apologetic things to him and Mr. Finley was saying polite things to reassure her and alone in the parlor, tense upright on the high-backed sofa, was Jerry Linton, shaking, shaking far down inside with a kind of savage joy and a desire for knowing, knowing, knowing —

"Mother. What was that other thing he did?"

"Oh, Gerald. I don't want you thinking about such things. We're civilized now. I don't see why, even if it is history, people have to go raking up all those horrible old things and making people remember them. People ought just try to forget things ever weren't as decent and quiet as they are now. I wish that Mr. Finley, even if he is a gentleman —"

"Mother. What did he do?"

"Well . . . I suppose you do have to know sometime,

Gerald. He, well, after his wife died — worried her into her grave, I'm sure that's what happened — he took up with, well, with an Indian woman. And he, well, he never even married her. There. I've told you. Now I want you to just put it out of your mind and not go around thinking about it . . ."

Out of mind?

So Jerry Linton had to wait until his mother was busy again picking up and tidying about upstairs, then go find the old man. He was not out behind the garage. He was in the basement, on his old chair in the recess by the coalbin. Jerry Linton, stretching and gangling into his fifteenth year, almost as tall already as his father, stood on the basement steps near the bottom and saw the old man sitting there sucking on a bubbly old pipe and was afraid, afraid of this suddenly strange-again old man, thinner and more stooped than when he first came, with old eyes dulled now, somehow even in his dwindling meager smallness looming tremendous and blotting out the whole neat horizon of accepted living.

Jerry Linton could barely get the word out. "Grandpa."

It was really one of the old man's good days. He did not turn his head but he heard. "Eh, boy?"

"Did you . . . did you really shoot that Indian?"

Long seconds of waiting then the old man's head turned slowly toward Jerry and nodded. "With that rifle a mine. That's a Sharps, boy."

"They . . . they don't believe you."

"That don't mean nothin'. How'd they know? Thing is, I know."

It was peculiar. Grown folks couldn't talk to the old

man. But a boy could. Jerry Linton sat down on the second step from the bottom. His chin fitted into the notch between his knees poking up with his arms around his legs holding them together, and by twisting his head just a bit he could look at the old man.

"That Indian woman . . . Why didn't you ever marry her?"

"Yer mother's been talkin'." The old man chuckled. "Fact is, I did. Injun style. Good enough fer her so good enough fer me. Stuck with me till she finished." He chuckled again. "Tell ye somethin', boy. She was more woman'n the first one . . ."

And after that Saturdays were special because in the mornings when Jerry's mother was uptown doing her household shopping and picking out the groceries that would be delivered in the afternoon he was with the old man, in the basement or out behind the garage, and there was no end to the questions that kept coming.

"Grandpa. Did you ever shoot a buffalo?"

"Buffler, boy? That's fer sure. Partner'n me worked hides two-three years. Toted in more'n 'leven hundred once. Worked out a Bismarck up in Dakoty . . ."

That was the way it was, simply the plain unslicked statements somehow more real and exciting because of their very matter-of-fact plainness, to be expanded in imagination and given meaning in the thinking over afterwards.

"But why won't you ever ride in the car?"

"Goldamned machine. Legs or a hoss's the way to get around. What good'd that thing be fer rough goin'? Up in the mount'ns? Ain't worth a buffler chip off a road. Me, I ain't never stuck to roads . . ."

"Did you ever see Jesse James?"

"Nope. Didn't miss much nuther. Saw Boone Helm once. Knife man, he was. Killed a lot of people. Folks got together an' used a rope up in Montanny. Used to see the place freightin' into Virginny City . . ."

"But, Grandpa, weren't you ever scared? Indians and wild animals and things like that?"

"Why, fer sure, boy. Lots a times. Bein' scared's all right. Backin' away ain't. I'd start shiverin' and I'd say, Jonas, ye goldamned mule, ye got yerself into this here fix an' so what comes ye can just take — an' after that it wouldn't be so goldamned bad . . ."

So Jerry Linton, in a sense, was living two lives, one neat and orderly, cushioned by security and the polite courtesies of respectability, bounded by school and family meals and the rules and almost unvarying routine of his parents' household, the other unruly and exciting, pushing haphazard into the long echoing past of an old man who had never stuck to roads, pushing in imagination outward into the open spaces of new land and of wild land not yet tamed but only being tamed where distance pulled at the mind and danger could be a frequent companion and a man could look along the barrel of a Sharps rifle and aim true. After a while the two lives began to merge in almost unnoticed small ways, unnoticed even by Jerry Linton himself. But one day in history class a picture of Andrew Jackson came alive on the page and he suddenly knew that the names in the book were not just names but people and not people apart and different but ordinary everyday-seeming people who ate meals and dressed and undressed and sometimes were tired and sick and just went ahead and did things and lived and in time grew thin and stooped and old.

Walking to school he saw the other houses in their neat rectangles of yards, the squared corners of the streets laid out in regular blocks, and he knew that almost everywhere out beyond the town were the neat sectioned farms with their neat cultivated fields and pastures, almost everything here and out there neat and decent and respectable. It was not always like that. Indians once roamed even this tamed land at will. And buffalo. Men had made it the way it was, men like his father, steady and dependable, careful with figures, planning ahead. And suddenly he knew, knew in real knowing not just as an idea taught in class, that other men had come first, men who didn't stick to roads and who knew Indians and fought them and sometimes even lived with them and could bring in eleven hundred buffalo hides in a single season. The wind drifting in from the west was not just the wind any more. Maybe that blowing against his cheek came from way off, beyond this Minnesota, from beyond the far Black Hills near the Devil's Tower where the old man had killed a mountain lion once or even from on up in the real mountains themselves where Boone Helm lay buried with a rope-broken neck.

In small ways. Even in games. When he was in grammar school he never played much with the older boys, except sometimes with the two younger ones who lived next door. The older boys stayed around after school and played on the grounds and on the athletic field beside the big building. His mother wanted him to come straight home, to play around the house and yard. She couldn't see why boys always liked to play such rough games anyway. There were so many ways they could be hurt, like the boy in the next block who broke an arm playing football. Now Jerry was in high school, even just the first year, it was different. His mother had one of her talks with him and told him he could stay around after school two or three days a week if he really wanted to because she was sure she could trust him not to be wild and rough like some of the boys. He stayed around and it was early fall and they were playing football and at first, for quite a few days, he just stood and watched. He wanted to play too but he couldn't help thinking about getting hurt. And one day he pushed in with the others and he was let be on one side just to fill in and then he was out on the field more frightened than he had ever been before and ready to run away. And suddenly he was telling himself without thinking how or why that he'd gotten himself into this fix so he'd just have to take what came and in a kind of savage joy almost as if he hoped to be hurt so he could show he could take it he plunged into the game and it wasn't so bad after all. In a little while it was even fun, to be running and yelling and bumping into other boys trying to block them and gasping for breath with the blood in him pounding strong.

It was spring and Jerry Linton was past the halfway mark of his fifteenth year when his mother came home one Saturday morning from her household shopping and called and called to him and at last he answered from behind the garage and then he forgot and she had to call him again.

"Gerald," she said. "I do wish you would come when

I call. Now carry these parcels upstairs. The least you can do is help with all the running up and down stairs that has to be done in this house." And when he had put the parcels in the upstairs hall and was back down and starting out the kitchen door she stopped him. "Gerald. It seems to me you're spending entirely too much time with Jonas Brandt. It's beginning to show in your talk. And you're becoming entirely too loud and noisy lately."

Jerry Linton stood in the doorway shifting from one foot to the other and his mother said: "Sit down, Gerald. I want to have a talk with you. I don't see how it can do you any good to have a man like Jonas Brandt filling your head with wild notions and horrible old stories that very likely aren't the least bit true anyway. I'm sure most of the time he's just trying to justify himself and make you think that after all he really was something. You know how old people are, getting things mixed up and getting to think maybe things are true that really weren't true at all. I'm sure you remember what happened when that Mr. Finley —"

"Oh-h-h, Mother. He really did shoot that Indian!"

So Jerry Linton had spoken back to his mother and spoken sharply too and his father had to have a talk with him, dry-voiced and precise, reasoning it out. "Jerry. I know you didn't mean to upset your mother but you did and that's that. I know when we're through here you will go and tell her you are sorry. What you have to realize is that she is right. No doubt there is some truth in the things your great-grandfather has been telling you. But he is nearly ninety years old and they happened a long time ago. Most people's memories, espe-

cially old people's, are very faulty as we keep finding out
at the bank. Trying to straighten out wills and property
deeds and things like that. Your great-grandfather has
not given much evidence in his life that he has much
sense of responsibility. And, after all, what happened
so long ago is not nearly as important to a growing boy
as what is happening right now. This is a practical world
we live in these days and it is run on business principles.
What you should be doing is tending to your lessons and
learning how best to get along in it."

So Jerry Linton told his mother he was sorry. But
his parents saw the stubborn look on his face and worried
about it and only a few days later his father brought
home a copy of the historical society's quarterly and
showed him Mr. Finley's article.

There it was, in the cold clear neat precise not-to-be-
questioned authority of printed words, the whole story,
very well told and with impressive footnotes, of sixteen
people fleeing for their lives under the leadership of a
Martin Schultz and evading the bloody-handed Sioux
for three days and on the third day sighted by an Indian
scout who never got word back to his band because of
the cool courage and unerring markmanship of Martin
Schultz. The only mention of Jonas Brandt was in a
footnote: *The fifth man was a freighter named Jonas
Brandt, who joined the group for added safety in reaching the fort.*

So his parents were right. There were no more Saturday mornings behind the garage for Jerry Linton. He
was too busy playing with the other boys. It wouldn't
be exciting listening to the old man anyway. Jerry Linton saw him in sensible perspective now and realized that

for quite a while his memory had been getting bad after all. He contradicted himself sometimes and when he tried to pin down a date he kept getting mixed up. He was just an old relic out of another time who didn't fit in the modern practical world.

Jerry Linton was fifteen, in his sophomore year at high school, when he woke one spring morning in his second-floor bedroom soon after the first light of dawn with a strange feeling that something was wrong. He found himself listening and not sure for what. Then he knew. There were no slow hobbling footsteps overhead. He lay quiet wondering about that and after a while slipped back into sleep and when his mother called him and he dressed and went downstairs there was a slight chill in the house and his father was in the basement rattling and banging at the furnace. While they were eating breakfast the doctor came and Jerry's father went off with him upstairs. In a few moments they were back down, the doctor bustling and good-natured, rubbing his hands together and saying: "Nothing to get too much upset about, Mrs. Linton. He's a bit feverish but that's to be expected. He's had some kind of a light stroke. A remarkably tough old constitution, I'd say. Wouldn't surprise me to see him up and about again in a few days."

But it was not a few days. It was the very next day, early in the morning with the first light of dawn. Jerry Linton woke and heard slow hobbling steps overhead, quiet and muffled, that faded away and then were heard again coming down the narrow attic stairway and going past his door and fading out again down the back stairway to the kitchen. A kind of warm feeling drifted through him and he slipped back into sleep and suddenly he was awake again. Wide awake. The footsteps were returning past his door and on up the attic steps, not slow and hobbling but quicker, lighter, hurrying. Jerry Linton lay still and listened and they came down the attic stairs again and were going past his door again. He eased quietly out of bed and tiptoed to the door and opened it a crack. The old man was just disappearing into the back stairway and he was carrying his old rifle.

Jerry Linton couldn't move at first. He was still, motionless, with his face pressed close against the door crack. Then he opened the door and went, soft and quick, along the hall toward the front of the house and stopped by the closed door of his parents' bedroom. He stared at the door almost a full minute. And suddenly he turned and hurried back to his own room and dressed as fast as he could and pulled on a sweater and went out and down the back stairs.

The old man wasn't in the basement. He wasn't on the back porch or anywhere in sight in the yard. He was behind the garage and he was standing straight, hardly stooped at all, with the heavy old rifle firm in one hand, and his old eyes were brighter, brighter than they had ever been, when he looked at Jerry coming around the corner of the garage.

"Time ye were out a blankets," he said. "There's things doin'." He looked at Jerry in a strange way, not the way he ever had before, in a strange and straight and piercing way almost as if Jerry were someone else who should have been out of blankets before this. "What's got into ye, Jed?" he said. "Can't ye sniff it? Injun smell." He pointed with his free hand off across the vacant lot behind theirs and the fields beyond to the slight rise that hid the town dump. In the growing light of dawn Jerry saw it, a last thin wisp of smoke floating upward and dissolving away. "That's just a fire over in —" he started to say but the old man was poking his old head at him and saying in a fierce whisper: "Tell me I don't know Injun sign! Someun's got to do some scoutin' or they'll be on us afore we know it!"

The old man started off, striding fast, across the vacant lot, and Jerry Linton wavered and turned to hurry back to the house and stopped. Slowly he turned around again and saw the old man striding away, head forward and intent, striding fast on old feet that must hurt him but he didn't seem to notice that, striding ahead with his heavy old rifle in his right hand, and far down in Jerry Linton a tingling started and shook him and would not stop and he was running to catch up.

The old man flicked one sideways glance at him as he came alongside. "Right, Jed," the old man said. "Two's got more chance 'n one."

They were across the vacant lot and they struck straight across the fields beyond, climbing fences as they came to them. Once a dog ran up barking at their heels and the old man swung around and down and snarled something at it that didn't seem to be words and it stopped barking and put its tail between it legs and dropped behind and away. They went over the rise that hid the dump and on past the dump itself where some fire still smoldered which the old man didn't even notice and he stopped and raised his left hand to shield his eyes against the sun just begin-

ning to show over the horizon and peered all around
studying the countryside. "They'll come snakin' down
that draw," he said and struck off again toward the
only rough land, the only untamed-to-farming land,
anywhere around, toward the far base of the huge wide
slow-sloping hill that rose west of town with its near
slope torn and eroded by an ancient dry boulder-strewn
stream bed. They reached the base of the hill and Jerry
Linton's legs were tiring from the pace but he couldn't
have stopped if he had wanted to. It was impossible how
the old man kept going on his old frozen feet, striding
forward, head swinging from side to side, old eyes bright
and intent under their heavy brows. He struck straight
up along the upper left side of the dry stream bed that
widened upward like a vast shallow funnel and Jerry
Linton followed and followed and his legs were aching
and the old man stopped. "Can't figger it," he said.
"Sioux ain't been liftin' hair lately." He started on and
they were near the top of the hill and Jerry Linton's legs
were aching and suddenly the old man clapped him on
the shoulder so hard he went forward on his knees.
"Down," said the old man in a fierce whisper, dropping
to the ground and scrambling over behind a boulder.
"Over here."

So there they were, Jerry Linton and the old man,
behind a boulder on the edge of a wide gully, really just
a wide stretch of rough eroded hillside, and far off down
the slope and across the level, like a neat picture in the
midst of neat surrounding farms, was the neat town with
its square-blocked streets where decent and respectable
people were still sleeping with maybe some of them already beginning to stir in their neat houses. And the old

man raised and peered over the boulder, intent old eyes studying the wide gully. "Take a peek, Jed," he said. "See 'im? Ahind that rock looks like a keg. Straight across an' down some."

Jerry Linton, aching and scratched but with a tingling inside that wouldn't stop, peered over the boulder too and at last he saw the rock that looked like a keg, way off across and up the other side of the wide gully. But it was only a rock and that was all.

"Got it," said the old man. "Pawnee. Sneakin' devils they are. Paint up like that." And then Jerry Linton, squeezing his eyes to sharp focus, saw showing above the rock in a small patch an outcropping of red sandstone in the ground beyond, bright and shimmering a little in the early morning sun.

"Likely a passel a bucks over the ridge," said the old man. He turned toward Jerry. His old voice was an urgent hoarse whisper. "Git amovin', Jed, an' rouse the folks. I'll slow 'm here while ye get help."

It was the tingling in Jerry Linton that pushed him up and started him a few steps away. Then he felt foolish and he stopped and looked around. The old man was beside the boulder, flat on his stomach, and he was shoving the old rifle forward and muttering to himself. He put a finger in his mouth and licked it and stuck it up to test the air. "Wind about ten mile," he muttered. "Figger the drop across there maybe thirty feet." His left arm was out, resting on its elbow, and his left hand held and steadied the heavy old rifle barrel and the stock was snuggled up against his right shoulder and he squinted through the strange old double sights and suddenly the old Sharps roared like a Fourth of July cannon and the recoil smacked shaking through the old man's body. He rolled over and behind the boulder again and sat up with the rifle still in his hands and yanked down on the trigger guard and the breech opened and he clawed in a pocket and took out a funny old linen cartridge and started reloading and his fingers fumbled and dropped it and the old gun fell too, down and across his legs, and his whole body seemed to stiffen into a kind of rigidness. Slowly his old head came up and eyes, dulling rapidly, looked around and stopped on Jerry Linton.

"What ye doin' up here, boy?" he said and his whole body sagged out of the rigidness into a kind of limpness and relaxed back against the boulder and slipped down sidewise to the ground.

Jerry Linton knew. He had never seen this before but he knew. He looked down at the crumpled still body a long time. He looked up and across the wide gully where a patch of red sandstone showed above a keg-shaped rock. Slowly he started down the rough eroded near side of the gully and then he was walking faster and then he was running, down and across the center dip and up the other side and then slowing, almost afraid to look.

There was the rock. There behind it, farther behind than it seemed from the other side, was the patch of red sandstone. And there, near the top of the patch where it would show over the rock, close to the edge but there, was the fresh, chipped, the shining gouge in the stone.

Jerry Linton stood with his back to the patch of sandstone. He started again across the gully, taking long steps, stretching them to what he judged the right length. Down and across and up. One thousand and twenty-seven. Taking into account the slope down and up that was still close enough.

Jerry Linton picked up the old rifle and looked at it. There was not a spot of rust on the metal. The old stock was sound. "Yes," he said. "Yes. I'm a Linton. But I'm a Brandt too." He said it to the body of an old man who had given him what no one else could, what no one could ever take away from him because always, simply by closing his eyes, he would be able to see, across a thousand yards of untamed land, a patch of red chipped sandstone.

He turned and went down the slope toward the town to get his father, who, in his own precise way, steady and dependable, would make arrangements to take care of what was left of the old man.

JACOB

A Big Deer That Walked in High Places

THOSE MOCCASINS? Mine. Though I never wore them.
Had them on just once to see if they fitted. They did.
A bit tight but I could get them on.

Don't touch them. The leather's old and dry and the
stitching rotted. Ought to be. They've been hanging
there a long time. Look close and you can see the crafts-
manship. The best. They're Nez Percé moccasins. Notice the design worked into the leather. It's faint now
but you can make it out. Don't know how they did
that but the Nez Percés could really work leather. A
professor who studied such things told me once that

design means they're for a chief. For his ceremonial appearances, sort of his dress-up footwear. Said only a chief could use that design. But it's there. Right there on those moccasins.

Yes. They're small. Boy size. That's because I was a boy then. But they're a chief's moccasins all the same. Kept them down the years because I'm proud of them. And because they mind me of a man. He had a red skin. Copper would be closer the color. A muddy copper. And I only saw him once. But he was a man.

That was a long way from here. A long way. In years and in miles. I was ten then, maybe eleven, maybe twelve, in that neighborhood, I disremember exactly. Best I can do is place it in the late seventies. Funny how definite things like dates and places slip away and other stray things, like the way you felt at certain times and how your first wild strawberries tasted, can remain clear and sharp in your mind. We were living, my folks and my older brother and myself, in a little town in eastern Montana. Not much of a place. Just a small settlement on the railroad that wouldn't have amounted to anything except that it had a stretch of double track where a train going one direction could pull off to let one going the other get past. My father was a switchman. Looked after track and handled the west-end switch. That was why we were there.

The Indian smell was still in the air in those days. People around here and nowadays wouldn't know what that means. It was a knowing and a remembering that not so far away were still real live free-footed fighting Indians that might take to raiding again. They were pegged on treaty lands and supposed to stay there. But they were always hot over one thing or another, settlers gnawing into their hunting grounds or agents pinching their rations or maybe the government forgetting to keep up treaty payments. You never knew when they might get to figuring they'd been pushed far enough and would start council fires up in the hills and come sudden and silent out of the back trails, making trouble. It was only a year or two since the Custer affair on the Little Big Horn southwest of where we were. No one with any experience in those things expected the treaty that ended that business to hold long.

Don't take me wrong. We didn't look for Indians behind bushes and sit around shivering at night worrying about attacks. The nearest reservation was a fair jump away and if trouble started we'd know about it long before it reached us, if it ever did. Matter of fact it never did. I grew up in that territory and never once was mixed in any Indian trouble past an argument over the price of a blanket. Never even saw any fighting Indians except this once I'm telling about and then they weren't fighting any more. It was just a smell in the air, the notion there might be trouble any time. Indians were quite a topic when I was a boy and the talk of an evening chewed it plenty.

Expect I heard as much of it as any of the boys around our settlement. Maybe more. My father had been in the midst of the Sioux outbreak in Minnesota in the early sixties. He'd seen things that could harden a man. They settled his mind on the subject. "Only good Indian," he'd say, "is a dead one." Yes. That's not just a saying out of the storybooks. There were men who really said

it. And believed it. My father was one. Said it and believed it and said it so often I'd not be stretching the
truth past shape to figure he averaged it couple times a
week and so naturally we boys believed it too, hearing
it all the time. I'll not argue with anyone wants to believe it even today. I'm only telling you what happened
to me.

Hearing that kind of talk we boys around the settlement had our idea what Indians were like. I can speak
for myself anyway. The Indians I saw sometimes passing through on a train or loafing around a town the few
times I was in one with the folks didn't count. They
were tame ones. They were scrawny mostly and they
hung around where white people were and traded some
and begged liquor when they couldn't buy it. They
weren't dangerous or even interesting. They didn't
matter more'n mules or dogs or anything like that clut-
tering the landscape. It was the wild ones filled my
mind, the fighting kind that lived the way they always
had and went on the warpath, and made the government
send out troops and sign treaties with them. Can't recall
exactly what I thought they looked like, but they were
big and fierce and dangerous and they liked to burn out
homesteaders' cabins and tie people to wagon wheels
and roast them alive over slow fires, and it took a brave
man to go hunting them and look at them down the
sights of his gun. Days I felt full of ginger I'd plan to
grow up quick and be an Indian fighter. Late afternoon,
before evening chores, I'd scout the countryside with
the stick I used for a gun and when I'd spot a spray of
red sumac poking out of a brush clump, I'd belly-it in
the grass and creep to good cover and poke my gun

through and draw my bead. I'd pull on the twig knob
that was my trigger and watch careful, and sometimes
I'd have to fire again and then I'd sit up and cut another
notch on the stick. I had my private name for that.
Making good Indians, I called it.

What's that got to do with those moccasins? Not
much I guess. But I'm telling this my way. It's all part
of what I remember when I sit back and study those
moccasins a spell.

The year I'm talking about was a quiet one with the
Sioux but there was some Indian trouble all right, along
in the fall and a ways away, over in the Nez Percé
country in Idaho. It started simple enough like those
things often did. There was this band lived in a valley,
maybe seven hundred of them all told, counting the
squaws and young ones. Biggest safe estimate I heard
was three hundred braves, fighting men I mean. Can't
remember the name of the valley, though I should. My
brother settled there. But I can recall the name of the
chief. That sticks. Always will. Not the Indian of it
because that was a fancy mouthful. What it meant.
Mountain Elk. Not that exactly. Big-Deer-That-
Walks-the-High-Places. Mountain Elk is close enough.
But people didn't call him that. Most Indians had a short
name got tagged to them somehow and were called by it.
His was Jacob. Sounded funny first time I heard it but
not after I'd been hearing it a while.

As I say, this trouble started simple enough. We heard
about it from the telegraph operator at the settlement
who took his meals at our place. He picked up information relaying stuff through his key. News of all kinds
and even military reports. Seems settlers began closing

in around Jacob's valley and right soon began looking
at the land there. Had water which was important in
that country. Some of them pushed in and Jacob and
his boys pushed them back out. So complaints were
being made and more people wanted to move in, and talk
went around that land like that was too good for Indians
anyway because they didn't use it right, the way white
men would, and when there was enough steam up a
government man went in to see Jacob. Suggested the
band would be better off living on some outside reservation. Get regular rations and have an agent to look after
them. No, Jacob said, he and his were doing all right.
Had been for quite a spell and expected to keep on doing
the same. Sent his thanks to the Great White Chief for
thinking about him but he wasn't needing any help. So
after a while the pressure was stronger and another government man went in. Offered to buy the land and
move the band in style to a reservation. No, said Jacob,
he and his children — he called them all his children
though he wasn't much past thirty himself — he and his
children liked their land and weren't interested in selling.
Their fathers had given up land too much in the past
and been forced to keep wandering and had found this
place when no one wanted it, and it was good and they
had stayed there. Most of them then living had been
born there and they wanted to die there too and that
was that.

Well, the pressure went on building and there were
ruckuses here and yonder around the valley when some
more settlers tried moving in and a bunch of young braves
got out of hand and killed a few. So another government man went in, this time with a soldier escort. He

didn't bother with arguing or bargaining. He told Jacob the Great White Chief had issued a decree and this was that the whole tribe was to be moved by such and such a date. If they went peaceable, transportation would be provided and good rations. If they kept on being stubborn, soldiers would come and make them move and that would be a bad business all around. Yes, said Jacob, that would be a bad business but it wouldn't be his doing. He and his children wouldn't have made the storm but they would stand up to it if it came. He had spoken and that was that.

So the days went along toward the date set which was in the fall I'm telling about. Jacob and his band hadn't made any preparations for leaving and the officer in charge of this whole operation thought Jacob was bluffing and he'd just call that bluff. He sent about four hundred soldiers under some colonel into the valley the week before the moving was supposed to happen, and Jacob and the others, the whole lot of them, just faded away from their village and off into the mountains behind the valley. The colonel sent scouting parties after them but couldn't make contact. He didn't know what to do in that situation so he set up camp there in the valley to wait and got real peeved when some of Jacob's Nez Percés slipped down out of the mountains one night and stampeded his stock. Finally he had his new orders and on the supposed moving day he carried them out. He put his men to destroying the village and they wiped it level to the ground, and the next morning early there was sharp fighting along his upper picket lines and he lost quite a few men before he could jump his troops into the field in decent force.

That was the beginning. The government wanted to open the valley for homesteading but couldn't without taking care of Jacob first. This colonel tried. He chased Jacob and his band into the mountains and thought overtaking them would be easy with the squaws and young ones slowing Jacob down, but Jacob had hidden them off somewhere and was traveling light with his braves. He led this colonel a fast run through rough country and caught him off watch a few times and whittled away at his troops every odd chance till this colonel had to turn back, not being outfitted for a real campaign. When he, that'd be this colonel, got back he found Jacob had beat him there and made things mighty unpleasant for those left holding the camp before slipping away again. About this time the government realized what it was up against and recalled the colonel and maybe whoever was his boss, and assigned a general — a brigadier — to the job and began mounting a real expedition.

We heard plenty about what happened after that, not just from the telegraph operator but from my brother who was busting the seams of his breeches those days and wanting to strike out for himself, and signed with the freighting company that got the contract carting supplies for the troops. He didn't see any of the fighting but he was close to it several times and he wrote home what was happening. Once a week he'd promised to write and did pretty well at it. He'd send his letters along to be posted whenever any of the wagons were heading back, and my mother would read them out to my father and me when they arrived. Remember best the fat one came after he reached the first camp and saw Jacob's valley. Took him two chunks of paper both sides to tell about it. Couldn't say enough about the thick green grass and the stream tumbling into a small lake and running quiet out again, and the good trees stepping up the far slopes and the mountains climbing on to the end of time all around. Made a man want to put his feet down firm on the ground and look out steady like the standing trees and stretch tall. Expect that's why my brother quit his job soon as the trouble was over and drove his own stakes there.

Yes. I know. I'm still a long way from those moccasins. I'm over in Idaho in Jacob's valley. But I get to remembering and then I get to forgetting maybe you're not interested in all the sidelines of what I started to tell you. I'll try to move it faster.

As I was saying, the government outfitted a real expedition to go after Jacob. A brigadier general and something like a thousand men. There's no point telling all that happened except that this expedition didn't accomplish much more than that first colonel and his men did. They chased Jacob farther and almost penned him a few times and killed a lot of braves and got wind of where his women and their kids were hidden, and forced him to move them farther into the mountains with them getting out just in time, not being able to carry much with them. But that wasn't catching Jacob and stopping him and his braves from carrying on their hop-skip-and-jump war against all whites in general and these troops in particular. Then a second general went in and about a thousand more soldiers with them and they had hard fighting off and on over a couple hundred miles and more, and the days drove on into deep winter and Jacob was licked. Not by the government and its soldiers and their guns. By the winter. He and his braves, what was left of them, had kept two generals and up to two thousand troops busy for four months fighting through parts of three states and then the winter licked him. He came to the second general under truce in what remained of his chief's rig and took off his headdress and laid it on the ground and spoke. His children were scattered in the mountains, he said, and the cold bit sharp and they had few blankets and no food. Several of the small ones had been found frozen to death. From the moment the sun passed overhead that day he would fight no more. If he was given time to search for his children and bring them together he would lead them wherever the Great White Chief wished.

There. I'm closer to those moccasins now even though I'm still way over in Idaho. No. Think it was in western Montana where Jacob surrendered to that second general. Well, the government decided to ship these Nez Percés to the Dump, which was what people called the Indian Territory where they chucked all the tribes whose lands weren't just cut down but were taken away altogether. That meant Jacob and his children, all that was left of them, about three hundred counting the squaws and kids, would be loaded on a special train and sent along the railroad that ran through our settlement. These Nez Percé Indians would be passing within a stone's throw of our house and we would have a chance to see them at least through the windows and maybe, if there was need for switching, the train would stop and we would have a good look.

Wonder if you can scratch up any real notion what that meant to us boys around the settlement. To me maybe most of all. These weren't tame Indians. These were wild ones. Fighting Indians. About the fightingest Indians on record. Sure, the Sioux wiped out Custer. But there were a lot more Sioux than soldiers in that scuffle. These Nez Percés had held their own mighty well against a big chunk of the whole United States Army of those days. They were so outnumbered it had got past being even a joke. Any way you figured, it had been about one brave to six or seven soldiers and those braves hadn't been well armed at the start and had to pick up guns and ammunition as they went along from soldiers they killed. Some of them were still using arrows at the finish. I'm not being funny when I tell you they kept getting bigger and fiercer in my mind all the time I was hearing about that long running fight in the mountains. It was notches for Nez Percés I was cutting on my stick now and the way I felt about them, even doing that took nerve.

The day came the train was to pass through, some time late afternoon was the first report, and all of us settlement boys stayed near the telegraph shack waiting. It was cold, though there wasn't much snow around. We'd sneaked into the shack where there was a stove, till the operator was peeved at our chattering and shooed us out, and I expect I did more than my share of the chattering because in a way these were my Indians because my brother was connected with the expedition that caught them. Don't think the other boys liked how I strutted about that. Well, anyway, the sun went down and we all had to scatter home for supper and the train hadn't come. Afterwards some of us slipped back to the shack and waited some more while the operator cussed at having to stick around waiting for word, and one by one we were yanked away when our fathers came looking for us, and still the train hadn't come.

It was some time past midnight and I'd finally got to sleep when I popped up in bed at a hammering on the door. I looked into the kitchen. Father was there in his nightshirt opening the outside door and the operator was on the step cussing some more that he'd had word the train was coming, would get there in half an hour, and they'd have to switch it and hold it till the westbound night freight went past. Father added his own cussing and pulled on his pants and boots and heavy jacket and lit his lantern. By time he'd done that I had my things on too. My mother was up then and objecting, but my father thought some and shushed her. "Fool kid," he said, "excited about Indians all the time. Do him good to see what thieving smelly things they are." So I went with him. The late moon was up and we could see our way easy and I stayed in the shack with the operator and my father went off to set his signal and tend his switch. Certain enough, in about twenty minutes the train came along and swung onto the second line of track and stopped.

The telegraph operator stepped out and started talking to a brakeman. I was scared stiff. I stood in the shack doorway and looked at the train and I was shaking inside like I had some kind of fever. It wasn't much of a train. Just an engine and little fuel car and four old coaches. No caboose. Most trains had cabooses in those days because they carried a lot of brakemen. Had to have them to wrangle the hand brakes. Expect the brakeman the operator was talking to was the only one this train had. Expect that was why it was so late. I mean the railroad wasn't wasting any good equipment and any extra men on this train, and it was being shoved along slow when and as how between other trains.

I stood there shaking inside and the engine was wheezing some and the engineer and fireman were moving slow and tired around it, fussing with an oilcan and a tin of grease. That was the only sign of life I could see along the whole train. What light there was in the coaches, only one lantern lit in each, wasn't any stronger than the moonlight outside and that made the windows blank-like and I couldn't see through them. Except for the wheezing engine, that train was a tired and sleeping or dead thing on the track. Then I saw someone step down from the first coach and stretch and move into the moonlight. He was a soldier, a captain, and he looked tired and sleepy and disgusted with himself and the whole world. He pulled a cigar from a pocket and leaned against the side of the coach, lighting the cigar and blowing out smoke in a slow puff. Seeing him so lazy and casual, I stopped shaking and moved into the open and closer to the coach and shifted around trying to find an angle that would stop the light reflection on the windows and let me see in. Then I stopped still. The captain was looking at me. "Jee-sus," he said. "Why does everybody want to gawk at them? Even kids." He took a long drag on his cigar and blew a pair of fat smoke rings. "You must want to bad," he said. "Up so late. Go on in, take a look." I stared at him, scared now two ways. I was scared to go in where those Indians were and scared not to, after he'd said I could and just about ordered I should. "Go ahead," he said.

"They don't eat boys. Only girls. Only at lunchtime."
And sudden I knew he was just making a tired joke,
and it would be all right and I went up the steps to the
front platform and peered in.

Indians. Fighting Indians. The fighting Nez Percés
who had led United States soldiers a bloody chase
through the mountains of three states. The big and
fierce redmen who had fought many times their own
number of better-armed soldiers to a frequent standstill
in the high passes. And they weren't big and they
weren't fierce at all. They were huddled figures on the
coach seats, two to a seat down the twin rows, braves
and squaws and young ones alike, all dusty and tired
and hunched together at the shoulders in drowsy silence
or sprawled apart over the windowsills and seat arms in
sleep. In the dim light they looked exactly like the tame
Indians I'd seen, and they seemed to shrink and shrivel
even more as I looked at them and there was no room in
me for any emotion but disappointment, and when I
noticed the soldiers sleeping in the first seats close to
me I sniffed to myself at the silly notion any guards
might be needed on that train. There wasn't the slight-
est hint of danger anywhere around. Being on that train
was no different from being off it except that it was
being on a stopped train and not being outside on the
ground. It didn't even take any particular nerve to do
what I did when I started walking down the aisle.

The only way I know to describe it is that I was in
a sort of trance of disappointment and I wanted to see
everything and I went straight down the aisle looking
all around me. And those Indians acted like I wasn't
there at all. Those that were awake. Each of them had

his eyes fixed somewhere, maybe out a window or at the floor or just at some point ahead, and didn't move them. They knew I was there. I could tell that. A feeling. A little crawling on my skin. But they wouldn't look at me. They were somehow off away in a place all their own and they weren't going to let me come near getting in there with them or let me know they even saw me outside of it. Except one. He was a young one, a boy like me only a couple years younger, and he was scrooged down against a sleeping brave — maybe his father — and his small eyes, solid black in the dim light, looked at me, and his head turned slow to keep them on me as I went past and I could sense them on me as I went on till the back of the seat shut them off.

Still in that funny trance I went into the next coach and through it and to the third coach and on to the last. Each was the same. Soldiers slumped in sleep, and the huddled figures of the Indians in different pairings and sprawled positions but the effect the same and then at the end of the last car I saw him. He had a seat to himself and the headdress with its red-tipped feathers hung from the rack above the seat. He was asleep with an arm along the windowsill, his head resting on it. I stopped and stared at him and the low light from the lantern near the end of the coach shone on the coppery texture of his face and the bare skin of his chest where it showed through the fallen-apart folds of the blanket wrapped around him. I stared at him and I felt cheated and empty inside. Even Jacob wasn't big or fierce. He wasn't as big as my father. He was short. Maybe broad and rather thick in the body but not much, even that way. And his face was quiet and — well, the only

word I can ever think of is peaceful. I stared at him and
then I started a little because he wasn't sleeping. One
eyelid had twitched a bit. All at once I knew he was
just pretending. He was pretending to be asleep so he
wouldn't have to be so aware of the stares of anyone
coming aboard to gawk at him. And sudden I felt
ashamed and I hurried to the back platform to leave the
train, and in the shadows there I stumbled over a sleeping soldier and heard him rousing himself as I scrambled
down the steps.

That started what happened afterwards. Expect I'm
really to blame for it all. Mean to say it probably
wouldn't have happened if I hadn't been hurrying and
wakened that soldier. He didn't know I was there. He
was too full of sleep at first and didn't know what had
awakened him. While I stayed in the dark shadow by
the coach, afraid to go out into the moonlight, he stood
up and stretched and came down the steps without
noticing me and went around the end of the train toward the wider shadow on the other side, and as he
went I saw him pulling a bottle out of a pocket. I felt
safe again and started away and turned to look back,
and the light was just right for me to see some movement
inside through the window by the last seat. Jacob was
standing up. All kinds of wild notions poured through
my mind and I couldn't move and then he was emerging
through the rear door onto the platform and I wasn't
exactly scared because I wasn't conscious of feeling
anything at all except that I couldn't move. Time
seemed to hang there motionless around me. Then I
realized he wasn't doing anything and wasn't going to
do anything. He wasn't even aware of me or if he

was I was without meaning for him and he had seen me
and dismissed me. He was standing quiet by the rear
railing and his blanket was left inside and the cold night
air was blowing against his bare chest above his leather
breeches but he didn't appear to notice that. He was
looking back along the double iron line of the track
toward the tiny point of light that was my father's
lantern by the west switch. He stood there, still and
quiet, and I stayed where I was and watched him and
he did not move and stood there looking far along the
westward track and that was what we were doing, Jacob
and I, when the soldier came back around the end of
the train.

Thinking about it later I couldn't blame that soldier
too much. Maybe had orders to keep the Indians in
their seats or not let them on the rear platform or something like that. Probably was worried about drinking
on duty and not wanting to be caught letting anything
slip with the tang plain on his breath. Could be too
he'd taken on more than he could handle right. Anyway
he was surprised and mad when he saw Jacob standing
there. He reached first and pulled some object off the
platform floor and when he had it I could see it was
his rifle. Then he jumped up the steps and started
prodding Jacob with the rifle barrel toward the door.
Jacob looked at him once and away and turned slow and
started to move and the soldier must have thought Jacob
moved too slow because he swung the gun around to
use the stock end like a club and smack Jacob on the
back. I couldn't see exactly what happened then because
the scuffle was too sudden and quick but there was a
blur of movement and the soldier came tumbling off

the platform to the ground near me and the gun landed
beside him. He was so mad he tripped all over himself
getting to his feet and scrabbling for the gun and he
whipped it up and hip-aimed it at Jacob and tried to
fire it and the breech mechanism jammed some way and
he clawed at it to make it work.

And Jacob stood there on the platform, still and quiet
again, looking down at the soldier with bare breast
broadside to the gun. I could see his eyes bright and
black in the moonlight and the shining on the coppery
firmness of his face and he did not move and of a sudden
I realized he was waiting. He was waiting for the bullet.
He was expecting it and waiting for it and he would not
move. And I jumped forward and grabbed the rifle
barrel and pulled hard on it. "No," I shouted. "Not
like that." And the soldier stumbled and fell against
me and both of us went down and someone was yelling
at us and when I managed to get to my feet I saw it
was the captain and the soldier was up too, standing stiff
and awkward at attention. "Bloody Indian," the soldier
said. "Trying to get away." The captain looked up
and saw Jacob standing there and jerked a bit with
recognizing who it was. "He was not," I said. "He was
just standing there." The captain looked at the soldier
and shook his head slow. "Jee-sus," he said. "You'd
have shot that one." The captain shook his head again
like he was disgusted and tired of everything and maybe
even of living. "What's the use," he said. He flipped a
thumb at the soldier. "Pick up your gun and get on
forward." The soldier hurried off and the captain
looked at Jacob and Jacob looked down at him, still and
quiet and not moving a muscle. "There's fools of every

color," the captain said and Jacob's eyes brightened a little as if he understood and I expect he did because I'd heard he could speak English when he wanted to. The captain wiped a hand across his face. "Stand on that damned platform as long as you want," he said. He remembered he had a cigar in his other hand and looked at it and it was out and he threw it on the ground and swung around and went toward the front of the train again, and I wanted to follow him but I couldn't because now Jacob was looking at me.

He looked down at me what seemed a long time and then he motioned at me and I could tell he wanted me to step out further into the moonlight. I did and he leaned forward to peer at me. He reached a hand out toward me, palm flat and down, and said something in his own language and for a moment I was there with him in the world that was different and beyond my own everyday world and then he swung away and stepped to stand by the rear railing again and I knew I was outside again, outside of his mind and put away and no more to him than any other object around. He was alone there looking far down the track and it sank slow and deep in me that he was looking far past the tiny light point of my father's lantern, far on where the lone track ran straight along the slow-rising reaches of distance into the horizon that led past the longest vision at last to the great climbing mountains. He was looking back along the iron trail that was taking him and his children away from a valley that would make a man want to put his feet firm on the earth and stretch tall and was taking them to an unknown place where they would not be themselves any longer but only some

among many of many tribes and tongues and all dependent on the bounty of a forgetful government. It
wasn't an Indian I was seeing there any more. It was a
man. It wasn't Jacob, the tamed chief that even foolish
kids could gawk at. It was Mountain Elk, the Big-Deer-
That-Walks-the-High-Places, and he was big, really
big, and he was one meant to walk the high places.

He stood there looking down the track and the westbound night freight came rumbling out of the east and
strained past, and he stood there watching it go westward along the track and his train began to move,
creeping eastward slow and feeling forward, and I
watched it go and long as I could see him he was standing
there, still and quiet, looking straight out along the back
trail.

Well. I've taken you to where I was headed. It's only
a hop now to those moccasins. I tried to tell the other
boys about it the next day and likely boasted and strutted
in the telling and they wouldn't believe me. Oh, they'd
believe I saw the Indians all right. Had to. The telegraph operator backed my saying I was there. Even
that I went aboard. But they wouldn't believe the rest.
And because they wouldn't believe me I had to keep
pounding it at them, telling it over and over. Expect I
was getting to be mighty unpopular. But Jacob saved
me even though I never saw him again. There was a
day a bunch of us boys were playing some game or
other back of the telegraph shack and sudden we realized
someone had come up from somewhere and was watching us. An Indian. Seemed to be just an ordinary everyday sort of tame Indian. But he was looking us over

intent and careful and he picked me and came straight to me. He put out a hand, palm flat and down, and said something to me in his Indian talk and pointed off to the east and south and back again to me and reached inside the old blanket he had fastened around him with a belt and took out a dirty cloth-wrapped package and laid it at my feet and went away and faded out of sight around the shack. When I unrolled that package there were those moccasins.

Funny thing. I never wanted to go around telling my story to the other boys again. Didn't need to. Whether they believed or not wasn't important any more. I had those moccasins. In a way they made me one of Jacob's children. Remembering that has helped me sometimes in tough spots.